# A
# FATAL
# FORTUNE

# A
# FATAL
# FORTUNE

A
MURDER BY THE
NUMBERS MYSTERY

# J.L. WINTERS

LeVeL
BEST BOOKS

First edition

ISBN: 978-1-68512-609-4

Cover art by Level Best Designs

This book was professionally typeset on Reedsy.
Find out more at reedsy.com

*To Lonna, my financial guru. Without you none of this would have been possible.*

# Chapter One

I f fortune favored the bold, I had a lot of catching up to do. Whether I was being reckless or merely determined, only time would tell. Either way, I had an important choice to make.

"I'm just going to do it," I said, making the declaration as I turned from my office window, a tenth-floor view of downtown Los Angeles sparkling below. It sounded fancy, having a view like that, but it was nothing more spectacular than concrete high-rise buildings with mirrored windows lined by neat rows of palm trees. Not a glimpse of the Pacific Ocean in sight. Only a freeway congested with smog and eight lanes of traffic. I could be anywhere, really, but at thirty-four, I was on the tenth floor of Wallace and Reed Consultants, Forensics Division. A career destination I never would have dreamed possible had I chosen to settle for the monotony of answering phones and fetching coffee at my father's small-town investment office.

"Are you sure this is such a good idea?" Grace, my assistant, lifted a wary, manicured brow, though the look of veiled amusement on her face told me she knew we hadn't gotten to the corner office by playing it safe.

Kate Abbott, fraud examiner, and numbers expert, was never one to avoid a challenge. Never one to quit. Never one to back down. And I had no intention of starting now. My promotion to Junior Forensic Associate happened on Friday; now it was Monday, and Grace and I had been whisked away to a new office over the course of a single weekend. While I appreciated the new title and the new view, it was really my boss's way of making me a glorified research assistant with an over-inflated paycheck so some other firm wouldn't steal me away. At least both of us knew I was worth the money.

But it wasn't money I was after. It was numbers. When I was buried deep in evidence, working on discovery for an investigation, scanning pages and pages of financial records, analyzing a crime from all angles, the numbers just magically clicked into place for me. My mind recognized the patterns and hidden clues in between all the decimal points and wire transfers. The numbers told me all of their secrets. I couldn't explain why I had this gift or where the talent had come from. I didn't understand it myself, except to say that numbers spoke to me.

Yeah, try sharing that little tidbit at the office Christmas party. My therapist prescribed a high dose of anti-anxiety meds with a disapproving frown. Apparently, the good doctor wasn't in line with the theory that numbers could speak to anyone. From then on, I tended to keep my gift a secret. It was sort of like having a superpower, and even Clark Kent chose to hide in plain sight.

"The meeting is getting ready to start," Grace said. "And you're on a plane out of here in..." She checked her silver Coach wristwatch. Practical and dependable, just like she was. "Four hours and sixteen minutes."

"Exactly why I can't waste any more time." I gathered up the files on my desk for the case I'd been working on over the last several weeks.

One Mr. Alex Jones was the head accountant at a tech start-up firm, and the board of directors suspected he'd been embezzling funds over the last year, which was eating away at their profits. Over the weekend, I'd finally found the fake work order accounts and deposits he made to an off-shore bank account in the Caymans, essentially solving the mystery of how a crooked accountant had managed to steal a bunch of money.

"Aren't you going to tell Mr. Reed about your discovery first?" Grace asked, ever the voice of reason.

"Not this time." I walked to the full-length mirror behind the door to re-tuck my white silk blouse into the waist of my gray pencil skirt. I turned from side to side to assess my reflection. My brown hair was still neatly swept behind my head in a loose bun, and my long-lasting makeup was doing its job. "Brandon and his team have had this case for longer than I have, and they didn't find the obvious. Why should I point it out to them?"

I'd proven myself more than capable on several of the firm's forensic accounting investigations, hence my most recent promotion. However, when it came to taking credit for the work done on the cases, that went to the men at the firm. Once again, proving my father right.

*Numbers are a man's world.*

He didn't believe a woman belonged in the upper ranks of the investment world. I intended to change that notion. If I had to do it one case at a time, so be it. The Alex Jones case would be my first major victory. I was tired of getting stuck with the research while my male colleagues patted each other on the back over a job well done. This time, I wanted the pat on the back. I was the one who'd discovered the fake work orders, and I intended to take the credit for my research.

"I suppose you'll need this." Grace handed me the black leather portfolio my boss had gifted me years ago that I never used. "You're in the big leagues now. You can't go waltzing in there with an armload of file folders. If you want to be taken seriously, you have to dress the part."

"What would I do without you?" I stuffed my files into the portfolio, then pulled the zipper closed and tucked it under my arm. "How do I look?" I threw back my shoulders and kicked up my chin, channeling my inner superhero.

"Like a woman about to make the biggest mistake of her career."

I frowned. "You're my assistant; you're supposed to be helping me, not making me feel worse."

"I'll be helping myself to that assistant job over in investments if you don't pull this off."

"Have a little faith." I took Grace's free hand and gave it a tight squeeze. "We made it this far, didn't we?"

She fixed me with her girl-be-for-real look, then said, "And who do you think helped you get here?"

"You did," I said, and I meant it. Grace was the best administrator at Wallace and Reed. That's why she worked for me.

"You'd better get going." She shooed me toward the door.

"I'm working up my nerve," I said, quickly checking my watch. I still had twelve minutes before the meeting started and wanted to catch the clients making small talk until the meeting officially got underway. That didn't leave me much time.

"What should I say if Mr. Reed comes looking for you?"

She could tell him I was on the Moon for all I cared. "Tell him I'm in the bathroom."

Grace's perfectly arched brows shot up to her hairline. "You're lucky you have me. I could think of a thousand better excuses than that one."

"Then tell him whatever you want. I don't plan on this taking very long. I'm going to get in, get the board president's ear, and tell him what I found. It's as simple as that."

"I'm sure that's exactly what Kim thought before she married Kanye."

"Don't worry, nothing will go wrong," I assured her. "The last thing I want is you going over to investments. I speak from experience when I say you'll be bored to death."

My father had owned an investment company back in my hometown in Minnesota, and I'd worked in his office all through high school. It's how I'd learned I have a gift for numbers. At seventeen, I was designing high-performance portfolios for his clients and making him a pretty penny in the process, not at all interested in the receptionist position he thought I deserved. When I got involved in a mock trial for my high school honors program, my team investigated a money laundering scheme, and a whole new world of numbers opened up for me, much to my father's disappointment.

*Get the skills that will get you a dependable job.*

He didn't believe a woman belonged in the business world. If I'd chosen to follow his dreams for my future, I'd be working as someone's assistant rather than gunning for the eventual title of Senior Forensic Partner. I was on my way to the top floor. If only he could see me now. Would my success have changed things between us?

"Should I even bother to keep unpacking?" Grace lifted the flap of one of the boxes stacked against the wall. "Or should I wait until you get back?"

I swiped my cell phone from the desk. "We're not leaving this office unless it's to move up."

"Good, because I'm getting used to the Starbucks kiosk in the lobby."

"So am I." It was definitely an improvement over sharing research on the fourth floor with the mailroom. "Wish me luck."

"Oh, I'll be praying for you."

I didn't need Grace's prayers when it came to Mr. Reed. My boss, I could handle. What I needed was for the client to take me—a woman—seriously. I knew what I was doing, and I had the numbers on my side. For this case, I'd found 22 deposits made to 2 fake accounts, broken down further into 11 equal deposits to one account and then the other before they were later sent to their final destination off-shore. I loved when the patterns were easy.

The rest of the office was quiet with that post-lunch slump as I scurried down the hallway towards the board room. Voices drifted out, and I slowed my pace, trying to get a feel for the room as I inched closer to my destination. This was my big chance. Time to take destiny into my own hands.

"Abbott!" The male voice startled me, and I jumped.

Drawing up short, I whipped my head around to see Brandon Cole right on my tail. Literally the epitome of tall, dark, and handsome in a charcoal gray designer suit, I'd secretly been dating him for the past two years. Brandon had long, slender sideburns, a neatly trimmed goatee, and a tribal tattoo on his left shoulder. His body was solid muscle, and his stamina never ran out. I'd never had such a perfect boyfriend, and right now, he was the last person I wanted to see.

"Where are you off to in such a hurry?" His perfect mouth spread into a playful smile as he came around and stood in front of the door to the boardroom, essentially blocking my path.

"I'm about to be late for a meeting." I glanced over his shoulder into the boardroom. So close, and still so far.

"I thought you were heading home to Minnesota for your father's funeral."

An unwelcome reminder. My father and I hadn't spoken in over ten years, and it was too late to fix any of that now. "My flight doesn't leave for a few hours."

"Working up to the last minute," Brandon said, loud enough to be heard by the entire accounting department. "I admire your dedication to the job."

"Is there something you need?" I didn't try to hide the annoyance in my tone, but I had a very short window of opportunity, and he was standing in my way.

He leaned close and whispered a wickedly erotic scenario in my ear.

"There's no way you're getting that here," I told him, trying to hide my embarrassment as heat rushed to my cheeks.

If I could say one thing about Brandon, it's that he was an exciting lover when he could manage to find time for me. We'd kept our so-called relationship a secret for two years, at Brandon's request, because he thought people wouldn't take me seriously if they knew I was sleeping with the head of forensics. He wanted to see me advance at the company on my own. In a way, the plan had backfired on him because I'd spent many lonely nights working on caseloads and had now surpassed him and his entire team when it came to streamlining my forensic analytical skills. Along with my gift for numbers, I could run circles around the rest of the associates.

"Maybe you could come by my place later," he suggested, a wicked gleam in his dark eyes.

"I can't blow off going home for the funeral," I said. "My mother and sister are expecting me. I have to be there."

"It doesn't mean I won't miss you." Brandon reached up, his long finger gently tracing my cheekbone before he tucked a stray lock of hair behind my ear. "We didn't get a chance to finish what we started at the quarterly social."

I remembered that night all too well. Brandon cornered me in the coat closet at the cigar lounge and had me up against the wall, dress pushed past my hips, before a poor old gentleman walked in on us, looking for his wife's coat. Mortified beyond belief, I'd cut the rendezvous short and hailed a cab back to my apartment, then briefly contemplated quitting my job.

"You can see me when I get back." The raspy quality of my voice surprised me, and I knew I was still blushing, my cheeks growing hotter. I slid a sideways glance at accounting to see if anyone was watching us over their gray cubicle walls.

"I don't know how much time I'll have," Brandon said. "I'm still stuck on the Jones case. My team has been at it for weeks and still can't find any evidence." He took a step back and shoved his hands into his pants pockets. "I know it's there; we just can't see it."

A wave of guilt washed over me as I clutched the portfolio tighter in my hand. I had all the evidence he needed. Words like *teamwork* and *cooperation* swirled around in my brain. I tilted my wrist to check my watch. Five minutes left. I needed him to leave before I changed my mind. The right thing to do would be to give Brandon my research, but I was afraid he'd turn around and do what was right for him, completely leaving me out of the equation. And I didn't want to give him a chance to show me that side of his character. This time, I figured it was my turn to shine.

"You look busy," he observed. "Will you come by my office before you leave?"

"Yes." I nodded emphatically. "Of course."

"I've got a meeting in five minutes." He walked past me, headed back to his office.

My way clear, I took a quick assessment of the people in the board room. Only the clients were there: the CEO, board president, and another member of their board. My mind told me to wait, to fully think it through one more time, but my legs were already carrying me into the room. The board president, Donald Wilson, was the first to see me. Short and round, with a shiny bald patch in the middle of his head, he watched me approach.

"Good afternoon, Mr. Wilson." I walked straight up to him, calling on a confidence I didn't quite feel. "I'm Kate Abbott, part of the forensics team assigned to your case."

We exchanged a polite handshake, while the CEO now turned his attention to me as well. "I think this meeting is about to get started," Mr. Wilson said. "Is there any particular place you'd like for us to sit?"

"I actually have something to show you first," I said. "I found a discrepancy while going over the company records."

That got his attention and he zeroed his focus in on me. "What have you got?"

"Kate, what is this?" Mr. Reed scuttled up to our group, placing himself in front of the client to scold me with a look. "Don't you like your new office?"

"I love it."

"Then why aren't you in it?" He forced the words out through clenched teeth and a tight smile. I sometimes found it hard to take him seriously because I was always thinking how badly he needed to groom his thick eyebrows.

"I was just showing Mr. Wilson how I found some fake work orders and traced those transfers from the business account through several shell accounts to get to an off-shore account opened by Alex Jones. I found the pattern, which was really quite obvious. He did the transfers in the same order for the same amounts each time."

Mr. Reed's nervous smile faltered. I knew my boss hated being put on the spot because it usually required quick thinking, which he tended to lack most of the time.

"Will you be joining us today?" Mr. Wilson looked hopeful and relieved to be making some sort of headway on the case.

"Kate is on her way out of town for a funeral," Mr. Reed said, sending me a warning look. "She was just leaving."

"Oh, I'm so sorry," Mr. Wilson said.

"Thank you, but—"

"Brandon, will you come and get Kate's presentation before the meeting starts?" Mr. Reed waved his hand over my head.

Great. Crash and burn, with Brandon here to witness the wreckage. It seemed fitting considering my next appointment was a funeral.

Mr. Reed gave me a stern look. "We'll talk about this later."

"Yes, Sir." I knew my chance was gone, and wasn't sure I'd ever get another one.

"What's this presentation?" Brandon stood beside me, hands in his pants pockets, rocking back on his heels. Totally clueless.

"It's nothing," I said, not sure if I wanted to cry, or hit something. I looked over at Brandon. It might feel good to hit him just for being a man. Born the right sex so everything just always worked out for him. All he had to do was show up and look good.

I stormed off in a mild huff while the clients began taking their seats around the large mahogany conference table. Grace was going to give me an earful when I made it back to my office. One I probably deserved.

"Wait, where are you going?" Brandon followed me out into the hallway.

"I'm going home for a funeral, remember?"

"But what about the presentation for the meeting?"

Something inside of me snapped. I don't know if the outburst was spontaneous or if it had been a long time in the making, but I let Brandon have the blunt end of my ire. "I'm not your secretary! Put a few brain cells together and do your own presentation. After all, isn't that why they pay you the big bucks?"

"Whoa, hold on." He put his hands up in surrender. "I'm just following orders."

As soon as the words had left my mouth, I regretted them. None of this was Brandon's fault. "I don't have anything to present. I still have to sort out my research."

"Are you going to tell me what's going on?"

I noticed a few interested glances from the accounting department. Apparently, we were going to fuel the drama for the day. "I solved the Jones case."

Brandon looked somewhat put off by my accomplishment. "How can that be possible? I've had my entire team working overtime to find even a scrap of evidence. You couldn't have done it alone."

"It wasn't all that hard. Once I found the pattern, it all fell into place."

"What pattern?" Brandon twitched with nervous energy. "Give me your research."

I should have been prepared for his reaction, but his cavalier attitude only made me angry. "Not this time."

His brows dipped in confusion. "Did I miss something?"

"I'm not giving you my research." I enunciated the words clearly for him in case his giant male ego had gotten in the way of his hearing.

"Any research you have is proprietary; it belongs to the firm. As lead on the case, you're required to turn all evidence over to me." He held out an expectant hand.

I frowned, not sure why I imagined he'd be proud of me. Maybe because he was my boyfriend. Although he'd never referred to himself as such. "I want to present it."

"That's not going to happen," Brandon declared. "Not the way you dropped it on Reed. You know he doesn't like surprises, and frankly, neither do I."

"Why are you so upset?"

Brandon narrowed his gaze, his dark eyes brimming with impatience. "I'm not upset. Just disappointed."

"Disappointed?" It was my turn to give him an annoyed stare. "I thought you'd be happy for me."

Brandon took a step closer. "You know I'm proud of your work. It's why I want us to finish the research together. There's still room for you on my team."

I bristled at the mention of joining his team. Of working under him. A part of me didn't know whether he wanted me to work on his team because he genuinely wanted to assist in my research, or because he wanted me to be convenient.

How could he make me feel so desired yet so insecure at the same time?

"I don't want to join your team. I want to make it here on my own. You know that."

Brandon retreated back a step. "Why do you have to be so damn independent? Can't you ever let people help you?"

"I thought you wanted to see me advance here without your help." I recognized the turbulent fire brewing behind his eyes, but I didn't regret throwing his words back at him. I wasn't going to play small so he wouldn't feel insecure. "Let's not argue about this."

"Fine." Brandon shoved his hands in his pockets. "They're waiting for me in there. Tell me what you have, and my team can do an official report later."

Something inside me didn't want to budge. Not one inch. "It'll be easier if I explain it."

"Easier for who?" Brandon didn't want to budge, either.

"This is my research, and I want the credit for it."

"What does it matter who presents the research? You might work alone, but at the end of the day, we're all on the same team."

I knew he was right. The desire to be an equal member of the team almost had me handing my findings over to him, but remembering all of the times they'd left me out kept my hands clasped on the leather portfolio. "If we're all a team here, why don't I ever get to take credit for solving a case? I help out just as much as anyone else, but I always end up fetching the coffee and putting in the lunch orders."

"Wow." Brandon shook his head back and forth. "I never realized how selfish you are."

Those words did it. They stung me, pricking my eyes with tears. How many times had I selflessly given my talents to the team, only to be overlooked in favor of a man? A thousand replies came to rise, but I wisely turned on my heel and walked away as fast as I could. If I said what I was thinking, I'd be a single woman.

"Wait, I'm sorry you're upset." Brandon hurried to keep up with me. "Would you just wait?"

I abruptly came to a halt and spun to face him. "Was that your idea of an apology?"

"What do you want me to say?" he asked, a sheepish look on his face. "You're the one who wants to take all the credit."

"Do your own research," I snapped. "I have a plane to catch."

"Don't leave like this," he pleaded. "Let me try to smooth things over with Reed. Meanwhile, you can get a report together. We can make this work."

His offer felt sincere, or maybe I simply wanted it to be. In any case, I didn't want to leave angry. "I'll put something together on the flight and send it to you later."

"That's my girl." He gave me a strong pat on the back. "I knew you'd do the right thing."

Watching him retreat and head into the board room left me questioning where this relationship was headed. Why did Brandon want me on his team? Why did he need my research? And what made me feel I needed to give it to him in order to make him happy? Shouldn't I be enough?

A wave of homesickness overwhelmed me, and I was suddenly glad I'd be getting on a plane in a few hours. I might be going home to bury a father I hadn't spoken to in ten years, but I'd also be returning to the friends and family I'd been away from for so long. To the people who thought I was enough. The life I'd been so eager to leave behind was now the one calling me home.

# Chapter Two

It was unfair to say I hated funerals. Just this one. I sat in the front row of the tiny Lutheran church with my mother and younger sister, mostly wondering about time and why we never seem to have enough of it. Wondering if my father thought the same thing before he died.

I didn't get up and say anything about my father. What could I say? The one person who could've lifted me up had handed me a bunch of limitations instead. He'd said the financial world wasn't the right place for me. I'd disagreed, and we'd both said things we shouldn't have. Things we couldn't take back. When he'd refused to pay for the rest of my college tuition so I could pursue a mathematics degree, I'd left my tiny hometown of Harmony Falls for the big city. Determined to prove him wrong, I'd chased after my dreams on my own, getting a job and putting myself through college. My father quit speaking to me after that, and the days and months of silence stretched into years.

Standing alone beside his grave, I still had nothing to say to him. I'd succeeded in a man's world. I'd done the impossible, according to John Abbott. Would it have been good enough for him? Would I always be striving to live up to his impossible expectations? What if I'd been born a son instead of a daughter?

I turned my face up to the heavens. The late September sun was shining high and bright in the clear, blue sky. The rays warmed my skin. I've always loved the fall. The last gasp of nature's beauty before it gave way to the harsh northern winter. The trees were dressed in magnificent autumn hues of rust, gold, and crimson and made a striking contrast to the eternally green foliage of Los Angeles I'd grown so accustomed to. From an overhead branch, a lone cardinal whistled its song. It would have been a perfect day had I not just buried my father. If only I could bury my regrets with him.

Back at my father's house, I helped my sister, Kylie, tackle the chore of hosting the funeral reception. We didn't have time to dwell upon what we'd recently lost and, instead, were kept busy putting out finger sandwiches and refilling wine glasses and cups of coffee for those who opted to attend the reception.

"I heard she inherited the whole fortune," said Mrs. Pearson, a retired librarian who loved to gossip almost as much as she loved to buy ridiculous and colorful hats.

"But weren't they divorced?" asked Mrs. Lee, who volunteered at the senior center and the church nursery on Sunday mornings. "Why would he leave his entire fortune to his ex-wife?"

"Kate, you know how a life insurance policy works," Mrs. Pearson said to me while I cleared a mess of abandoned paper plates and crumpled napkins from the fireplace mantel. "How did your mother get all the money?"

I paused my cleaning, a smile lighting my lips. *It's none of your business*, I wanted to say, but unlike Mrs. Pearson, I had manners. "You also know how a life insurance policy works, Mrs. Pearson, since you were the beneficiary on your late husband's policy."

The old woman pursed her lips, her hat looking like a peacock, ready to take flight from the side of her head. "But you're a financial expert. Why wouldn't your father want to leave his money to you girls? Or to poor Janice?"

Mrs. Lee nodded her head in agreement. "I heard Janice will be living on the streets now that you're selling your father's house. Don't you think she should inherit something? After all, she was your father's girlfriend."

The two women awaited an answer from me, and I knew I had to choose my words wisely, because whatever I said would be all over town before the evening news. "I have to help Kylie in the kitchen."

On my way to the kitchen, I stopped by the cafe table we'd brought in from the back patio and placed under the large picture window next to the front door. My father's business partner, Larry Stone, and the office receptionist, Hannah, had taken up residence in the sunny spot, along with a newcomer I didn't recognize. The man was younger than Larry, closer to my age actually, mid-thirties. And he was good-looking, in a movie star quality way, complete with perfectly tousled brown hair and a strong, chiseled jaw. Their table was littered with an array of Kylie's freshly baked scones and cookies, along with empty wine glasses, and I decided to take advantage of the opportunity to discover the identity of this handsome stranger.

"The business will be better off now to say the least," Larry made the snide comment, unaware I was standing behind him.

I'd only just met Larry at the funeral that morning, but I didn't like the man. Something about him put me on edge. Maybe I could blame it on his horrible man-perm and limp, clammy handshake. Or the way he was in such a hurry to get his hands on my father's share of the business.

"There you are, Kate." Hannah, the pretty blonde receptionist, put on a smile. "We were wondering if we'd get a chance to tell you again how sorry we are for your loss."

"Yes." Larry cleared his throat in an attempt to disperse the awkwardness. "Your father will be missed."

"It sounds like it," I remarked, then proffered the bottle of white wine in my free hand. "More wine?"

"I'd love some." The handsome stranger held up his empty glass.

"This is Damon," Hannah made the introduction. "Larry's nephew. He's in town to help with the –"

A stern look from Larry stopped her midsentence.

"Hello." Damon beamed a smile at me as I filled his wine glass.

Close up, he was almost too good-looking. His face was all hard lines and sharp angles, with a dusting of stubble along his strong jaw. How could a man this disarming possibly be related to plain, ugly Larry?

"Thank you for coming." I gave the standard reply I'd been using most of the day. It was easier than thinking of something new to say to each person. I was tired of thinking at the moment.

"It's lovely to meet you." Damon extended his hand to me in greeting.

15

I put my hand in his much bigger one and he closed strong fingers around mine, giving a firm squeeze. The man had quite a handshake.

"I'm sorry I missed the funeral," Damon said. "I just arrived in town this afternoon."

Hannah practically had stars in her eyes as she stared at Damon. "He's going to be helping out at the office. With your father gone, we could really use an extra hand."

Larry shot Hannah a withering stare. "This has been difficult on all of us."

"How are you holding up?" Hannah asked me, concern burning behind her blue eyes.

What did I say to that? My father died without warning, my mother showed up to the funeral wearing white, my boss probably intended to fire me at any moment, I'd had a fight with my boyfriend and left him almost two thousand miles away, and now I'd inherited a share of my father's business, in addition to the house we all currently occupied. I was going to have to extend my stay in order to get it all settled. Meanwhile, my life in LA was in danger of falling apart.

"I'm fine." I managed an appeasing smile. "Life goes on. Isn't that what they say?"

I added a generous pour of wine to the rest of their crystal glasses. At first, I'd hesitated when Kylie suggested we use our father's good glasses and the fine China, afraid something might get broken, but then I figured, what did it matter? He was gone now. The dishes spent most of their time locked away in a cupboard, so we might as well get some use out of them.

"Your father's death was so sudden," Hannah said. "It must be very overwhelming to inherit a business and a house, especially when you don't even live here. What are you going to do?"

"Hannah," Larry said, his voice dripping with annoyance. "Weren't you going to powder your nose or something?"

Looking contrite, Hannah silently rose from the table and disappeared down the hallway.

"Since we'll both be in town for a while, I hope to see more of you." Damon's smile was all arrogance, as if he knew the effect his looks had on the opposite sex. "I'm looking forward to it, actually."

Good thing for me, men like him were a dime a dozen in Los Angeles. Damon might have the ability to make women fall at his feet, but I wasn't the swooning type. "I'm hoping I won't be here for long. I have to get back to my job in LA. I don't think I'll have much free time."

"Speaking of free time," Larry said. "Have you had a chance to look over my proposal? I'm ready to sign the papers."

There was no doubt Larry was in quite a hurry to buy out my share of the business. It would certainly make my life easier. I'd only have the house left to deal with, and I could handle the sale through emails and phone calls. "I haven't even looked at your proposal yet, but I plan to go over everything after I'm done with the funeral."

"I was hoping we could get everything signed today," he pushed.

"I'd like to read the papers before I sign them," I pushed back.

He'd only given me the papers this morning in the reception line during the visitation. When was I supposed to read them? While sitting in the church, surrounded by friends and family, mourning my father? What a jerk.

"It's a standard buy-out contract," Larry said. "Let me save you the trouble of trying to figure out all the complicated legal terms and tell you the offer was drawn up by your father's own lawyer. You can leave the business to the men and concentrate on how many pairs of shoes you can buy with a check that large."

Larry and Damon shared an amused look and chuckled with each other.

They obviously had no idea who they were dealing with. I stiffened, standing taller as I faced him down. "While I may not be up to your standards, don't treat me like I'm some little girl confused by all the books and smart talk. I will leave you in the dust."

Larry flinched, his eye twitching ever so slightly. That was good enough for me.

"Now, I'm very busy, and I have other guests to greet." I walked away before my temper got the better of me.

Being spoken down to by a man was something I encountered on a daily basis in my profession, and though I wanted to slap the smirk right off his ugly face, I was proud for remaining professional. I might work in a predominantly male field, but I deserved respect. Besides, I held more securities licenses and accreditations than most of my male colleagues.

I went into the kitchen and tossed my collected trash and the empty wine bottle in the garbage bin. Kylie was taking a break, sipping from a glass of wine as she leaned against the butcher block island in the middle of the kitchen, more treats baking in the double ovens behind her. The clock on the stove read 2:22. A harmonious number for sisters.

"How is the food holding up out there?" Kylie asked, her blonde ponytail swishing over her shoulder. She wore her white catering jacket over her black funeral clothes.

I joined my sister at the counter and poured myself a generous glass of wine. "The scones disappear as fast as you put them out."

"Dad always loved them," she said. "I brought him a plate from the shop every Saturday."

Kylie was the golden child of the family. When she'd wanted to start her own catering business, our father not only approved of her choice in professions but put in a new kitchen with industrial double ovens, a state-of-the-art range, and a French door stainless steel fridge to give her a proper place to get started. He'd also given her start-up money to open her cake shop downtown. Quite a contrast to me asking for a mathematics degree and getting the silent treatment for ten years.

I took a deep swallow of my wine. It wasn't Kylie's fault our father believed a woman belonged in the home, taking care of men, but my sister had cleverly figured out a way to use his prejudice to her advantage.

"I'm sorry I couldn't get here sooner to help you out," I said.

"You are helping me. Having you serve the food and do the mingling means I can hide in the kitchen and avoid all the awkward conversations. I swear, if Larry Stone pats my ass one more time, I'm going to let Logan deck him."

"I'd pay to see that." I laughed.

Logan was Kylie's buff, firefighter boyfriend. He got called away during the funeral for a semi rollover on the interstate, saving him from having to mansplain to Larry why he was getting punched in the face. Too bad.

"I don't know how Dad worked with that guy," Kylie said. "He's such a sleaze. You should see how he treats the receptionist. Going into that office was like passing through a time warp into the fifties where men stared at your breasts instead of looking you in the eye."

"Now you know why I left. When Dad wanted me to start working for him, I thought he wanted me doing research and running statistics, not answering phones and booking his tee times."

"You shouldn't have been so hard on him. He didn't know any other way."

I set down my wine glass and looked at my sister, completely stunned. "I shouldn't have been hard on *him*? He was the one who refused to talk to me."

Kylie let out a heavy sigh. "I wish you two could have worked out your differences before he died. It would have been nice to have you home for more than a few days over Christmas."

"Well, I'm stuck here now," I said, complaining. "At least until I handle Larry and get the house cleaned out and listed for sale. I'll never understand why Dad left everything to me. He hated me."

Kylie put her hand over mine and squeezed. "He didn't hate you."

I held onto her hand. "It would have been nice to hear him say that."

"He did." Kylie's eyes flooded with tears. "In the only way he knew how."

I didn't always share my sister's positive outlook on the world, but I appreciated her optimism. Leave it to Kylie to take someone in the ditch and show them the stars.

"I can't believe how many people showed up today." I scanned the faces of the various people crowding my father's small Victorian house. "I don't know who half of these people are."

"You haven't been home in a long time," Kylie commented.

In a far corner of the living room, a man was speaking with Larry in hushed tones, and then he stabbed a finger into Larry's chest. "Who's that with Larry?"

Kylie looked up from the timer on her cell phone. "That's Nick Callahan. You should recognize him because you went to high school together."

"Of course, I thought he looked familiar."

Nick Callahan had been a high school senior when I was a sophomore, and no one in town would ever forget the seventy-five-yard Hail Mary pass he made to cinch the win at that year's homecoming game. He was practically a town hero. And he looked angry enough to shove Larry through a wall.

"What do you think they're arguing about?" I watched Larry lean in towards Nick and offer some harsh words of his own.

"Business stuff probably, I don't know." Kylie shrugged it off. "Nick owns the only other financial office in town. He was always fighting with Dad and Larry over clients."

I continued watching the men argue when an incoming call on my cell phone buzzed from the far end of the counter.

"Would you take this thing?" Kylie plopped the vibrating phone down in front of me. "It won't stop."

I scanned through several missed calls on my phone. All of them were from Grace. "It's work. I have to get this."

The urgency to return Grace's calls didn't match my desire to continue watching the argument between Nick and Larry unfold. "What if they get into a fight?"

"Well, then, I won't have to listen to you complain about Mom wearing white anymore. Two grown men throwing fists at a funeral would definitely surpass a fashion faux pas."

"I'm being serious." I found it difficult to keep a straight face when Kylie started to laugh.

At my frown, she covered her laugh with her hand. "Sorry. It's not funny."

I let out a small laugh. "Yes, it is."

It felt good to laugh and smile again, like sisters. Like old times. It reminded me of how much I'd missed my home and my family. The relationship I'd had with my father might have been strained, but things hadn't always been bad. I held many good memories of growing up in Harmony Falls and being together as a family. Then I'd wanted to go to college, and my parents had gotten divorced, and everything seemed to fall apart after that.

"Hello, girls." Vivian Abbott, my mother, breezed into the kitchen, the billowy white pantsuit she'd purchased for the funeral fluttering around her lithe and slender figure. With her silver-blonde hair cut into short layers and a minimal amount of makeup, some special magic kept her looking younger than her sixty years. "What a beautiful party. You two have done a great job."

"It's not a party." I bristled. "It's a funeral."

"A funeral should be a celebration of life." Vivian appropriated an open bottle of wine from the island counter and replenished her empty glass.

"Is that why you wore white?" I fought to keep my tone civil. It wouldn't do any good to start a fight with my mother and incite further rounds of gossip.

Vivian plunked the bottle down and stuck a hand on her slender hip. "Why does it bother you so much that I'm wearing white?"

"I told you, it seems disrespectful." I'd pleaded with my mother to go along with tradition and wear black, to no avail. The woman was determined to make a statement.

Vivian looked to her youngest daughter. "Is that what *you* think?"

"I'm not getting involved." Kylie pushed away from the counter, putting her hands up in surrender. "But I don't think Dad would care."

"That's exactly right." Vivian pounded her fist on the counter with enough verve to slosh some wine over the rim of her glass. "Your dad never cared about the things that were important to me. It's why I divorced him."

I cast Kylie a wary glance, afraid we were going to have to bring Vivian in from the edge. Alcohol and conversations about the divorce made a toxic combination for our mother. Kylie shrugged it off and checked the batch of scones she had baking in the oven. Our mother's flair for the dramatic didn't bother Kylie as much as it aggravated me.

"All the time we were married, I thought he never appreciated me enough," Vivian carried on, crossing one arm over her chest. "Then he went and left me a million dollars. Who does that?" She threw up her hand in exasperation.

"He must have wanted you to have it," I said.

I couldn't explain it any more than I could explain why I'd inherited his house and business.

"Everyone expected you girls to inherit all the money, or even Janice, but not *me*. The evil ex-wife." She paused to take a sip of her wine. "I loved your father at one time, but things between us had been over long before the divorce. The way I see it, I kept up his house and raised his children. I gave that man the best years of my life. I deserve to enjoy this money, and if Janice doesn't like it, she can go jump in a lake!"

Picking an inopportune time to wander into the kitchen, my best friend, Alex, stopped in her tracks, her long red hair making a perfect cascade over her shoulders. "I think I'll need more wine for this discussion."

"Nonsense, come and join us." Vivian waved her up to the counter. "You've always been like one of my girls." She wrapped a loving arm around Alex's shoulders.

Dressed in a skin-tight black dress and ridiculously high heels, Alex embodied a level of confidence I would never achieve. Where Alex was comfortable in sexy dresses and stiletto heels, happy to be in the spotlight, I preferred twin sets and flats with a book to hide behind. However unlikely it seemed, we'd been best friends since grade school when Alex's family moved to Harmony Falls. Not always the easiest community to fit in with, a boy at school had been giving Alex a hard time about being new, and then dared to make fun of her red hair. She'd walloped him over the head with a math textbook, Anne-Shirley-style, and that's when I knew we'd be kindred spirits.

Alex now ran a successful interior design business in town, she was tall and slender, with long waves of auburn hair, striking blue eyes, and she had the greatest laugh. Even though I lived in LA and Alex called Harmony Falls her home, our friendship continued as if no time or miles existed between us.

"Thanks for your help with the house," I told Alex, seizing the chance to steer the conversation away from my mother's dramatics. "Having you do the staging and take the pictures for the real estate listing will save us a lot of time."

"Don't thank me." Alex picked up another full plate of cookies to pass around to the funeral-goers. "I got to do what I love and help my best friend in the process. What could be better than that?" She plucked a chocolate chip cookie from the plate and took a dainty bite.

Kylie swooped in and placed two baking sheets of fresh scones on the counter. "Are you sure you don't want to keep the house?" she asked, tugging off her monogrammed oven mitts. "Dad did so much work fixing up the place. I almost hate to let it go."

"What am I going to do with a house in Minnesota?" While I loved the two-story Victorian home my father had so carefully restored through the years, all I had left of the place were bad memories, and I was tired of living with those. "Let's stick with our original plan and sell the house. I still have to figure out what to do with Dad's half of the investment business."

"I thought you were going to sell to Larry." Vivian reached for one of the fresh cinnamon and sugar scones Kylie was arranging on a platter. "He seems to think it's a done deal."

"I want to go over the paperwork he gave me this morning before I decide." I'd thought it would be an easy decision, sign on the line, but what if Kylie was right? What if my father leaving his business and his house to me was his way of apologizing? Should I at least consider the reasons he wanted me to have them?

"Your father was in business for a long time, and he had a lot of loyal clients." Alex finished the last bit of her cookie. "You'd be off to a great start if you wanted to move back and take it over. We'd be working across the street from each other. How cool would that be?"

"I would love that," I admitted, letting myself entertain the idea for the briefest moment. "But I want to be working on forensics cases and putting criminals behind bars, not signing off on forms and fielding phone calls. How many financial crimes happen in a town this small?"

"Why couldn't you branch out to surrounding areas?" Alex got that knowing twinkle in her eyes, and her mouth spread into a sly smile as she twirled the plate of cookies in her hands. "Last time I checked, you were a brilliant, successful career woman kicking ass in the big, bad city. Why not relocate? Get a fresh start?"

"I don't want to get stuck coddling a bunch of little old ladies inheriting life insurance policies." I slanted a careful glance at Vivian. "Sorry, Mother."

"Don't apologize," Vivian said. "You're right. You're so smart and so talented, if your clients are in the big city, then that's where you belong."

"You could always market to the Twin Cities," Alex parried playfully. "That's two big cities for the price of one, at only an hour's drive from here." With a wink of her eye, she swept out of the kitchen with the plate of cookies, swerving to miss a bunch of laughing children bounding down the stairs and chasing each other out the front door.

I tried to picture what a life in my hometown could look like, commuting to Minneapolis or St. Paul, but there was also Larry to consider. He owned the other half of the business, and in my dream, I'm running my own company, not sharing one with a partner. Then there was the money aspect to think about. I made six figures at my job. Granted, most of it went to rent for my apartment, my car payment, and gas, but what would I live on back here? No, I was going to find my dream back in LA, not in Harmony Falls. All I had to do was play nice with Brandon on the Jones case and get back in my boss's good graces. My focus back on track, I picked up my cell phone. "Excuse me for a minute; I'm going to return this call."

"I hope I'm not interrupting anything." A short, petite woman with a black netted hat inched her way into the kitchen like a jackal approaching leftover kill. "I wanted to say hello to the girls."

"Hello, Janice." Vivian managed to keep her tone civil. "I see you're looking as fabulous as ever."

"Vivian." Janice issued a curt nod. "I admire your courage."

Vivian turned to face her straight on. "Is that supposed to be an insult?"

The sparks flying between my mother and my father's girlfriend had me coming around to the other side of the counter. "How about some more wine?" I filled my mother's glass, but Janice didn't have one. "You know this is the wine Logan makes. He gave us three cases for the funeral. Wasn't that nice?"

"It certainly was." Vivian sipped from her glass. "He's going to be a wonderful son-in-law."

"Mother!" Kylie screeched loudly. "I wish you would stop telling people I'm getting engaged or married. Look how well that went for you and Dad."

I knew to keep my mouth shut on this topic. Kylie had always wanted to get married and have children, but our father had routinely insisted women can't have it all. They can't run a successful business and a successful family. They had to choose one or the other, so Kylie was under the belief she had to give up running her own business if she wanted to have a family. That was her issue to work out. I had my own to deal with.

"Our marriage wasn't all bad, until the end." Vivian looked at Janice. "One woman's junk is another woman's treasure, isn't that what they say? Do you know your dad wore sweater vests and dorky glasses when I met him? I pretty much saved that man's life by marrying him."

"Mom, that's enough," I tried to stop her tirade. "Let's not forget this is that man's funeral."

"You're absolutely right," Janice said, her mouth set in a thin line. "I'm leaving. No one wants to listen to her misery."

"Misery?" Vivian's eyes went wide. "Honey, I just inherited a million dollars. That man has never made me so happy."

"Well then, that makes one of us." Janice spun on her heel and stormed out of the kitchen.

"Nice going." I grabbed the wineglass from my mother's hand. "You've had enough to drink."

Vivian snatched her glass back. "I haven't had enough." She took a defiant drink. "Not nearly enough. It's not my fault Janice convinced your father to invest in another one of Larry's get-rich-quick schemes that left her with no inheritance."

Kylie continued arranging her platters of scones. "Is she really so upset about Dad not leaving her anything in the will?"

"She's furious," Vivian confirmed in a hushed voice. "She hasn't exactly kept it a secret. My book club group thinks your father just forgot, but I think it was his way of cutting her off after she spent so much of his money while he was alive."

"Does your book club also discuss books?" I wondered, knowing my mother's propensity for dishing the dirt on the latest scandals. Small-town gossip was her specialty.

"Yes, we discuss books," Vivian remarked snidely. "This month, we're reading a very steamy romance. I could loan you my copy. It might do you some good."

I barely had time to roll my eyes before my father's lawyer stepped into the kitchen, dressed in a suit and carrying a leather briefcase.

"Mr. Byron, thank you for coming by," Kylie said. "Would you like something to eat or drink?"

"No, thank you." He strode up to the counter and set his briefcase down, then popped the locks and flipped it open. "I've only come by to deliver something to Ms. Abbott." His bright eyes landed on me.

*Great, now what?* I wasn't sure I could take any more surprises.

He withdrew a simple white envelope and handed it to me.

"What's this?"

"That's for you to find out." Mr. Byron closed and locked his briefcase. "My instructions were to hand deliver this to you in the event of your father's death."

I saw Kylie's eyes go round as saucers. Mr. Byron took his briefcase and left as quickly as he'd appeared.

"Aren't you going to open it?" Kylie bounced with excitement.

More curious than worried, I tore open the envelope and dropped a brass key in the palm of my open hand.

"What's it for?" My mother peered over my hand to inspect the key more closely.

Along with the key, I found a business card for the local bank with a three-digit number written on the back. "It's for a safe deposit box."

# Chapter Three

The next morning, I entered the bank the moment they opened to access my father's safe deposit box. My name was listed on the signature card. All I had to do was show my key, present my driver's license for identification, and sign a form.

The soft-spoken woman working in the vault led me through rows of secured boxes, all of them holding their own secrets. I'd spent a sleepless night wondering what was so important my father had to hide it away. And why he wanted me to be the one who unlocked his secret. I didn't know my father well enough anymore to have the first clue what might be waiting for me.

The woman stopped at an end row of locked boxes and put her key in the lock for box 555. A high-pitched ringing sounded off in my ear. The numbers were already talking. Asking me to take notice and pay attention. It was common for me to see patterns and sequences in the numbers, most notably triple-digit numbers. I didn't always know what they were trying to tell me, but I had devised my own system for deciphering the messages. Number 5 was the number of change.

I slid my key into the adjacent lock, and in seconds, the woman had retrieved the box. She led me to a private cubicle and left me alone to access the contents. My hands hovered over the metal lid of the box. It was truth time. Kylie thought our father was hiding a load of cash or secret stock certificates. My mother believed he had an antique gun collection. Out of left field, Alex had suggested he might be hiding evidence of a long-lost love child or some clandestine affair. Whatever I found would change my life in some way, according to the numbers.

I took a deep breath, then threw back the lid. Stored in the box were a laptop computer and a business card. The card had an official government seal and belonged to an Agent, Mason West, working with the U.S. Treasury Department in the Financial Crimes Enforcement Network. That was a bit intense. A FinCEN agent would only investigate major crimes like money laundering schemes and bank fraud. Why did my father have a Treasury agent's business card? The hair on my arms stood up as little bumps of gooseflesh broke out on the surface of my skin. Whatever the reason, it couldn't be good. I turned the card over and found something written on the back in all capital letters. PHOENIX.

I felt like I'd entered the plot of some high-stakes espionage novel. Had my father been in some kind of trouble? My gaze darted to the laptop computer. I'd bet the answers were all there. After agonizing over what could be in this box, I wasn't leaving until I found out why my father had gone to such great lengths to keep it a secret. I pulled the metal folding chair out from under the table and looked for an outlet to plug in the computer. If I'd known I'd be crawling around on a cold, linoleum floor, I wouldn't have worn a skirt and heels, but I managed just fine and got the computer plugged in, then sat in the chair and turned it on.

The login screen required a password. On a wild hunch, I typed in PHOENIX and waited for the home screen to load. A single file folder titled Real Estate Group popped up in the top left corner of the screen. I heard a ringing noise in my left ear as my gift stirred to life. The numbers were starting to talk. There was something here I needed to see, and I clicked on the file to open the contents. At first glance, the files resembled the basic documents required to open an investment account. There were ninety accounts in total. The accompanying marketing materials promoted a hedge fund investing in foreclosed real estate, which would later be resold for a profit and huge returns paid back to the group of investors.

It sounded easy enough, but the ringing in my ear grew louder, and I knew the numbers had more to tell me. I clicked open one of the client files and found the account paperwork and a copy of the check written for the initial investment, but nothing else. No performance statements or follow-up documents to prove the investment had been made or that the hedge fund even existed.

Something didn't add up. There should be more to the file, but there wasn't. I had to look beyond the numbers if I wanted to find the discrepancy. The evidence was there, and if I listened, the numbers would tell me where to find it. I opened a few more files and scrolled through the documents. They were all exactly the same. Paperwork and checks. And then I caught it. All of the checks had been made payable to Harmony Wealth Partners, my father's business.

The ringing in my ear wasn't a fluke; it wasn't imagined. My gift for numbers was real. I didn't know why the numbers had chosen to speak to me, but I'd learned to trust them. Numbers didn't lie. They were reliable. Predictable.

I searched through the rest of the files to confirm what I'd found. Every single client check had been written to Harmony Wealth Partners. To an untrained eye, it might not seem out of place. Even I'd missed it at first.

The problem? Investment checks were never paid directly to the advisor's personal business. Commingling funds and all that jazz. Checks had to be payable to the bank managing the investment. And with no additional paperwork to confirm the money had been invested, I had to wonder where it had ended up. If it had been a simple mistake, and the funds had been deposited with Harmony Wealth Partners and then forwarded to the investment company, the business might get by with a warning. But anything else, any signs of fraud or misdirection, and the business could face hefty monetary fines. The advisors could be banned from ever working in the securities industry again, or even serve jail time. In federal prison. I know because I'd sent a few crooks there myself.

What kind of business had I inherited? I busted these types of people. I didn't become one of them. All this time I'd doubted whether I had the integrity to live up to my father's expectations. Now I was searching through his files for possible fraud. Why would he leave me this information? Why not give it all the to the FinCEN agent? I was nothing but a disappointment to my father.

It didn't make any sense. By leaving me this evidence, he had to know I'd discover the crime, and what I would be compelled to do once I did. Unless he'd wanted me to find the evidence. Had he been directly involved in the crime, or did he expect me to go after Larry?

The answer fluttered in my gut like anxious energy. The numbers didn't like Larry any more than I did, and it wouldn't surprise me to find out he was a crook. People thought it was easy to get away with crimes in a small town. Lots of times they did. Perhaps there was a reason, aside from guilt, that I'd been compelled to come home.

I ran my fingers through the length of my hair and tied it up in a loose bun as I contemplated my next move. Larry was expecting me at the office so I could sign over my share of the business. If I did that, I'd lose access to any evidence I might find at the office and in the files, but I could also become an unwilling accessory to a crime. On the table next to the laptop, I looked at Agent Mason West's card again. Was it possible he knew something? Had my father been actively working with the Feds? Maybe they'd found him out and forced him to turn evidence for a plea deal. I saw it happen all the time.

Was my father nothing more than a small-town crook?

Another thought began to form in my mind. One I didn't want to entertain, but knew I had to. My father had stashed away evidence of a possible crime. What if his death wasn't due to a bad heart? What if someone murdered him to avoid getting caught? I had no idea how much money was at stake. Thousands? Millions? Enough to kill someone over? It might sound crazy, especially in cozy little Harmony Falls, a town where nothing ever happened, but it wasn't impossible.

My whole world shifted, and my next step suddenly became very clear. I'd never earned my father's approval in life, though not for a lack of trying. If he'd been in trouble for what he'd done, or what he'd known, leaving behind evidence with the hope I'd investigate, then maybe he was trying to make amends for the past. Whatever the reason, he'd put his faith in me, and I had to finish what he'd started.

That's where things got tricky. If I left the bank to go sign away my share of the business to Larry, I'd have no way to investigate further. Of course, I could turn it all over to the authorities and let them handle it—that was the smart thing to do—but now that I was involved, I wanted to get to the truth. It was a professional habit to chase the money and then chase the crime underneath the money. It's how I was wired. I turned everything into numbers.

As confrontation wasn't my strong suit, I'd rather let the authorities handle it than back out of my deal with Larry. I also had no proof any crime had been committed. A few checks written to the business weren't worth getting excited over if the money had been invested and everything was kosher. My father could have died of a bad heart. He'd been taking meds for years. Then there was my job in LA. They were expecting me to return tomorrow. If I wanted to investigate, I'd have to stay in Harmony Falls, and my boss would not be pleased.

The easy thing to do would be to meet with Larry, sign over my share of the business, and get back to my job. But then Larry would have full control of the office and sole access to all of the records and files, making it easy for him to bury any evidence. And I just couldn't let him get away with that. What could it hurt to ask to see the financial records before I signed his contract? If I knew the money had gone where it was supposed to, I could go back to LA with a clear conscience. Not knowing would drive me crazy.

It was time to get another opinion. I checked my watch. Half past nine. I told Larry I'd be in first thing, and I didn't want to delay, which meant I had to come up with a plan before I got to the office. I powered down the laptop and tucked it into my shoulder bag, along with the agent's business card, then left the bank and headed down Main Street.

The crisp morning chill had worn off and the temperature was somewhere in the sixties, the breeze light, and I was comfortable in only a short-sleeved blouse and a skirt. Foot traffic on the sidewalk was heavy as I made my way into the heart of the downtown business district. The closer I got to my destination, the heavier the weight in my gut settled in, and I glanced back over my shoulder, having the strangest feeling someone was watching

31

me. Not in a friendly way, either. More like a hunter-stalking-its-prey-and-waiting-for-the-right-time-to-pounce kind of way.

I scurried past local businesses, many of which had propped their doors open to welcome the beautiful day inside. Storefront windows were decorated with colorful fall leaves and autumnal displays of pumpkins, mums, and Indian corn. The outdoor café tables in front of the Central Park coffee shop were occupied with people enjoying their drinks and baked treats, soaking up the morning sunshine. Fall in Minnesota, though brief, was my favorite time of year.

The next store entrance was Alex's design studio, and I ducked through the door, which stood propped open by an antique metal umbrella stand.

Inside Monroe Design Studio, the open floor plan was arranged as a showroom displaying a staged kitchen and dining room area, along with a living room, a bedroom, and a children's bedroom. Each room had been artfully staged in Alex's signature design style, a perfect blend of modern and vintage. I loved tagging along on shopping trips with Alex to source items for her business, browsing the air-conditioned interiors of trendy furniture stores, and hunting through boxes at estate sales and flea markets until Alex's van overflowed with the perfect finds to fill the mock rooms of her studio.

Along with being meticulously arranged, the studio was also a celebration of fall, giving a generous nod to the season with rusts and golds bursting forth from throw pillows, blankets, rugs, and intricate floral arrangements in pottery vases or woven baskets. Square tables were set with dinnerware, linens, crystal glasses, and gourds of all shapes and sizes. It was an artful way to showcase all the accessories available in the studio while also demonstrating Alex's skill for design down to the last detail. The studio even smelled like fall, and I didn't have to see the spiced pumpkin candle burning off in the distance in order to know it was there.

Back at the sales counter, Alex handed off a handled white bag to a lady while thanking her for stopping in. I scrambled up to the counter, nodding a rushed yet polite greeting at the customer as she left.

As soon as Alex saw me, her eyes lit with excitement, and she asked, "What did you find in the safe deposit box?"

I figured it was best not to mince words with time ticking by. "It appeared my father might have been working with the Feds to bust Larry for investment fraud, and he might have been murdered to cover it up. That's one theory anyway."

Alex's smile faded.

"How's that for a surprise?" I dropped my shoulder bag on the sales counter and collapsed over it, groaning in dramatic fashion. "What am I going to do?"

"Oh, dear." Alex moved the jar with a burning candle off to the side to avoid catching the ends of my hair on fire. "I should've known it would be something like this. Mercury is in retrograde for another week."

I lifted my head and gave her a look. "That has nothing to do with anything."

"You can turn up your nose at astrology all you want, but considering we're all sitting on a planet spinning through space, trying to figure out how to survive the ride, it's only logical to conclude the movements of the stars and planets not only affect us, but might offer up some help. Remember that time in high school when Venus and Mars clashed in your chart and the next day Tommy Wilson dumped you?"

Okay, maybe she had a point. "Next, you'll be telling me it's a Full Moon."

Alex's mouth tilted up in a sly smile. "That was yesterday."

I dropped my head into my hands with another groan. "I'm supposed to be meeting Larry to sign the paperwork, but if I do, I'll lose access to all the files. If I don't sell, I might become an accessory to a crime or, worse yet, partners, with a murderer." I stepped away from the counter and paced back and forth. "I'm sorta freaking out a little bit."

"What surprises you more?" Alex asked. "That Larry Stone is a no-good crook, or that something like this could happen in Harmony Falls?"

I stopped my pacing. "This isn't what I expected to find in that box."

"What else was in there?"

I reached into my bag and pulled out the agent's card, smacking it down on the counter in front of her. "This."

Alex picked up the card and studied it closely. "This guy sounds interesting." She set the card down and pulled on a cardigan sweater over her navy sheath dress. "I'm thinking pocket protector, thick glasses, bad haircut. He probably speaks fluent nerd. The two of you would probably hit it off great."

"He might be able to help me," I said. "Although the Feds aren't prone to sharing information. The card was in there for a reason."

"Then maybe you should call him." Alex locked the cash register drawer and put the key in a jar behind the counter.

"But what if my dad is guilty, and he made some kind of deal to rat out Larry and save himself?"

"Then don't call him."

I inhaled a deep, cleansing breath, then let it out and gave myself a quick pep talk. "I can figure this out. I know I can. I do it all the time in LA."

It wasn't helping.

"How many forensic accounting cases have you lost?" Alex wondered.

"None." I knew that didn't mean anything. It was a statistical probability I would have to lose a case at some point. I just didn't want it to be this one. This one mattered. It was personal. "What am I going to do?"

"What do the numbers say?"

Alex was the only person who knew about my gift. We'd been trusting each other with our secrets ever since we were eight-years-old. "They say strange things are afoot at the Circle K." I referenced our favorite quote from one of the eighties movies we loved with Bill, Ted, and an adventure through time.

"Do you want to know what I think?" Alex leaned her hip against the counter and folded her arms over her chest.

"Yes!" I practically shouted. "It's why I rushed over here, and now you're involved, so you have to help me. It's part of the best friend code."

"I think this is the perfect opportunity for you to take over your dad's share of the business. It's not like you don't know what you're doing when it comes to money and investments, and you have all the licenses you'd need to do it."

"That's not an option." I shook my head in disagreement. "I need to get back to LA before I lose my new office, my career, and my boyfriend."

"You don't really have to take the business over," Alex elaborated. "Just let Larry think you are to buy yourself some more time. He'll have to draw up new paperwork with the lawyers, and that should give you at least another day or two to snoop around and see if you can find the evidence you need."

"I'm not sure I want to be in the same office with someone who might have killed my father. Shouldn't I go to the cops?"

"With what? A crazy story and a laptop?" Alex looked doubtful. "You need proof if you want them to take you seriously."

I leveled a stare at Alex. "Do you think it's possible my father could have been murdered?"

Alex blinked and started to say something, then stopped.

"What is it?"

"I wish I could tell you it's impossible," she said. "I don't know what to think anymore. If Larry has been defrauding his clients, he seems like the kind of guy who would do anything to keep it a secret."

"So, in the meantime, I should start going to the office like I own the place and get my hands on some hard evidence."

"Yeah." Alex's face lit up. "That's exactly what you're going to do."

"You've got that look," I said. "I don't like when you get that look. It means I'm going to get in trouble."

"I need my mid-morning latte." Alex picked up her purse and drew the strap over her shoulder, then came around the counter and laced her arm through mine. "Let's get to work on your plan."

"I don't have one."

"Of course you do," she said, scooping up her set of keys from the counter. "You're going to nail the bastard." She leaned down and blew out the candle.

I was grateful Alex drove us to the office because my high heels had become almost unbearable. I wasn't used to covering so much ground in them and didn't want to walk two more steps, let alone two more blocks. We climbed out of Alex's minivan and walked up to the front door of Harmony Wealth

Partners. Alex gulped from her cup of takeaway coffee as she waited behind me.

"Are you sure this is going to work?" I asked, hesitating at the office door.

Alex had given me a quick rundown of our plan on the drive over, but I didn't think it would be so easy to walk into my father's office and start acting like I owned the place. Even though, technically, I did.

Alex put a hand on my shoulder and turned me so we faced each other. "You're going to tell Larry you've changed your mind about selling your share."

I nodded. "Changed my mind."

"And you want to fix the office up a bit to attract more clients," Alex coached.

"Because you know a guy."

"I'm an interior designer, and I have a guy to paint the lobby." Alex smiled to herself. "Javier will be perfect. He loves power tools and Latin radio. If Larry can concentrate in the midst of all that chaos, I'll be impressed."

"The noise will drive Larry crazy; he'll leave the office, and I can snoop for clues."

Alex smiled proudly. "It's as simple as that."

"Yeah, simple." I readied myself to go inside and hoped the guilt I felt wasn't evident on my face.

"You've got this." Alex urged me on with a thumbs up.

Resolved, I grabbed the handle on the door to open it. "It's locked."

"How can it be locked?" Alex peered through the front window. "It's after ten, and the office hours say nine to five."

I tried the door again, but it didn't budge. "It's definitely locked."

"Use your key."

"I can't just go in there."

"Sure you can," Alex insisted. "You own half the place."

I rifled through my bag to find my father's set of keys and went through them until I found the one for the office. I was worried Larry might have changed the locks already, but the key turned the lock and opened the door.

When we stepped into the dark office, the mess didn't immediately register.

I hadn't been inside my father's old office since the last day I'd worked there, over ten years ago, and not much had changed. A ratty pair of industrial chairs and a water cooler were the only items to fill the tiny lobby. The paint had peeled away from most of the gray walls and a wooden sign with the business name provided the only decor. Once I located the light switch panel on the wall, I flipped on all three switches. Bright light illuminated the office and the pieces of paper strewn all over the floor. "Oh my God, look at this mess. What happened?"

The worn brown carpet was hardly visible under the cover of thousands of papers and turned-out file folders.

"Are these all the files?" I crouched down to scoop up one of the papers and couldn't make sense of it. The mess would take days to clean up and sort through.

"Do you think Larry did this?" Alex stared at the chaos in disbelief.

"I don't know." I dropped the sheet of paper and rose from the floor, my gaze roaming over the paper-covered office. Deep in my gut, I got an ominous feeling, a warning that something was wrong. Someone didn't just toss files like this unless they wanted to send a clear message.

"Do you want some help cleaning it up?" Alex went down on one knee and started gathering some of the papers.

"What's that?" I pointed to the doorway of the first office. A flicker of apprehension coursed through me. We weren't alone.

"What's what?" Alex rose to her feet and stood right behind me. "I don't see anything."

"It's right there." I pointed my finger again.

Alex peered over my shoulder and her harsh intake of breath told me she saw it too. "Oh no, that is not good. That is so not good."

"What do we do?" I didn't want to panic, but it wasn't every day I came upon a pair of shiny shoes attached to perfectly creased pant legs, lying in a doorway.

"Go over and check on him." Alex gave me a not-so-gentle nudge.

"I'm not going over there." I shook my head, digging in my heels.

"He's your partner."

"How do you know it's Larry?" I asked, though I knew the chance of some other man lying on the floor, unmoving, was highly unlikely. Besides, who else had keys to the office?

"You're the one who wanted to come in here like you own the place."

I shot Alex an annoyed glance over my shoulder. "This was your plan."

"I warned you. Two words. Mercury. Retrograde."

I rolled my eyes, then called out to the motionless man on the floor. "Larry?"

"He's not taking a cat nap," Alex chided. "You have to check his pulse."

"Check his pulse?" My eyes went wide. "Check it for what?"

"To see if he's dead, duh." Alex took a large gulp of her coffee. "I should have gotten a triple."

Steeling my nerves, I threw back my shoulders and lifted my chin. I could do this. I could go over and see if Larry was *dead*.

This was my office for the moment, my business, and Larry was my partner. Perhaps I was about to learn he had some strange quirks, like taking morning naps on the floor. Or maybe this was all my fault. What if he'd keeled over from a heart attack? He knew what I did for a living. Had he panicked, afraid I might have found out what he'd done? Had it driven him mad enough to dump his files all over the office and commit suicide rather than go to prison?

"You're coming with me." I grabbed Alex's free hand, and the two of us crept across the sea of scattered papers over to Larry's office. Slowly, the rest of the body came into view. It was Larry, alright. And there was no need to check his pulse. A large red blotch spread across his chest, staining his white shirt a dark crimson, and his eyes were open and unblinking.

"Oh. Holy. Jesus." Alex dropped her coffee, the light brown liquid spraying across the papers strewn at our feet. "He's... he's..."

"Dead?" I supplied the word.

Behind me, Alex slowly shook her head. Her face had gone pale white. I wasn't feeling so hot myself, and a cold knot formed in my stomach. Larry Stone wasn't just dead. He'd been murdered.

# Chapter Four

"What's going on in here?" A voice crept up behind us. Alex screamed and practically jumped out of her skin, giving me an unnecessary fright. I'd had enough of those for the day. It was only Hannah who'd come into the office without making a sound.

"Don't sneak up on people like that." Alex placed a hand over her heart.

Dressed in a pink skirt and blouse, complete with matching high heels, Hannah waited with a hand resting on her hip. "Why are these papers all over the floor?"

"I think we need to call the police," I concluded, figuring the authorities would know best what to do with a dead body. "Nobody touch anything."

"Is that Larry?" Hannah's eyes filled with shock as she saw her boss lying dead on the floor of his office. "Is he hurt? Why isn't he moving?"

"Why don't you go call the police?" I placed both of my hands on Hannah's shoulders and tried to gently turn her away from the horrific sight. "Can you do that?"

Larry's young secretary nodded her head vehemently, though her eyes weren't focusing. She hovered on the verge of tears as she stared at Larry's lifeless body.

"Go on, Hannah. You don't need to see this." I urged her toward her desk in the front of the office.

Alex leaned against the wall in the hallway and cast her gaze up at the ceiling, avoiding the awful sight Larry made. "Someone killed him, didn't they?"

"I don't think Larry shot himself in the chest." I was overcome with the sudden urge to get far away from the body while at the same time feeling a need to watch over it until the police arrived. We were now standing in the middle of a crime scene. "The question is, what were they looking for?"

Ever since I'd retrieved the laptop from my father's safe deposit box, the idea that he'd been killed haunted me. It felt like someone was watching me, and now Larry had been murdered. I didn't want to overreact, but something was rotten in Harmony Falls.

On the phone at her desk, Hannah connected with the police and relayed the morbid details of our situation. "My boss is dead. I don't know. I can't do that. Please, just send help." She hung up the phone and swayed in her chair, a lost, haunted look on her face.

"Are you supposed to hang up on them like that?" Alex asked.

"I don't remember." Hannah brushed an errant blonde lock out of her face.

"What did they ask you to do?" I wondered, curious about the one-sided phone conversation.

"They wanted me to check for a pulse. I'm not touching a dead body. There's so much blood." She sobbed, the tears streaking down her face.

"It's going to be okay." I went over to her and knelt beside her chair. Not sure how to comfort her, I took one of her hands and held on to it. "I didn't want to do it either. We can let the police handle things when they get here."

Hannah nodded, crying silently to herself, then her head snapped up and she looked past me to Alex. "This is all your fault! None of this would have happened if you'd minded your own business."

"What's she talking about?" I rose and waited for an answer from Alex.

"How would I know?" Alex narrowed her eyes at Hannah. "Neither one of us had anything to do with this mess."

I noticed movement outside the lobby window. Three black and whites slid up to the front curb, their lights flashing but without the noise of sirens. Car doors slammed, and a small army of men in light blue shirts with brass badges and heavy utility belts charged for the office entrance.

The next part of the morning passed in a blur. As more authorities arrived at the scene and the police stretched lengths of yellow tape to section things off, they took the three of us into my father's old office and had us answer questions about who found the body, what time, and how we all knew the victim. Larry was no longer Larry; he was *the victim*. We all gave the police our full names and contact information in case they needed to ask any more questions later. Then, we were informed we would have to go down to the station and give formal statements.

Damon arrived at the office next, blowing into the front lobby like a force-four hurricane. "Where's my uncle?" he shouted. "I want to know what happened! Nick Callahan is responsible for this! I want him arrested!"

I couldn't blame Damon for being upset, and I had seen Nick and Larry arguing at my father's funeral. I wished I knew what their conversation had been about. What would make a person angry enough to resort to murder?

Things in the lobby quieted down, and I assumed the police were talking to Damon in hushed tones in an attempt to calm him. Another officer came into the office where we were waiting next. He had the classic cop stance, full of confidence and authority, as he stood in the doorway, his hand low on his hip.

"Good morning, ladies," he said in a firm but kind voice. "I'm Detective Jake Matthews with the Harmony Falls Police Department." He took a quick assessment of each of us, his gaze landing on me.

I was surprised to be met with the warmest pair of light brown eyes I'd ever seen. It wasn't just the color, but the kindness and openness behind them. They pulled me right in, made me feel like I could tell him anything.

"Who does the white van parked out front belong to?" he asked.

"That's my car," Alex said.

"We need to search the vehicle, ma'am."

Alex shot a nervous glance at me and then looked back to the detective. "Why do you need to search my van?"

"It's part of a murder scene."

All the color drained from her face. "Go ahead. The keys are in it."

After Matthews had gone, Alex fell into the office chair and dropped her head down on the desk. "Why do they want to look in my van? There's nothing in it but dried flower arrangements I was going to take to the chamber office."

"Don't worry." I slipped into the chair in front of the desk while Hannah remained squeezed in the far corner, streaks of mascara running down her wet cheeks. "It's probably just procedure."

"They didn't ask to search Hannah's car." Alex lifted her head, her face clouded with uneasiness. "Why do they only want to search mine?"

Her question was answered a few short minutes later when Detective Matthews returned with two officers flanked behind him.

"Ms. Monroe." He looked directly at Alex, his expression serious. "Where were you between the hours of ten and two last night?"

Her mouth dropped open, then she answered, "At home, in bed, asleep."

"Can anyone vouch for that?"

Alex's gaze darted around the room in frustration.

"Where are you going with this, Detective?" I jumped up in defense of my friend. He was treating Alex like she'd been the one to kill Larry Stone.

"What is your name?" He shot me a stern glance, but his eyes had little crinkles at the corners, like maybe he smiled a lot. Just not at work.

Overall, Matthews had a wholesome, hometown appearance. His face was freshly shaven, and he had short, dark hair, cut clean on the sides but longer on the top. He looked like he would be as comfortable manning a barbeque as he was a crime scene.

"I'm Kate Abbott," I said, although I suspected he already knew the answers to the questions before he asked them.

He returned his focus to Alex. "Ms. Monroe, how well did you know Larry Stone?"

"I didn't know him."

"Are you sure about that?" Matthews raised a doubtful brow.

"Wait a minute," I interrupted again. "Do you think she killed Larry?"

"Anything's possible at this point."

"What motive could she possibly have?" I argued. "Why would she want to kill Larry?"

"That's what I intend to find out. Down at the station."

Alex's lovely face blanched with shock at his statement. "Am I under arrest?"

"Not yet, but your cooperation would be much appreciated."

Alex implored me with panic-filled eyes. "This is insane. I didn't do anything. I didn't kill anybody."

"I know you didn't." My mind scrambled wildly for a way to help my friend. Murder was way out of my league.

Matthews held his palm open to the officer flanked on his right. The officer placed a plastic bag in his hand, and he held the clear bag aloft for all of us to see the black pistol inside. "Do you have a permit for this weapon?"

Hannah gasped from her corner of the office and shot me a dirty look. Did she somehow think this was my fault? A pretty, young blonde with lots of potential, Hannah looked visibly upset over Larry's death, truly mourning his loss. I couldn't figure out for one moment why. No matter what Larry had done, he didn't deserve to die, but I wasn't going to lose sleep over his death either. Did Hannah maybe have feelings for her boss that extended beyond a professional relationship?

That was a visual image I was never going to get rid of.

"That's not mine," Alex declared, rising to her feet.

"I can vouch for that," I added. "Alex hates guns and violence. She'd never learn to shoot a gun."

"Then how did it come to be in the backseat of her car?" Matthews asked, a tic working along his smooth jaw. "Two shots have been fired. My guess is this is the gun that killed Larry Stone."

Hannah burst into another quiet round of sobs.

"You have the wrong person," I informed him, infusing my voice with conviction. "Why would she return to the scene of the crime with the murder weapon conveniently stowed in the back of her van? The real killer would have gotten rid of it."

"We're going to hold her on suspicion of murder."

"This is absurd!" I walked up to the detective. "Alex couldn't have killed anyone. I'm sure one of her neighbors could verify she was home last night, and she's been with me this morning."

"All morning?" The detective asked.

"Well, no, but—" I was terrible at lying. Always had been.

"Then until someone who was with Ms. Monroe comes forward to provide an alibi, or we get an explanation for the gun we found in the backseat of her van, we have enough evidence to take her in."

The two uniformed officers stepped forward and one asked Alex to go with them. She complied with the order and gave a final, helpless look to me as they led her out of the room.

"I think we have everything we need," Matthews said. "I'm sure we'll have more questions for you later."

Hannah seized the opportunity to rush out of the office in a flurry of tears, but as I moved to follow, Matthews stepped further into the room and blocked the doorway. Obviously, he had more questions.

"Do you know if Ms. Monroe had any reason to dislike Larry Stone?"

"I think the question you should be asking is did anyone in town have a reason to like him," I said. "I can't say I'll miss him. He was kind of a jerk. Aren't you going to test her hands for gunshot residue?"

"We have to do that back at the station."

"What else do you have connecting her to the crime?"

He shifted his weight to one foot. "For now, just the murder weapon."

"Are there any witnesses?" I pressed on. "What made you decide to search her van? What other proof do you have?"

Matthews rubbed a hand over his cheek, his warm eyes sparkling with amusement. "I'm the one asking the questions here, ma'am."

"Then ask me the right questions." I blew out an exasperated breath. "Like who else might have wanted Larry Stone dead?"

I could think of a few people. Nick Callahan was top of that list.

He reached into the breast pocket of his blue shirt and drew out a notepad with a faded leather cover. He flipped through several pages until he found the right one. "What do you know about his nephew, Damon Stone?"

"Nothing," I said. "My father's funeral was the first time I'd ever met him."

"So, you weren't aware that Damon was Larry's sole heir? Or that he would inherit the business upon Larry's death?"

It appeared Damon had a very good motive to kill his uncle. Getting his hands on the business. Or a load of pilfered money. I wondered if Damon was in on Larry's scheme. Did he get greedy and kill his uncle in order to get his hands on all of the money? What would he do if I refused to sell my share? Would he kill me, too?

I knew I should tell the detective about what I'd discovered that morning, but everything was happening so fast, I couldn't make sense of it all. For all I knew, Larry's murder could have nothing to do with the business. "I had no way of knowing Larry's personal affairs, but Damon didn't strike me as a killer when I met him."

"They never do." Matthews jotted something down on his notepad. "Unless you have any questions for me, I think we're done here."

This was my chance to tell him everything. But what would he do with a laptop and a crazy story? All I had were maybes and possibilities, and those wouldn't get Alex off the hook for murder. If I wanted to help my friend, I needed to follow the money and find some evidence. It's what I did best.

Matthews tucked his notepad and pen back into his shirt pocket. He handed me his card next. "If you think of anything else we should know, or if any new information comes up, you can call me anytime."

I took his card and slid it into the front pocket of my skirt. "Alex isn't a killer." I gave him a defiant stare. "Someone else murdered Larry Stone."

"That's what I intend to find out." He lingered for a brief moment, his smile almost apologetic. "You have yourself a nice day, ma'am." After a concise nod of his head, the detective turned and strode out of the room.

Back out in the lobby, the handsome and mysterious Damon Stone spoke with an officer who scribbled furious notes to keep up. Dressed casually in jeans and a black T-shirt, the tight cotton hugging the well-defined muscles of his biceps and chest, my newest partner brought an impressive body of work with him, but I couldn't let his attractiveness sway my suspicions.

When Damon spotted me emerging from the office, he made his way through the flurry of activity and right over to me. "I heard you found the body."

My God, I had. I'd found the body. I nodded, numb with the shock seeping into my veins. Tears sprang to my eyes. I wanted all of this to be a bad dream. Larry might have been a jerk, but had he deserved to die? How long had he been dead on the floor before we stumbled upon him?

"Thank you for calling the police right away," Damon said. "I'm hoping they can find some evidence on Nick Callahan. He was always jealous of my uncle's client base and constantly pressured him to sell the business. I know he's responsible for this." He spoke fast, like maybe he'd had too much caffeine. Which would be fitting for the morning we were all trying to get through. I could use a triple mocha latte about now.

"I'm very sorry for your loss." I offered the same condolence I'd received yesterday at my father's funeral. "But how can you be sure Nick Callahan killed your uncle?"

"His actions toward my uncle haven't exactly been friendly. He's the obvious suspect. Even the police say so."

"I didn't get that impression from the detective."

"It had to be him," Damon insisted, the earlier agitation returning to his voice. "He's the only one who stands to benefit from my uncle's death."

I didn't hide my surprise. "Really? The only one?"

I wasn't going to point out the obvious to him.

"They want us all to go down to the station and give our statements," he said. "My car is parked out back. Would you like to ride together? I don't blame you for not feeling safe around here with all that's happened, and understand if you don't want to be alone. There's safety in numbers right now."

Safety happened to be the first thing on my mind where he was concerned. If Damon had keys to the office, he could have easily snuck in last night, shot his uncle, and locked up afterwards. A killer could be lurking behind that charming smile, and I felt it would be wise to keep my guard up. "Thank you. I appreciate the offer, but I have some other things I need to take care of this morning." I edged past him and stepped around the photographer shooting photos of the crime scene to make my way out the front door.

What exactly was Damon Stone doing in Harmony Falls?

To my mind, that was as much a puzzle as Larry shot to death in his office. Maybe he hadn't seen his uncle in quite some time and had come to pay a long overdue visit. Maybe he had thought to help with the business now that my father was gone. Or maybe he was after a fortune.

I found it rather suspicious that a bizarre and gruesome murder had occurred at my father's place of business, just when a mysterious nephew had turned up to inherit it.

The numbers might find that suspicious, too.

# Chapter Five

It would have been impossible for me to head down to the police station to give my statement without first stopping by my sister's cake shop. Not only did I need to rest my aching feet, I knew Kylie and my mother would be going out of their minds trying to speculate what disaster had befallen the investment office and what exactly I'd found in the safe deposit box.

Kylie opened her shop, A Piece of Cake, at nine o'clock every morning except for Sundays. On her drive through the downtown business district along Main Street, she passed shops, restaurants, and office spaces, where flowerpots overflowing with vibrant blooms hung from the light posts lining both sides of the street. Central Park stood in the heart of town, its green and white gazebo decorated for fall with orange pumpkins, colorful gourds, and golden bales of hay.

A Piece of Cake was located on the last block south of the park. When Kylie had driven by the Harmony Wealth Partners office that morning, past flashing lights from police cars, an ambulance, and a fire and rescue truck, she'd called me, and when I didn't answer, she'd made a panicked call to her boyfriend, Logan, the firefighter and winemaker extraordinaire. He couldn't talk since he'd been called to the scene, so she finally called our mother, who naturally rushed right over.

When I walked into the cake shop close to lunch, I found my mother and sister in the kitchen. They heaved great sighs of relief, grateful nothing bad had happened to me, and then attacked me with a barrage of questions regarding the latest scandal in Harmony Falls. The gossip was flying, so

I gave them the quick and ugly—and honest—version of what happened, including what I'd found in the safe deposit box that morning.

"Murder?" Vivian said from her perch on one of the kitchen stools. Her manicured hand flew to her mouth, her face full of shock and outrage. "We've had our share of vandals and robberies and that stabbing at the local bar last year, but there hasn't been a murder in Harmony Falls as long as I've been alive. It's positively dreadful knowing someone in this town is capable of such a terrible thing. What's next? One of those methamphetamine labs?"

"There's no need to overreact. I don't think it was a random killing." I kicked off my heels and sank onto one of the kitchen stools at the stainless steel work table. "I think Larry was a specific target. Maybe someone found out he was stealing money. Like one of his clients."

Kylie stood at the end of the table, rendered speechless, a dusting of flour on the end of her petite nose and a cake baking in the industrial oven behind her. "Someone was murdered in Harmony Falls. The words don't even sound right. I'm going to have to start locking my doors."

"I still can't believe it," I said. "And I'm the one who found Larry with two bullet holes in his chest."

"How awful," Vivian said. "To be in that office all morning with a dead body right down the hall. I don't know how you managed it."

"What's awful is that someone was killed." My stomach rumbled with hunger as the sweet smell of the baking cake filled the kitchen, but the thought of eating didn't appeal to me when I could still picture Larry, dead and bloody, on the floor of his office.

"How did the gun get in the back of Alex's van?" Kylie asked. "Do you think the killer had some reason to frame her for Larry's murder?"

"I have no idea." I shook my head, appreciating another scenario to consider, but at the same time, I felt overwhelmed by the scope of possibilities. "I just know Alex isn't a killer. We're talking about someone who catches spiders in the house and lets them go outside, and she cries when she sees a dead animal on the side of the road. You should see her try to run the deer hunters into the ditch during hunting season. She couldn't kill anything."

"I always thought Harmony Falls was a safe town," Kylie said. "It's small and boring. People are genuinely happy. Things like this don't happen here."

"It doesn't matter how big or small the town," I said. "People are people, and they get greedy or set on revenge whether the population is ten or ten thousand."

Harmony Falls wasn't the same town I'd left all those years ago. Times had changed, and my home was no different. While most people who lived here were happy and content, someone among them harbored enough darkness inside their soul to pull the trigger and end a man's life.

"Our little town will never be the same after this." Vivian reached for her coffee mug, the saying *"I'm only here for the cake"* across the front.

"Do you really think Larry was stealing money?" Kylie looked distraught over the idea.

"If what I found in the safe deposit box means anything, his murder only makes it more believable. There could be a lot of money at stake. Maybe an entire fortune."

"Money makes people do crazy things." Vivian sipped from her coffee. "What are the odds that both your father and Larry died within days of each other? It seems odd now."

"Yeah, but Larry was murdered," Kylie pointed out. "Dad died of a heart attack. It's just a weird coincidence."

"Is it?" I bit down on my lip, my gut urging me to say what was on my mind and my heart afraid to even consider any other truth. "I know Dad died of natural causes according to the autopsy report, but the timing of his death and what I found in the safe deposit box makes me wonder if something else is going on here. What if he was part of the whole thing? And someone murdered him for the money?"

Kylie shifted and placed her hand on the counter. "You think Dad was stealing from his clients?"

"No." Vivian's firm denial held conviction, and she crossed her legs. "Your father couldn't have been murdered. Maybe he wasn't a good husband, but he certainly wasn't a crook. He would never be involved in something like this. The man was honest to a fault."

Didn't I know it. When he told me what a disappointment I'd turned out to be, he hadn't minced any words.

"Why would Dad leave the evidence for you if he was part of the crime?" Kylie drummed her fingers methodically on the stainless-steel counter. "Wouldn't it make more sense that he found out about it and died before he could do something to stop Larry?"

"Or he was killed, so he couldn't do anything to stop Larry," I added.

"And now Larry is dead." Kylie stopped her fingers and slid on an oven mitt. "But if someone killed Dad, wouldn't they have shot him like Larry?"

"Good point." She had me reconsidering my theory.

"Just stop with all this talk of murder." Vivian scissored her hands. "Your father died of a heart attack. End of story. If you think he had something on Larry, you should tell the police and let them investigate."

I didn't like seeing my mother upset, and knowing I was the cause made me feel that much worse. "I think you're right. I have to go to the station and give a formal statement, so I'll give everything I found to the detective." I glanced at the clock on the wall. Each hour was marked with a different colored cupcake, and it was half past noon. I didn't have much time.

"Have you eaten anything today?" Vivian scrutinized my waistline. "You've lost weight since the last time you were home."

"No, I haven't," I argued. If anything, I'd gained weight from adding a pastry to most of my coffee breaks, thanks to Grace and her persistent sweet tooth.

"I hope you don't decide to become one of those vegetarians. You know, the ones who don't eat dairy."

"Those are vegans." Kylie supplied the correct term.

"I'm not going to become a vegetarian. Where do you get these ideas?" I made that my cue to leave. "I'll see you later." I slid off my stool, shoved my blistered feet back into my heels, and gave Vivian a kiss on the cheek.

"Do you need a ride?" she asked.

"No, I want to walk. It's a nice day outside." My feet were burning, but the police station was only a block away, and I needed a few minutes to take care of something before going there.

"I'll come by the house after work," Kylie said as she opened the oven behind her. "I'll bring something to eat so Mom doesn't have to worry about you becoming a vegetarian."

"Or worse, a vegan." I winked at my mom, grabbed my bag off the floor, and gave a wave on my way out of the kitchen.

"Let us know if anything else happens," Vivian called after me.

My mother was more likely to have fresh gossip to share before any new information came my way. Unless I stumbled upon another dead body.

I passed through the front of Kylie's cake shop, where glass cases displayed muffins, cookies, scones, and intricately decorated cupcakes, all of the baked goods like works of art. They were almost too pretty to eat. With two large front windows and white floor tiles, the place looked clean and bright and was a perfect reflection of my sister. But Kylie's earlier question, wondering if Alex had been deliberately framed for Larry's murder, still nagged at me. I couldn't think of one person who would want to go after Alex, or a reason why.

Stepping out onto the sunny street, I put on my sunglasses and walked over to Central Park, where I took a seat on one of the public benches. There were a few suits from nearby offices having their lunch in the gazebo, but aside from them, the park provided a quiet, shady refuge. I hated to do this in broad daylight, where anyone could see me, but it would only take a minute. From inside my bag, I took out the laptop and fired it up, then found a spare flash drive I had stashed in a zippered pocket. Yes, I carried flash drives in my bag. They came in handy, especially if I was going to turn the laptop over to the police. I wanted a copy of the files for my own investigation.

What my mother didn't know wouldn't kill her.

While I waited for the files to transfer, my phone started buzzing and vibrating. I extricated my cell from the depths of my bag, and the screen flashed with Wallace and Reed's office number.

"I got your email," Grace said, her voice calm and unwavering. "When will you be back?"

"I'm still booked on a flight out tomorrow," I told her. "If that changes, it could be Friday at the latest."

"The clients want to meet on Friday," Grace said. "And Mr. Reed is here.

He'd like a word with you."

I heard a shuffle, and then my boss came on the line. "Abbott, I want that presentation on the Alex Jones case."

"I can work on it from here and be back as soon as I can."

"Look, the client is getting nervous, and I can't blame them."

"Yes, Sir, I understand. I'll have it right away."

"I certainly hope so. I need you to get back here in time for the meeting."

"I'll be back by the end of the week."

"Good. Grace will get you the details."

"Great," I said, but he'd already hung up.

An email from Grace immediately came through listing the details my boss wanted to see in my report, along with a suggestion I contact Brandon with an update. I waited for the file transfer to finish, then packed up the laptop and flash drive and sent Brandon a quick text before I forgot.

*Still working on the report. How are you?*

I waited a moment for a reply, but I never got an instant one from Brandon. I always had to wait for him to respond. Sometimes until the next day.

In this case, it would buy me more time to focus on helping Alex get out of jail. Heading for the police station, I greeted the people I passed on the street, but my thoughts traveled to LA and how realistic it was to think I'd be back there in time to make the client meeting. Would I be able to get on a plane tomorrow and leave my best friend sitting in jail for murder? Alex would never leave me hanging. I wasn't about to do that to her.

Before I knew it, the police station on Grove Street loomed before me. It was a square brick building and resembled a box with rows of arched windows. Both sides of the front walk were bordered by green courtyards, and out front they flew the American flag and beside it, the blue flag with the state seal of Minnesota.

Inside, a robust, intimidating woman manned the front desk, and she never smiled once as I politely informed her that I was there to give my formal statement.

"Ms. Abbott?" Detective Matthews emerged from some secret door, a Styrofoam cup in his hand. "Are you here to give your statement?"

The policewoman handed me a visitor's badge. "Do you want me to give her to Peterson?"

"I'll take her," Matthews said, holding my gaze. "Do you want to come with me?"

It wasn't like I had a choice in the matter, so I followed Matthews to his office. Not knowing what I expected to find, his office was small, a framed smattering of accolades hung on the wall behind the desk, and the only mess was a pile of case files sitting atop a metal cabinet. There were no personal items, no photos, not even an obligatory plant. I noticed he had no wedding ring on his left hand, but he did wear an Omega Chronograph watch. Very impressive. I recognized expensive wrist wear. My own watch was a Cartier Tank with a black leather band. It was something I'd bought for myself after my first large promotion. Watches told a story about the person wearing them, and Jake's watch told me there was more than meets the eye when it came to the kind, patient detective.

"Please, have a seat." He motioned to the chair in front of the desk.

I sat on the edge of the chair and clutched my bag in my lap. Matthews tossed his cup in the trash bin beside the desk and walked around to sit in his chair.

"Would you like something to drink?" he offered. "Coffee? Water?"

"No, thanks." I was nervous, but for some odd reason, I found the detective's presence comforting. He seemed to have that effect on me. I was so used to being on the defensive with Brandon, it was a welcome change.

"Thank you for coming in. I know this can't be easy for you."

"Let's just say I've never found a dead body before."

"Hopefully this will be your last." He switched on his computer and prepared to take my statement.

"You must have seen so many dead bodies in your line of work that you're used to it by now." I scanned the service awards and professional certificates on the wall behind him. "How long have you been a cop?"

"I've been serving for fifteen years." His expression stilled and grew serious. "And you never get used to it."

How did I manage to sound so insensitive? If the ground wanted to open up and swallow me, now would be the perfect time. Making small talk with law enforcement wasn't one of my stronger skills, even knowing I was on the right side of the law. "Have you investigated many murders, or put a lot of killers behind bars?"

"Not in Harmony Falls." He typed an entry into his computer. "I got my fill of violent crimes back in Buffalo. Moving here has been a nice change of pace."

"Not anymore." I let out a nervous laugh.

He met me with another serious stare.

"You're from New York?" I tried to steer the conversation back to friendly territory, while also wanting to find more confidence in his ability to nab Larry's killer. People got murdered in New York every day, so it was safe to say Matthews had experience in the matter.

"Born and raised." He eased into one of his warm smiles. "Should we get started? I don't want to keep you from your day."

What was left of it, anyway. No matter what else happened, this would always be the day of Larry Stone's murder. I settled back into the chair and readied myself to rehash the morning's events.

Matthews readied his fingers over the keyboard. "Let me know at any point if you need to stop or take a break."

"Let's just get it over with."

He led me through several rounds of questions, repeating many of them so he could write my words exactly as I'd stated them. He had a professional, courteous manner, and we eventually fell into a rhythm with each other. Matthews was easy to talk to, and I found myself warming to him the longer I sat in his office. There was something about him that made me want to be open and honest with him, so I did my best to give as many details as I could remember in the hopes the information would be useful. The whole process took about an hour. When we were finished, he printed the statement for me to sign.

"When will I be able to get back into my office?" I signed the statement and slid the paper and pen back across the desk. "I have a big mess to clean up, and I don't know if anything else is missing."

"If you find anything was stolen, report it to us right away. Otherwise, once forensics has gathered all the evidence, you're free to return to work." He picked up the pen and tucked it back in his shirt pocket. "I can call to let you know, if you'd like."

"That would be great." I wanted to get my hands on the files covering the floor of Harmony Wealth Partners before Damon had a chance to get there first.

"I think we're finished here," Matthews concluded.

"I do have one more thing." I pulled the laptop out of my bag and set it on his desk. "My father left this for me. There's a chance the files hold evidence of a possible crime. An investment fraud, to be exact. It might be the reason Larry Stone was murdered."

His eyes dipped to the laptop, then back up at me. His lips tightened. "Why didn't you tell me about this earlier?"

"I didn't know if I should say anything." I gave an insecure shrug. "What I found would require further investigation, and maybe it'll turn out to be nothing at all. Mostly I want to help my friend get out of jail."

Matthews looked at me in silence, sizing me up, perhaps wondering if I was sane enough for him to spend valuable time chasing down my lead. "I'll have my team take a look at it."

His disinterest brought the same disappointment that came when you failed a test. To him, I was just a crazy story and a laptop. That didn't mean I would give up. "How long are you going to keep Alex?"

His expression grew guarded, the no-nonsense detective intensity returning to his features. "We're going to hold her at least until the ballistics results come back. She has no alibi, and her texts to you and her mother last night could have been sent from anywhere." He showed no signs of relenting with a probable suspect already in custody.

"So that's it?" I fumed, not wanting to be brushed under the rug, my skills constantly underestimated. "You have your suspect and case closed? Don't you want to know what's on that laptop, or what Larry's killer might have been looking for?"

He took my signed statement and placed it in a file folder on top of his desk. "We have to follow the evidence, and right now, we don't have much to go on. If there's any evidence on this computer, you can be sure we'll find it."

I wasn't sure they'd find it, not at all. I'd barely noticed it, and I was an expert. But what did I say to convince the detective? I had a feeling Larry's murder was somehow connected to the investment. I just didn't know how. That someone wanted to see Alex hang for murder, but I didn't know why. I wouldn't listen to me either. "Have you spoken with any of Larry's clients yet?"

His expression turned weary, but he remained patient. "Should I have reason to speak with any of them?"

"I wonder if any of them had a grudge against Larry, or a reason to be angry with him. Things like that happen in business, especially when money is involved."

"Would you be referring to someone in particular?"

I could only lead him far enough down the path to start putting the pieces together on his own. "I can't say for sure it's a client. I'm just curious. I work in forensic accounting back in LA and I see people lie, cheat, and steal all the time. It wouldn't be unheard of. And what about Nick Callahan? He was Larry's business competition."

"That doesn't automatically make him a killer."

"Would it help if I told you I saw Nick and Larry having an argument on the day of my father's funeral?"

"It would." Matthews jotted something on a notepad by his phone. "Is there anything else you forgot to mention?"

*Like the federal agent, my father might have been working with?*

"No." I gulped past the lump forming in my throat. The lie didn't go down well, but he'd brushed aside everything I'd given him so far. Why hand him all of my cards?

Matthews leaned forward in his chair, sending an imploring look across the desk. "I appreciate what you're trying to do, Ms. Abbott, but this is my investigation and I'll handle it my way. What I don't need is you jumping to conclusions or making accusations against innocent people because you want to help your friend."

I didn't like this feeling. Desperation. I didn't know how to make the detective understand. It was clear he wanted evidence, so it was clear I'd have to find some. "Forget I said anything," I relented, maybe too easily, but he didn't seem to notice. "I'm probably making something out of nothing."

The intercom on the desk phone beeped, and a voice crackled through. "Detective Matthews?"

He never took his eyes off me as he answered, "What is it, Regina?"

"The lady about the utility pole is here, and she's fit to be tied."

He cast the phone an annoyed look, his jaw clenched. "I'll be right out."

Relieved our meeting had come to an end, I stood, and Matthews grabbed the file folder from his desk, then motioned to the door with his hand. He escorted me back to the entrance of the station in silence, and I was grateful for the finality of our meeting.

"Thanks for coming in, Ms. Abbott." He held the door open for me.

"Good luck with the investigation, Detective."

He issued a polite nod before letting the door go.

I don't know what I'd expected from the detective. Maybe appreciation for the clue I'd dropped in his lap, or a belief in Alex's innocence. I left the station with neither, only the resolve that if someone was going to dig deeper for the truth, it would have to be me. I suspected Larry's murder had to be connected to money and one of his clients. Find the connection, and I would find the murderer.

# Chapter Six

The cab pulled to a stop in front of my father's house, and though it had never felt like home to me, I was glad to be back. I handed a twenty to the driver and told him to keep the change. With my shoes in hand, exhaustion carried me up the front path, and I wanted nothing more than to change into some comfortable clothes and hide from the world. The image of Larry's bloody corpse kept flashing through my mind, and I needed a distraction from my morbid thoughts.

Dealing with my father's girlfriend was not what I had in mind. Janice stood outside the front door, hands cupped to her face as she looked through the thick pane of leaded glass. I guessed she'd already knocked on the door and now waited impatiently for someone to answer. What did she want now?

"Hi there," I said when I reached the bottom step of the front porch.

Janice spun around, her purple flowered skirt and orange tunic top clashing wildly with her short, rust-tinted red hair. Gold hoops dangled from her ears. She looked like a deranged gypsy. "Kate! What lucky timing. I was hoping to catch you at home."

I came up the steps and dropped my bag and shoes on the porch. My poor feet throbbed in agony. "How are you, Janice?"

"I hope this is a good time." She watched me lean against the porch rail to massage one of my sore feet. "I just came from the sale at that new clothing boutique downtown, and then, of course, I had to run to the shoe store to get a new pair of sandals when I ran into Connie Pearson, and she told me all about what happened at the office this morning. So, I thought I just have to stop by and see how poor Kate is holding up." Janice stopped talking long enough to take a breath. "You look like you've been put through the wringer."

I felt like it, too. "The day hasn't gotten off to a good start."

"Is it true Larry Stone was *murdered?*" Janice whispered the word.

"I hate to say it's all true."

"Do the police know who killed him? Do they know why? I heard they arrested Alex Monroe. Do you think she did it?"

"They have to check the gun for fingerprints." I switched feet and massaged the blisters forming on my heel. "They don't have a motive, or much evidence, or even any witnesses." The only thing I knew anymore was that Alex was not a murderer.

"It's all so frightening." Janice brought her hand up and nibbled one of her nails. "None of us are safe with a killer on the loose. Who do you think they're after next?"

I had a hunch the person who murdered Larry hadn't struck at random, but if the town gossips got too out of control, everyone in Harmony Falls would be on the run from psycho killers. "I don't think you have to worry. The police will find out who killed Larry. They have a good detective working the case."

Janice didn't appear reassured. "I'm glad to be staying with a friend. I wouldn't want to be alone with all of this going on. Anything could happen."

And thanks to Janice, I was reminded of just how alone I happened to be at the moment. Alex and I had barely gotten started on a plan to bust Larry before she landed in jail for murder. None of it sat right with me. Not one bit.

"I hope they find whoever did this soon," Janice said. "I finally found a place I can afford to rent on my social security check, but I don't want to move out of my friend Evelyn's house until it's safe. This whole thing is terribly upsetting. I wish I had enough money to move away and start over somewhere new." Her tone was mild enough, but there was an edge underlying her words.

My father might have died and left Janice no inheritance, but she didn't need to be upset with me over the fact, and I had no intention of apologizing because I wanted to sell the house rather than let Janice continue to live there rent-free. "You're lucky to have a friend who will let you stay with her until you get back on your feet. Especially with a killer out there."

"We've had to cancel the Ladies' Aid bridge club. Nothing in Harmony Falls will be the same after this."

"Can I ask you something?" I wondered.

"What's that, dear?"

"Do you know if Larry and my father had a falling out, or a disagreement before he died? Did my father ever mention anything about one of the investments Larry sold to his clients?"

Janice blinked, her stare going blank. "What makes you ask a thing like that? They were partners. They got along splendidly."

It would seem Janice wasn't as involved in my father's affairs as I'd suspected, or she would have known they were having trouble. "That's a relief to hear. I'd hate for there to be any bad blood with Larry's nephew since it looks like we'll have to share the business."

After a brief silence, she asked, "But aren't you going back to California tomorrow?"

"With my father and Larry both dead, I imagine it will take some time to get the paperwork figured out with Damon. I also don't feel right leaving while Alex is in jail. I might have to stay longer."

"For how long?" Janice's calm disappeared, replaced by an earnest fidgeting of her hands, like wringing out a cloth that wasn't there. "Aren't you afraid you'll jeopardize your job? After all, you gave up everything to get it. You left your home, left your friends and family behind. It's your whole life."

I wanted to argue with her, she always provoked a desire to be contrary in me, but I found I had nothing to throw back at her. Without my job, what did I have? "I have my laptop, and I can work from here. It should only be a few more days before everything gets sorted out, and it gives me the chance to help Kylie finish cleaning out the house and organizing the estate sale. My dad had so much stuff."

"Most men do." Janice hefted her chin. "Hope you don't end up a fool like me, thinking he might have left you some of what he had."

"I'm sure my father didn't mean to hurt you. His death was rather sudden; maybe he didn't have time to get his will changed."

Janice frowned, deepening the lines around her mouth. "We were together six years. That should have been enough time."

"Maybe he just forgot." I was running out of excuses.

"It's too late to worry about it now," she said, a certain determination in her voice. "I have to move on with my life. I just hope you know what you're getting yourself into. That business with Larry drove your father to an early grave. I'd hate to see you go down the same path."

"What do you mean?" I asked, anxiety doing a flip-flop in my stomach. "Do you think Larry had something to do with my father's death?"

When Janice shook her head, her gold hoop earrings swished from her earlobes. "Your father was under a lot of stress before he died. That's all I know."

I studied Janice the way I studied subjects in depositions, and while my father's girlfriend appeared sincere, there was something she wasn't telling me. I could see it hiding behind her eyes as they darted around, barely stopping long enough to meet my own.

"I suppose I shouldn't talk about it," Janice said. "I don't want to start any more rumors, God knows we have enough of those floating around, and your father isn't here to defend himself. He'll never be here again." Her chin wavered slightly, and if she was on the verge of tears, she did a good job at concealing it.

A small part of me did feel sorry for Janice. She'd lost her partner and her security, all in one, fateful night. Starting over wasn't easy for anyone, and I figured at Janice's age, it had to be even harder to adjust.

"I wish there was something I could do to help," I said, mostly because I didn't know what else to say. "It must be difficult trying to get settled in a strange, new place."

"Well, thank goodness for Evelyn. If it wasn't for her, I'd be living in my car. She's giving me some things to help me get started in the new apartment, though most of it is covered in cat hair."

I didn't notice any errant tufts of animal fur clinging to Janice, but my gaze kept going back to her hair. Who was in charge of her color these days? The dye job had obviously been botched, with two unseemly shades of red clashing over the gray roots. Janice had worn a hat to the funeral so most of her head had been covered, but from what I remembered, she normally got her hair professionally colored on a regular schedule to keep any of the gray from showing. She appeared to have relaxed some of her beauty standards. Or she simply couldn't afford professional beauty services any longer.

"I have an idea," I said. "Why don't I put together some things from here? I imagine you could use some dishes, or bed sheets, some lamps, or even some of the furniture. I'm sure my dad would have wanted most of his things to go to you anyway, and Kylie and I don't need any more stuff."

Janice caught me in a dumbfounded stare and didn't need to give voice to the elephant sitting on the front porch. What she'd really wanted from my father was his money.

"It's the least I could do." I kept on, aware I'd struck a raw chord with Janice, but it was too late to stick my foot in my mouth now.

"Well, I would like to have the set of fine china, and the pots and pans," she admitted, then she got on a roll. "I do need some furniture, like a bedroom set, and the living room sofa, and the big television, the kitchen table, oh—and the desk from his office, if it will fit in my spare room. I'll have to measure first."

Okay, so she wanted it all. I don't know why it surprised me. "I'll keep you in mind as I'm packing everything up. We'll get you off to a nice start in your new place."

"I knew you'd do the right thing." Janice swiped a tear from the corner of her eye. "You remind me so much of your father. He was a good man. I don't know what I'm going to do without him."

I reached out with an affectionate pat on her arm. "Everything will be all right. Just wait and see."

"You have no idea how much this will help me out," she said. "I want to have my new place ready for next month's art circle. We're making crystal sun catchers. I should make one for you and Kylie."

I didn't have the heart to tell Janice I kept all of the handmade gifts she'd given me in a box at the back of my closet. I could only take so much glazed pottery and crocheted potholders. "That would be nice of you."

"I want to see you again before you go back to California. I just hope you aren't putting your job at risk. Your dad wouldn't have liked that." Janice tugged at the hem of her orange blouse. It had a stain on the breast pocket, and her makeup hadn't been applied as precisely as usual. Janice was one of those people who liked to draw their eyebrows on with a dark pencil, and today they were almost non-existent. Between that and the bad dye job, the always-put-together Janice appeared to be coming apart.

"My father didn't like any of the choices I made," I remarked blandly. "I do think he wanted me to stay and settle his business. I'm not sure he trusted Larry."

Janice cocked her head to the side. "Why would you think that?"

The wild look in her eyes gave me pause. "Just a hunch."

I got the distinct feeling Janice knew something she wasn't saying. Until I found out what she was dancing around, it might be smart to keep my suspicions about Larry quiet.

"I guess I don't have to worry if you're going to be around for a while." Janice took a few steps back toward the porch steps. "I'd better dash. I want to stay off the streets until the police find the killer. Let's talk soon. Bye-bye." She blew an air kiss before leaving.

I didn't give the weirdness of our conversation a second thought because conversations with Janice were always weird. Once she'd gone, I scooped up my shoes and bag and dug out the house key. Completely worn out, I let myself into the house. The afternoon light poured in from the row of tall windows in the living room, spilling across the glistening oak floors. My father refinished the floors as one of his first renovations. He'd restored the charming Victorian house from old and withered to classic and elegant, able to see the potential when he'd bought the run-down property after the divorce.

His renovation projects had always fascinated Alex, given her love of interiors, and she'd assisted with a few of his projects toward the end, also picking up some basic construction skills in the process. Much to her delight. If only I'd been lucky enough to earn some of his favor.

The wooden floorboards creaked under my feet, and piles of boxes greeted me in the entry, with more stretching into the living room and kitchen. I'd taken over the task of going through my father's things while I was home so Kylie could concentrate on her cake shop and catering business. We'd decided I would stay in the guest room upstairs, and seeing a project started, it went against my nature to leave it unfinished. I'd made some good headway on getting things boxed up after the funeral, and there was still so much to be done.

I moved silently through the living room. Even with the sunlight coming in through the windows, the interior of the house was dark. Painted in moody shades of greens and blues, most of the furniture consisted of dark leather sofas and club chairs. A tree trunk topped with a sheet of thick glass served as the coffee table. In the tiny den, my father had constructed and installed custom bookcases on all four walls and filled them with books. Past the den, in the back office, stood a lonely mahogany desk and, behind it, a deer head mounted to the wall. The sweet scent of pipe tobacco still lingered in the air, and bittersweet memories flooded my mind. I could picture my dad sitting at the desk smoking his pipe, wearing his Sunday sweater, reading the newspaper, and poring over the stock market quotes and the sports page.

The rift between me and my father had grown so large that I'd stopped coming home as much as I used to. It got uncomfortable being in a small town and trying to avoid the one person I wished would be proud of me. If I did visit, it was only for a few days over Christmas, always staying with Kylie, and I was usually back in LA by New Year's. I kept busy with my job and working my cases, never taking a break, never slowing down, and now I worried I'd lost track of what was important. I'd neglected the people I loved, taking the fact that they'd always be around for granted.

With my father gone, the awkwardness that usually surrounded my visits home wasn't there anymore. I didn't have to worry about running into him and Janice at the grocery store, or seeing him at family events. He was no longer a valid excuse to avoid coming home, and I made a promise to visit Kylie and my mother more often in his absence. If I could get away from work.

I set my shoulder bag on the desk in the office before going upstairs to change out of my nice clothes. The high heels went in my suitcase under the bed, where I vowed to leave them for the rest of my stay. I had no one to impress and was more comfortable in jeans and casual tops, and my black ballet flats went with everything.

Back downstairs, I got settled at the giant mahogany desk in my father's office with my laptop, and after a quick check of my emails, I pulled up the files on the flash drive to recheck they'd fully transferred. With that out of the way, I got to work on my report, when my cell phone chirped. The text was short: *Waiting on your report.*

No greeting, no asking how things were going, just business. Was Brandon my boyfriend or my boss?

I shot back an even shorter reply: *Working on it.*

Like a trained dog, I waited a few seconds for a response, and got nothing. Brandon and I hadn't parted on the greatest terms, but why was I always the one who had to apologize in order to smooth things over? And why did I feel the need to keep doing it?

I suddenly didn't feel like working anymore, and I closed my laptop. I looked at our brief text exchange again. Seven words. No feeling. It bothered me more than I wanted to admit. If life was made up of anything, it should be full of feeling.

Restlessness stirred me to get up and get moving. I had a lot to process, and sitting with it and ruminating didn't seem to be doing me any good. I passed through the den, dreading having to pack up all those books stacked in the cases. Coming into the living room, I looked at all the knick-knacks and magazines and stacks of newspapers that needed to be cleared out. The clutter felt like a reflection of the thoughts cramming my mind to capacity. I closed my eyes to breathe, and it brought up images of Larry in a pool of blood.

I had to move, to get out of my head, so I got to work. Armed with my air pods and my angry chicks playlist, I filled my head with the fury of Liz Phair, Garbage, Meredith Brooks, Fiona Apple, and Alanis Morissette, their lyrics calling the world out on its bullshit and helping me grind out some indignation with a long bout of rage cleaning.

The first chore I tackled was sorting the random piles of boxes into orderly stacks of keep, donate, or sell. As I worked, I wracked my brain for where to start looking for evidence, what I thought were dead ends, and who I could get to help me.

Then, I cleared the place out. Load after load of useless junk met its end in the rented dumpster parked in the driveway. A lifetime of clutter. A mess left behind for someone else to deal with. Like the laptop in the safe deposit box and the card upstairs on the dresser. Why did it have to be me? I didn't want any of this.

The anger finally surfaced. Each load I carried out to the dumpster met its end with a violent toss and a ferocious crash. I was angry at the police. Angry at Larry Stone for getting killed. Angry at whoever had killed him. Most of all, I was angry that my friend, who'd never hurt anyone, was sitting down at the local jail, waiting for the police to wrap up their investigation and charge her with murder. I hurled a box full of glassware into the dumpster. I suppose I should have left it in the pile I'd started for Janice's new apartment, but I found a greater satisfaction from the shattering sound of breaking glass. It was all I could do not to scream.

I wanted to take action. To come up with a workable plan to help Alex. But what could I do with the time I had left? Tomorrow, I'd be boarding a plane and heading back to Los Angeles, and life in Harmony Falls, though forever changed, would go on without me. And for the first time in a very long time, I didn't want it to.

How much longer would I run away from home? From the people who knew me best? From myself?

My therapist wanted me to face the demons of my past. Well, here I was, filling an entire dumpster with regrets. It only made things worse.

I had a life in LA. I was happy there. And as I carried dining chairs and lamps and end tables out to the garage, I couldn't remember the last time I'd truly laughed or let go and had fun. I didn't know fun. I only knew work and caseloads and corner offices. Once I made it to the top of my game, then I'd be happy. Then I'd have time for fun.

I took the nature-themed oil paintings off the walls and pulled all the nails and hooks from the plaster. Not ready to stop, I found myself standing in the office, staring down the deer head mounted to the wall. The black, lifeless eyes stared back at me. Dark pools of doubt, fear, and unfinished dreams. Not so gently, I took it down by the rack of antlers and tossed it out in the garage.

"I didn't shoot you," I told the thing, its blank eyes full of judgment.

Having worked up a good sweat, my emotions raw, my feelings laid bare, I decided that talking to a stuffed deer was a clear signal I'd had enough. My work for the day was done. Covered in dust and debris, with two broken nails, I finally knew what I had to do. This mess had been dumped in my lap because I was the only one who could handle it. Someone thought they could get away with a fortune and let Alex take the fall.

Not on my watch.

The setting sun hung low in the sky as amber light angled in through the windows, and with the hint of a fall chill in the air, I closed the garage. Kylie would be on her way over with dinner soon, and I had just enough time to go upstairs to take a shower and change my clothes. Then it was time to put my plan into action.

# Chapter Seven

Kylie showed up at seven, a pepperoni pizza from our favorite local joint in one hand, and a bottle of white wine in the other.

"You're my hero!" I took the cardboard pizza box from her and carried it into the kitchen. "I've been dying for a Wise Guys' pizza."

"You wanna pizza me?" Kylie imitated their sales gimmick on the side of the box with a Brooklyn mobster accent.

I put a roll of paper towels on the kitchen island next to the pizza box and threw the lid open to grab a slice. My stomach rumbled with hunger.

Kylie laughed at me. "Haven't you eaten today?"

"This is so delicious," I said through a mouthful of greasy, thin crust pepperoni. "It reminds me of Salvatore's up in Dinkytown."

I'd spent my early college years waitressing at the famous basement pizzeria in the Twin Cities. The quirky neighborhood of Dinkytown was a popular student hangout made up of second-hand clothing stores, bike shops, and used bookstores, along with tons of eclectic bars and cozy cafés overflowing with indie bands and upcoming songwriters. Those had been some of the best, and worst, years of my life. Rather than take on student loans when I ran out of money, I moved to Los Angeles, got a job, and finished my degree at UCLA.

"I miss Salvatore's," Kylie said. "That place was so cool. I heard they turned it into a Chipotle."

I scrunched up my nose at the thought of my fabled underground hangout going mainstream. "Those college kids don't know what they're missing."

Kylie set her tote bag on the counter and drew out a stack of paper plates, some napkins, and a bundle of plastic silverware. "Be civilized and use a plate."

I transferred my slice of pizza to a plate and wiped the grease off my fingers with a napkin. Meanwhile, Kylie opened the bottle of wine and filled two clear plastic cups. She lifted her cup to take a drink, then paused as she looked around the kitchen. "Wow, look at this place. You've been busy."

"I needed to work so I wouldn't keep seeing Larry's dead body in my mind." I wondered if I'd ever be able to sleep with the troubling vision burned into my brain.

"Do you want me to stay with you tonight?" Kylie offered. "I wouldn't want to be alone if I found a dead body. It gives me the creeps."

"That's not necessary. I'll be fine." I didn't want to overreact to the situation. It was important to stay calm. I had bigger things to worry about.

"At the rate you're going with all these boxes, we'll be able to have the estate sale sooner than I thought. I should put an ad in the paper."

"I also packed up some things for Janice to use in her new apartment," I said. "I thought it would be nice to help her get started. She has nothing."

Kylie snagged a slice of pizza from the box and placed it on her plate. "Why would you want to do that? After the way she acted when Dad died, I wouldn't give her anything. She was a real—"

"She means well." I couldn't believe I was actually defending Janice. "She's just a bit odd."

"If she gives me one more macramé plant hanger, I might use it on myself."

Inwardly, I laughed. The sun catcher would be a welcome change for my sister then. "We want to get rid of the stuff. What's the harm in letting Janice take some of it?"

Kylie spotted my notebook lying open on the counter and reached out to grab it. "What's this?"

"It's a mind map," I explained. "I use it to brainstorm ideas."

"You're trying to figure out who killed Larry." She scanned the wild scribbles. "It's a murder mind map."

"Something like that. I'm not letting the cops put the blame on Alex because it's easy. I want to do a little more research at the office."

70

"So, what are you going to do exactly?" Kylie pulled her pizza crust apart. "Find the killer on your own?"

"Yes."

She went slack-jawed, her pizza held in midair. "I was kidding."

"I'm going to start by finding out what happened to all the checks, where the money went, and that might lead me to the killer. I think one of Larry's clients killed him out of revenge. I need to go through the list of investors in this real estate deal and see who had the most money to lose."

"You're serious about this." Kylie dropped her slice of pizza before she could take another bite. "Do you realize how crazy this sounds? I mean, you're going back to LA tomorrow. I've got Mom watching the shop so I can drive you to the airport."

"I'm not ready to go back yet. I canceled my flight." I reached for my wine glass and took a long swallow. "I believe the gun was planted in Alex's van by the real killer so she would take the fall for Larry's murder, giving the killer time to get away. The best way to get Alex off the hook is to find out who killed Larry, and fast."

"You really want to go looking for a murderer?" Kylie brushed the crumbs from her hands. "Isn't that, like, dangerous?"

"I know Alex didn't kill Larry, and the cops don't have any leads. When I was down at the station this afternoon to give my statement, they seemed to think they've got the case wrapped up. I can't just sit around and do nothing."

"That's exactly what you should do. From what I heard at the shop today, most people think Hannah caught Larry with another woman, got jealous, and killed him in the heat of passion." Kylie plucked a pepperoni from her pizza and popped it in her mouth. "Cheaters always get their comeuppance."

"I wondered if there was something going on between Hannah and Larry." I put my slice back on the plate and slid my notebook over to scribble Hannah's name next to the others. "She was really upset over his death, but that could have been an act. She also got to the office late this morning and came in through the front door, which gave her plenty of time to stash the gun in Alex's van." I circled her name. "How did I not see that before?"

"I wouldn't be surprised if she killed him," Kylie said. "It's a motive, right?"

"It sure is, and I'm not ruling anyone out. Hannah has access to the office and the files. She could have easily killed Larry, planted the gun, and then turned on the waterworks for the police."

"I heard she was expecting Larry to propose. I imagine she'd be pretty upset to find out she wasn't his only girlfriend."

"You got all this gossip from the cake shop?" I took another substantial swallow of my wine as I watched Kylie continue to dissect her slice of pizza, one pepperoni at a time.

"And from Mom. She had water aerobics this afternoon, and Connie Pearson is in her class."

"That old gossip has something to say about everyone." And none of it was good. "I wonder what she has to say about us."

"People know not to believe half of what she says."

"Yeah, but which half?"

Kylie dabbed at her mouth with the corner of her napkin. "What did the police say when you told them about the laptop, and how do you think Larry was stealing money? Are they going to question any of the clients?"

"They said they'd look into it."

"That's it?"

"My thoughts exactly." I went into the box for another slice. "Now you know why I have to do some digging of my own. They think because they found the gun in Alex's van that she did it. I won't sit by and let her go to prison for a murder she didn't commit."

"Can't you get the police to listen to you instead of going behind their backs?"

"The only way they're going to listen to me is if I give them some hard evidence," I said. "I know more about financial crime and investment fraud than the police. It only makes sense for me to investigate and let them know what I find. This is what I do for a living."

"I don't think it's a good idea." Kylie shook her head, her blonde ponytail swaying.

"Do you have a better one?" I bit into my pizza while I waited for her argument.

Nothing she had to say could change my mind. I was the only person in town qualified to investigate a possible investment fraud without attracting any notice, and it was the least I could do to help Alex. If our situations were reversed, I knew Alex would move Heaven and Earth to get me out of a jam.

"How about this?" Kylie had an idea. "Let the police handle it."

"I am letting them handle it," I argued. "I'm just not satisfied with their job, and I want to ask some questions of my own. There are a few people who might have the information I'm looking for."

"Like what people?" Kylie slid the notebook back over to her side of the counter. "Damon, that's obvious, but why Nick Callahan?"

"I saw him arguing with Larry at the funeral. I think he was mad about losing business to Larry. He might have killed him to get rid of the competition." The lead was worth tracking down, and if I could eliminate Nick as a suspect, I'd be one step closer to finding the real killer.

"I think you're crazy." Kylie peeled a chunk of topping from her pizza and chewed thoughtfully. "If the murderer thinks you're on to them, they could come after you next."

"No one is going to find out." I snatched my notebook back.

"You'd better not tell Mom what you're up to. She's already upset about Dad and the murder. If she finds out you're looking for the killer, she'll go ballistic."

I took the last bite of my pizza and dropped the crust on my plate. "Don't you go telling her, either. I know how you let things slip once in a while."

"I can keep a secret." Kylie finished chewing, then asked, "Do you really think Nick Callahan could have killed Larry? He seems so clean-cut and by the book. He belongs to the chamber of commerce."

"In my experience, those are the ones to watch out for."

"You have three people on your list. What happens if none of them did it?"

"One of them is hiding something and Dad left it up to me to find out who."

"Yeah, but that's before someone got murdered."

"I can't let it go," I confessed. "It's my job to find the truth."

Kylie tore off another piece of her crust, not looking convinced. "This isn't the greatest plan you've ever had."

"It might have a few holes, but I'm not changing my mind." I watched her nervous fidgeting. "You're the only person I know who mutilates their pizza before they eat it."

Kylie's brow creased with worry. "What's wrong with the way I eat my pizza?"

"Nothing." I laughed as Kylie tossed what was left of the crust down on her plate. I knew she picked her pizza apart piece by piece because she was a big thinker, and she liked to break things down into manageable parts. It was one of the many things I loved about my sister. "There's no wrong way to eat a pizza. I just realized how much I've missed being home. I'm really glad to be back."

"I'm glad to have you back." Kylie raised her cup of wine. "Let's have a toast."

"What should we toast to?"

"To home."

I bumped the rim of my plastic cup with Kylie's. "To home."

Kylie exited the toast first and drank down the rest of her wine in one swallow, while I lingered, each sip of my wine filtering in a new thought.

I loved being home.

The trouble was, I wasn't sure if I knew where home was anymore. Was it Los Angeles, where I had my career and my life? Or was it found in good old Harmony Falls, with the places and the people I cherished most? I'd been in such a hurry to leave after the falling out with my father that I never stopped to consider what I'd be giving up by moving away. And how hard it might be to get it back.

"What are you going to do if the killer finds out you're looking for them?" Kylie grabbed the wine bottle and refilled our cups.

"The killer won't know I'm looking for them. I'm simply looking for a few answers. No harm ever came from asking questions."

Kylie put the bottle of wine down on the counter. "Maybe if you tell the cops what you do for a living, they'll let you work with them, or something. Like a consultant."

"I'm not going to take the chance that they'll give me the brush-off again. I'm doing this to help Alex." I had to stay focused and handle the investigation the same way I handled financial crimes. The evidence was there, and all I had to do was put it together. "Even if I don't find the real killer, I'd at least be helping all the clients Larry might have defrauded. That's what Dad would have wanted."

"What will you do about Damon and Hannah?" Kylie asked. "You might be working in the same office with a murderer."

I set my cup down and reached into the box for another slice of pizza. "I've already thought of that. I have to assume everyone is a suspect until I can rule them out."

"I wonder if you missed your calling, and you should have become a real cop, chasing down killers instead of investment fraud."

"I could never be a cop," I said. "It's too dangerous."

Kylie gave me a deadpan stare. "And this whole idea of yours isn't?"

"I know what I'm doing," I insisted. "And I can call for backup."

"Okay, Columbo, tell me what you've got up your sleeve."

I had Agent Mason West's card by my cell phone and I held it up. "I'm going to call *him*."

Kylie snatched the card from my fingers and studied it. "This is the first smart thing I've heard you say all night. Who is this guy? How do you know he can help?"

"I found the card with the laptop. Dad must have been in contact with him, and I should find out if he knows anything. It's worth a shot."

"What if he doesn't know anything?"

"I'll have to go to the authorities with what I discover at some point. I figure he's the best place to start."

"His name sounds hot, but he's probably a bigger nerd than you are." Kylie handed the card back to me. "Complete with pocket protectors and a calculator."

"A nerd is just what I need." The ace in my back pocket. "The bigger the brain, the better."

"Let's just hope he doesn't arrest you for obstruction of justice."

"I'm more worried about being charged as an accomplice to Larry's fraud. When I inherited Dad's share of the business, I inherited Larry and all his under-the-table dealings along with it. I need to be as forthcoming with this federal agent as possible. I have to show him I'm willing to work with him."

Kylie crossed her arms over her chest. "So, let me get this straight. You're willing to work with the Feds, but not the police?"

"The Feds scare me more."

"I'm worried you might be getting in too deep." Kylie tore another piece from her crust and popped it in her mouth. "Mom will kill me if I let anything happen to you."

"I'm the older sister. Let me handle Mom."

"You might be the older sister, but I'm the smarter one." Kylie grinned, and it turned into a bubbly laugh.

I didn't argue with her. She might be right. "I'm calling him right now."

Kylie sucked in a quick breath as I entered the agent's number on my cell phone and waited for him to answer. After four rings, the call went directly to his voicemail. Mason West had a surprisingly smooth, deep voice. For a nerd. I left a brief message with my name and cell number, then slipped his card in the back pocket of my jeans. "Let's hope he calls back."

Kylie brushed her hands together to get rid of the crumbs. "What can I do to help you avoid getting yourself killed?"

"You can do two things," I said. "I need you to keep your ears open at the shop and listen to what people are saying. In the midst of all the gossip, someone might share some information that can actually help us, or you might happen to overhear something of interest."

Kylie nodded her agreement. "What's the other thing?"

It was time for me to cast the net wider. "Let me borrow your car."

# Chapter Eight

My mind clear and a plan in place, I was ready to face whatever a new day might bring. I'd gotten up early to take a morning walk and then used my father's old French Press to make some coffee. I'd become fond of the little contraption and had to decide whether I wanted to give it to Janice or add it to the box of stuff I wanted to keep. I was leaning toward the latter.

As soon as eight o'clock rolled around, I called Nick Callahan's office and made an appointment to see him as soon as possible. My meeting was at ten. Shortly after, I received a call from Kylie letting me know the real estate agent would be showing the house later in the morning. Agent West hadn't called me back yet, but I knew he would. If he was anything like me, he got a special thrill at seeing white-collar criminals sitting behind bars instead of behind a desk.

Not able to go to the office until the police cleared the crime scene, I had some time to kill before I had to get ready for my meeting with Nick. I dug my father's cozy fisherman's sweater out of the box of things I'd been putting aside and pulled it on, then went out to sit on the front porch with another mug of steaming coffee. The crisp fall air was fresh, the skies clear. Gold and scarlet leaves let go of their branches and tumbled on their final dance to the ground, while from overhead came the honking calls of geese flying south. I sat in one of the wooden rocking chairs with my feet tucked under me, wishing I had a pair of thick, woolen socks to keep me warm.

Last night after Kylie left, I made some more notes on my mind map. I only had three suspects: Damon, Nick, and Hannah. I believed I'd find more after I got access to the office files. My plan was to start ruling out suspects and see who was left standing. That would be the killer.

Not long after making my notes, I'd drifted off to sleep watching a late-night talk show. I'd dreamed of blood and death and lies disguised behind handsome smiles. Later, I'd been woken up in the middle of the night by a phone call. My father still had a landline, and when I finally found the phone down in his office and answered the call, no one was there. It seemed odd to get a call at three a.m. and find no one on the other end. I laid awake in bed for a while after that, my mind tumbling over all my thoughts, and finally fell back to sleep, where no more dreams plagued me.

Now, I went over my list while I sipped my coffee. Nick should be able to supply me with basic information on Larry and his business practices, along with what the men had argued about, and his alibi, if he had one. Hannah was the gatekeeper. She would know passwords and security codes, and she could have information on the real estate investment and records of bank statements, as well as access to Larry's files, so I had to tread carefully around her. From Damon, I wanted to know why he was in Harmony Falls and where he'd been on the night of Larry's murder. I was sure the police had questioned him, but what was his alibi?

My investigation had solid footing, and I finished my coffee in quiet contemplation. What if all of my mornings could be like this one? Taking a walk along a trail, surrounded by nature, only having to share it with a few other early risers. Enjoying a mug of coffee while sitting on the porch, rather than sipping it from a takeaway cup, spending hours in traffic. And it wouldn't only be the mornings I'd reclaim. My evenings could be spent cooking new recipes I'd always wanted to try reading books, or binge-watching a television series.

Had my father known what he was doing by leaving me his share of the business? Being back home forced me to consider a different kind of life. To question the path I was on and if I wanted to stay on that path or forge a new one. If I walked away from my life in LA, I'd be giving up a six-figure salary with benefits and access to an endless amount of shady accountants, but I'd be gaining something much more important in return. Time. People

I cared about. I avoided coming home because I wanted to avoid my father, and now that he was gone, there was nothing left for me to run away from.

For the past ten years I'd worked hard at building the perfect life. One designed to keep me busy and on the run. I filled every moment of my time with tasks and distractions, because if I slowed down, my past would inevitably catch up with me. I never paused to question whether my life was moving in the right direction. It was moving, and that had been good enough.

Breathing deep, I cleared my mind and allowed the thoughts to dissipate, until it was just me, in the moment, enjoying the last sips of my coffee. The caramel creamer I'd added was the perfect treat for a cool morning. I lingered on the front porch while the neighbors rushed out of their houses to load briefcases and kids laden with backpacks into cars. There was something nice about slowing down and not always being in a rush. To savor the minutes instead of getting through them. Larry Stone's murder was a harsh reminder that life could be cut short when we least expected it.

How did I want to spend my time? Living a busy, hurried life full of material things and empty relationships? Or finding a slower, more meaningful life filled with things and people that really mattered? My father had given me an opportunity with his business. All I had to do was choose the life I wanted. I'd made tough decisions before. This time, I wanted to make the right one.

I stepped into the shiny, clean front lobby of Callahan Capital Management and checked my watch to verify I had indeed arrived ten minutes early. It was strangely liberating to be early for a meeting. Not having to do the little walk-run while trying to beat the clock, all the while rehearsing an excuse or a profuse apology in my head as to why I was late. *Traffic.* I didn't miss the dash. In fact, I liked this slower, on-time version of myself much better.

There were three front desks separating the lobby and the back offices, with women working diligently behind all of them. Two men in matching red shirts with buckets and squeegees cleaned the office windows, while two older couples sat waiting in the lobby with me.

As I waited, my gaze roamed the lobby. The office was a stark contrast to Harmony Wealth Partners. It was open and spacious, with a color scheme of royal blue, gray, and white. All of the chairs were blue, the walls were clean and white, and Callahan Capital Management was painted in gray block letters across the back wall. The rest of the walls were filled with pictures that featured people in all stages of life laughing together, traveling, hiking in forests, and walking along beaches with running dogs. The collage of ideal lifestyle pictures on display in the lobby was enhanced with three interspersed words in matching dark wood frames: Dream. Plan. Enjoy.

The entire marketing program they showcased was professional and effective, if the number of clients moving through the office was any indication. Two older couples emerged from the back offices, thanking their advisors before stopping at the front reception desk to book subsequent appointments, while the other two couples waiting in the lobby were called back to take their place. An odd quiet descended, and I was the only one left waiting. The place didn't seem to be hurting for business. I grew more and more curious about Nick Callahan as the hands on the wall clock over a coffee station hit the top of the hour.

I'd known him from afar back in high school and had only met him briefly in the reception line at my father's funeral. The town football star turned successful financial advisor. From what I could gather, I'd bet he was one of those guys with the Midas touch, where everything in his life was golden. It would make sense he'd be able to get away with murder.

"Kate Abbott?" A man called my name.

I rose from the comfortable chair and turned around to see Nick Callahan coming out of his side office, just to the left of the lobby. His black polo shirt with the company logo and khaki pants, along with his bronzed glow, gave me the distinct impression he spent most of his time on the golf course.

"Thank you for meeting with me." I approached the blond, tan, broad-shouldered Nick and shook his outstretched hand.

"Thank you for coming in to see me." His return handshake was firm and practiced. "It saves me from having to track you down."

Confused, I asked, "Track *me* down?" What could he possibly want with me?

"Let's talk in my office." He led the way into his spacious office.

Instead of guest chairs in front of his desk, a round meeting table was tucked into the corner and surrounded by three chairs. I joined him at the table.

Outside the window, sunlight dappled through the reddened leaves of the tree growing from the manicured green grass, and little brown swallows chirped and flitted between the branches. It was a nicer view than my father's office provided. His window looked out on a parking lot.

"I hear you've become a business owner." Nick leaned back in the chair and folded his hands in his lap.

"People in this town sure hear a lot of things," I commented dryly. "But, yes, I inherited my father's share of Harmony Wealth. I'm still trying to get my bearings."

"You've had an interesting start to the week." He chuckled, his smile flashing his perfect white teeth.

"I guess you could say that if you find murder interesting."

"It's a shame about Alex. Have you heard if they plan to formally charge her? I know you two are close friends."

"The cops know the gun was planted in her car by the real killer." Sure, I stretched the truth, but I wanted to see what his reaction would be. He didn't even flinch. "Alex didn't shoot Larry Stone. The killer is still out there, and the police are close to finding them."

"You're probably right." Nick ran a hand over his short hair, gelled perfectly into place. "We have a great law enforcement team. Besides, I know Alex couldn't kill anyone. She's not the type."

"Do you know her well?" I wondered what connection Nick shared with my friend. It couldn't be romantic. He wasn't Alex's type. She went for the bad boys with leather jackets and tattoos, not the town jock.

"We see each other at the monthly chamber of commerce events, usually the after-work happy hour," he explained. "My wife, on the other hand, has Alex redecorating a room in our house every year it seems like, and now she's moved on to the lake cabin."

I took a wild guess that Nick's wife spent his money as fast as he made it.

"You said my coming in this morning saved you from having to track me down," I said. "What did you mean?"

He opened a leather folio on the table, pulled out a thick envelope, and put it on the table in front of me. "I know the timing isn't great, but I've got my own business to think about."

Not sure what he was getting at, I opened the envelope and took out the documents. I quickly scanned them, then my gaze shot up to meet Nick's green-eyed stare. "You're suing me?"

"I'm suing Harmony Wealth Partners," he said, as if that was any better. "A few days ago, I would have been suing Larry Stone."

"You mean Harmony Wealth Partners?" I corrected snidely. "Let's not tiptoe around the fact that I know you're trying to put the competition out of business."

"Turnabout is fair play." He gave me a hard stare, unwilling to relent.

I was so angry, I had to fight the urge to kick his shins under the table. "Is this what I can expect from you if I decide to keep the office open? Getting sued if a client chooses to invest their money anywhere but with your firm?"

"Larry was openly soliciting my clients –"

"That's not illegal," I cut him off. "Larry never worked for your firm. Without a non-solicitation clause, your case has no merit." Was I going to have to defend Larry's nefarious actions to save the reputation of Harmony Wealth Partners?

"Hannah Younger worked for our firm," Nick said. "And she took our client list with her when she left to work for Larry. She signed a contract with a non-solicitation clause. The case has merit."

His revelation rendered me speechless. I couldn't argue my way out of that one. If what he said was true, Nick Callahan had a solid case. I'd have to find another angle, and Larry hadn't left me much to work with. The scumbag. "I heard Larry had some new investment his clients were interested in, but I can't find much information on the product. Do you have any idea what exactly he was selling?"

"Lies, that's what he was selling." Nick's eyes flashed with anger. "It's no wonder someone killed him. I'm surprised it didn't happen sooner."

I pressed on despite his obvious agitation. "How do you know his investment was a lie?"

"Larry promised them outrageous returns on their money. You know as well as I do that guaranteed returns are about as real as fairies and unicorns. I don't care what you're selling, the guarantee doesn't exist, and anyone who offers it should know better."

"But the clients bought it?"

"Of course, they bought it. People in town trusted your dad, so they believed Larry was trustworthy. They all had stars in their eyes, and none of them would listen to me."

"It must have been hard for you to lose so many clients to Larry." The lawsuit in my hand proved he hadn't taken the loss well.

A menacing look came to his eyes. "I don't have to worry about it anymore, do I?"

I couldn't rule out motive with Nick staring daggers at me, not the least bit sad over Larry's death. Now would be a good time for me to leave, because he was seriously creeping me out. Instead, I thought of Alex sitting alone and scared in jail, and it gave me the courage to keep going forward.

"Maybe you decided to get rid of the competition on your own," I suggested. "Where were you on Tuesday night?"

Nick sat forward in his chair and looked at me intently. "I've already talked to the cops."

"Did you tell them about the lawsuit?"

"No." He challenged me with his stare.

"Did you tell them you argued with Larry on the day of my father's funeral?" Before he could say anything, I added, "And don't try to deny it because I saw you."

"I argued with Larry." He gave a casual shrug, as if to say he was unconcerned. "He refused to acknowledge any wrongdoing or even discuss the situation. I warned him I'd pursue legal action if he didn't settle with me and he was the one who flew off the handle. Just because we argued, it doesn't mean I killed him. Do you expect to prove me wrong?"

83

I gulped. Was this the part where he'd strangle me for trying to uncover his secrets?

"Do you think one of Larry's clients found out he was running a scam and killed him because of it?"

"I wouldn't be surprised by that in the least," Nick said. "If Larry's investment had paid out like he promised, then we should have a lot of rich people walking around Harmony Falls."

"And if he made so much money for people, then why would any of them have a reason to kill him?" I concluded.

"Exactly," Nick confirmed with a decisive nod.

I wasn't sure what to make of Nick. He frightened me enough to the point I believed he was capable of murder, but he also seemed like a regular, honest guy. Not counting the lawsuit.

"Is a lawsuit really the way you want to handle this?" I hoped we might come to some better arrangement. "I'm not Larry. We could talk about solutions. What if we gave the clients back?"

"This isn't a game of marbles, Ms. Abbott. This is business. I want to be compensated for my losses."

I couldn't wait to find out how much he expected those losses would add up to. Even if, in some alternate universe, I decided to keep my share of the business, Nick's lawsuit would bankrupt me and completely destroy the firm's reputation. Along with my father's. If Larry and his scam didn't take care of that first. "Did you know Larry's nephew inherited his share of the business? You're essentially suing two people who had nothing to do with Larry poaching your clients."

"If the two of you want to put your heads together and try to come to a settlement out of court, I'm open to the proposition."

"Basically, all you care about is the money." I'd discovered the thing that made him tick.

"It's about recovering my losses." Nick gritted his teeth. "I deserve to be made whole."

"You know what they say. Money can buy happiness, but it can't buy character." I didn't care if I offended him with the unvarnished truth. Nick

Callahan was greedy and shameless. I stood up, ready to leave.

"I suppose you think I should just forget the whole thing? Turn the other cheek?" he said, looking up at me. "What do you expect me to do?"

I stared down at him. "I don't expect anything from you. Not after this." I shoved the thick envelope into my shoulder bag.

"I didn't want it to come to this. I'd hoped to talk some sense into your dad, but that's no longer an option."

"If that's true, why didn't you try to talk it over with me before slapping the business with a lawsuit? Damon and I can't even get back into the office until the police have collected all the evidence from the scene." I winced at the last word. Harmony Wealth Partners would forever be the scene of a deadly crime, just like Larry would forever be *the victim*.

"There is one thing I'd agree to." Nick stood to face me directly. "Sign the business over to me, and I'll drop the lawsuit."

*Whoa.* Sign the business over? First Larry had been after my share, and now Nick was making a move, albeit an underhanded one. If I still wanted to walk away and be done with the whole mess, this was my chance. I'd be leaving the clients in capable hands with Nick, and some of them had been his in the first place. I could get back to LA and leave Nick in the uncomfortable position of having to explain Larry's fraud to the authorities. It would serve him right.

My gaze was drawn to the framed photos on Nick's bookshelf next to his desk. He had the perfect pictures of the perfect family—a beautiful wife, two boys, one girl, and a smiling golden retriever. They probably lived in a perfect house and drove perfect cars and went on perfect family vacations. Everything about Nick was a little too perfect.

I knew I had to turn him down. I couldn't purposely ruin a man's life. And I wasn't handing my father's business over to anyone. Not even to the perfect Nick Callahan. "I'll have to discuss this with my partner, and we'll let you know."

"My offer is good whenever you decide."

"I'll keep that in mind." I'd tell him where to shove his offer later. For now, I wanted to leave all of my options open.

"Is there anything else you wanted to speak with me about?" Nick opened the office door to show me out.

"Actually, there is one more thing I want to know," I said. "You never told me where you were the night Larry was murdered."

A shadow fell across Nick's face, as if he hadn't expected me to continue pressuring him for an answer. "My son had a football game, and after that, we were all at home. My wife was getting the kids ready for bed."

Just as I expected, he even had the perfect alibi.

"Do you really think I had something to do with Larry's murder?" The look on his face told me maybe.

"I don't know you well enough to say either way." I did know that everyone had a few skeletons in their closet. Some were just bigger and scarier than others.

"If you really want to know who killed Larry Stone, why don't you ask his nephew?" Nick suggested. "Damon Stone rolls into town, his uncle gets murdered, and he inherits a profitable business. That's quite a coincidence, isn't it?"

"It certainly is," I agreed, more and more convinced I'd become business partners with a murderer and that he might be coming after me next. "Let's hope the police get the investigation wrapped up soon. I think we'll all sleep a little better at night once the killer is behind bars."

"I'm sure they're doing their best, but these things take time," he said. "Now, if there's nothing else you want to accuse me of, I have to get ready for my next meeting."

"I have somewhere I need to be anyway." I followed Nick back out to the lobby and stopped dead in my tracks when I came face to face with Detective Matthews.

"Ms. Abbott, what are you doing here?"

# Chapter Nine

"Detective, so nice to see you again." I hoped the guilt wasn't evident on my face. Here I stood, playing detective, and the real cop had caught me red-handed.

He did not look happy to see me there.

"Jake, good to see you." Nick exchanged a friendly handshake with him. "I'm still waiting for that rematch. You can't wipe the court with me and not give me a chance to redeem myself."

"I'll call you on my next day off," the detective said, then slid his gaze back to me. "Can I see you over here for a minute?"

Without waiting for me to answer, he steered me over to a deserted corner of the lobby. What was he doing at Nick's office anyway? Did he have more questions about the murder? Was Nick a suspect?

I whipped around on him. "Why are you here? Are you following me? Am I a suspect now?"

"Why are *you* here?" he asked. "I'd hate to think you might be interfering in my investigation."

"Not at all," I lied. "I was just—"

"Because if the killer finds out you're looking for him, he could come after you." Matthews looked more worried than upset with me.

"What makes you think the killer is a man?" I raised a brow in challenge. "And what makes you think I'm looking for anyone?"

"I talked to your sister before I came here."

"You *are* following me!" I pointed a finger to his chest. It was hard as a rock under his uniform.

"What else could you be doing here?" he asked in a tense whisper.

"Getting slapped with a lawsuit, apparently." I took the envelope out of my bag and smacked it against the wall of his chest. "See for yourself."

"You're not kidding." He folded the papers and shoved them back into the envelope. "That should keep you busy and out of my way."

I snatched the envelope from his hand. "Some help you are."

"I'm a cop, not a lawyer," he teased, smiling. "Though I could recommend a few if you need one."

"Only guilty people need lawyers."

"And you're innocent?"

"Well, yeah. Of course, I am." I smiled brightly, then wavered.

He looked me straight in the eye. "I assume your business here is finished."

I nodded, embarrassment heating my cheeks. His look went through me like a laser, and I began to think I'd seriously underestimated the detective. Up close and personal, I also had the chance to notice he was rather attractive. In a law enforcement type of way.

"Let's not have this conversation again." He put a gentle hand to my shoulder for emphasis. "Am I clear?"

"Crystal," I conceded.

I had no intention of giving up. I simply had to be more discreet now that he was on to me.

"Good." He turned and went over to where Nick waited, watching our interaction with a flare of interest. "Have a nice day, Ms. Abbott."

"I doubt it can get any worse." I stuffed the envelope in my bag and bid them both farewell, but curiosity nagged me. What was Matthews there to see Nick about?

"Can we talk?" Matthews asked him as I headed out the door.

"We can go to my office." Before Nick closed the door, he said, "Remember my offer."

I flipped him a mental bird. I wouldn't take his offer if he slapped me with a thousand lawsuits. Harmony Wealth Partners was not for sale. Not as long as I was alive.

When the two men disappeared behind the closed door, I stormed out of the office and walked across the parking lot. It would be impossible to wrangle any information out of Matthews now that he was aware of my meddling. I only wanted some answers. Unfortunately, I was still keeping secrets of my own, and until I was ready to give them up, how could I expect the detective to share any details?

I couldn't rely on the check copies saved to the laptop for evidence because it wasn't strong enough to prove Larry was a fraud.

The agent hadn't returned my call. If he even existed.

And then there was the incredibly convenient coincidence of Damon inheriting a business while he happened to be in town. And Hannah, jealous of Larry's other girlfriends, walking into the office behind Alex and I, which gave her enough time to plant a gun. What could I tell Matthews that he didn't already know? That I had a hunch?

Nick being upset over losing some clients and his lawsuit might be suspicious, maybe even motive, but it didn't make him a killer.

All I had were theories and maybes, and I was sure Matthews had enough of his own, so really, what could I tell him?

Out in Kylie's Honda SUV, I tossed my bag on the passenger seat. I pulled out the lawsuit paperwork and gave it another glance. Between Larry's scheming and what Hannah did to Nick, I didn't know if the business would have a chance at survival, or if it was headed for ruination. Hannah stealing the client list was wrong and unethical. I wouldn't argue that, but Nick didn't have to sue over it. Demanding Harmony Wealth Partners as a settlement offer was just as dishonest. His clients chose to leave him. Taking over the business was the only way he could save face and get them back under his management at the same time.

Golden boy Nick Callahan couldn't be as perfect as he wanted people to believe. I'd bet he had a skeleton or two in his closet. It might be time to snoop around and see if I couldn't dig one up. Give myself some leverage to negotiate. Turnabout was fair play. He'd said so himself.

Casting the paperwork aside, I pulled out my notebook next. I crossed Nick's name off my list. Matthews could be talking to him about anything, plus, he had an alibi for the night of the murder. I wasn't finished with Mr.

Perfect, not in the least, but I could safely say he was no longer my main suspect.

My meeting with Nick had confirmed one thing though. The theory that an angry client had killed Larry seemed to be the most logical. If only I knew where to start. The firm must have hundreds of clients. How would I whittle the list down to one person?

I started the car and backed out of the parking space next to what must be the detective's blue Blazer. There was a police badge decal on the bottom corner of the back window. What were his leads on the case?

I could drive myself crazy trying to speculate, and since I'd promised to check in with Kylie after my meeting, I let it go for now and headed to the cake shop. It was quiet when I entered. Two women were seated at a table by the main window, talking in muted tones over their coffee and cupcakes. Behind the front counter, Kylie leaned on her elbow as she flipped through a magazine. She looked up when I came through the door.

"It's nice to see things have settled down here," I said. "You were running when I left this morning." People were looking for any chance to congregate and discuss Larry's murder. It was literally the talk of the town, and Kylie's shop had become a popular spot.

"It'll pick up again around lunch." Kylie closed her magazine. "Mom stayed to help serve coffee and catch up on the gossip. The murder is all anyone can talk about. It's so out of place for Harmony Falls. Things like that just don't happen here."

"Any new leads?" I plopped my bag on the counter.

"Not at the moment," she said. "You?"

"Oh, nothing but this little lawsuit." I handed the papers to Kylie. "Nick Callahan is suing Harmony Wealth Partners for poaching his clients."

"Get out!" She slapped her hand on the counter. "Dad is barely in the ground, and Larry's still down at the morgue. Has he no respect for the dead?"

"He was the first to admit it was bad timing."

"I'll show him bad timing." Kylie dropped the papers on the counter. "Brooke Taylor dated him in high school, and she said his sport cup was extra padded, if you get my drift. Wait until that gets around."

Just what I didn't need. "Let's not do anything to piss him off more than he already is. I need to figure out how to make this go away."

Inside my bag, my phone vibrated with a new call. Now what?

Wallace and Reed popped up imploringly on the caller ID, and I answered.

"Mr. Reed would like to know when you will be here," Grace said.

Before I could say a word, my boss came over the phone. "You have to deliver that presentation so Brandon can approve it."

"Yes, I've done all the research and the prep."

"Exactly when are you coming back?"

"I should be back soon."

"Look, you've had plenty of time to get everything cleared up. What's the delay?"

*Oh, nothing. Just a little murder.* "I've run into a few snags, but I'm almost finished with my report."

"I want you at that meeting on Friday. That's tomorrow. Understood?"

"No need to worry. I'll make sure the client has what they need in plenty of time." It was the best I could offer under the circumstances.

Mr. Reed hung up.

"Thank you, Sir. Bye." I gusted out a long sigh.

Kylie slid me a curious look.

"That was my boss. It looks like the rest of my afternoon is shot. I'd better get something to tide me over until dinner." I started browsing the display cases in search of a sweet treat. "I think I'll have that one." I pointed to a vanilla cupcake with white lattice frosting and delicate green leaves made from icing.

"Can you pick me up for dinner at Mom's tonight? Logan got called in to cover a shift and since you have my car, I need a ride."

"Sure, then I don't have to walk into whatever ambush she has planned for me alone."

"It's not an ambush. She wants to have the family together for dinner, that's all."

"Is that why she told me to wear something nice?"

"Do you want a coffee?" Kylie put the fancy cupcake on a plate and handed me a fork and napkin along with it.

I'd filled up on enough coffee before my meeting with Nick. "Did you brew the iced tea yet?"

"It just finished." Kylie served her iced tea in fountain shop milkshake glasses with a long stick of sugarcane, a lemon wedge, and a mint leaf for garnish.

"This is amazing," I said through the first bite of the cupcake. It was moist and delicious, and the frosting was never too sweet. I might be biased, but my sister made the best cupcakes in Minnesota.

"You'll never guess who came in here this morning." Kylie watched me warily, sinking her teeth into her bottom lip.

"Detective Matthews," I said, then took a long swallow of the iced tea.

Kylie sputtered. "How did you know?"

"I ran into him at Nick's office. He said you told him I was trying to find the killer and that I went to Nick's office to question him."

"It just sort of slipped out."

I didn't need an explanation. I knew my sister. She couldn't keep a secret to save her life. "What else did you tell him?"

"He asked if I could give you an alibi for the night Larry was murdered."

"An alibi?" I crammed the last bite of cupcake in my mouth. "Does he think *I* killed Larry?"

"I also told him you were working with a Federal agent."

"Why did you go and tell him a thing like that?" My voice rose an octave. Had Kylie lost her mind?

"What did you want me to do? Lie to him?" She leaned across the counter and whispered hotly, "That's *your* department."

"I didn't lie to him." I became all too aware of the ladies at the table by the window and tried to keep my voice down. "I just haven't told him everything."

The door to the shop opened and a woman in yoga pants made her way up to the counter and asked about ordering a birthday cake.

I took my iced tea to an empty table and let Kylie wait on her customer. I didn't like knowing Matthews had put me on his own list of suspects. If he wanted an alibi, why didn't he ask me? Why go to Kylie?

While I considered my next move, my phone chirped with an incoming email from Grace asking for the status of my report. I typed a brief reply and let her know I'd run into a few complications settling my father's estate, and I had to extend my stay another day or two, which meant I wouldn't be able to make the client meeting tomorrow. I didn't imagine it would go over well with Mr. Reed, but as long as he had something to show the client, it should work out. It had to.

When Kylie finished with her customer, I brought my empty glass up to the front counter. "Thanks for the snack."

"Anything for my big sis." Kylie placed the dirty dishes in a plastic tub behind the counter.

"Do you think the detective suspects me?"

"Not really." She tore the top order sheet off her invoice pad, breaking into a mischievous smile. "If he did, he wouldn't have accepted Mom's invitation to dinner tonight."

"He what?" I exploded. "I knew this was a set up. What is Mom thinking? I have a boyfriend, and never in a million years would I want to date a cop."

"Did you know he's single?" Kylie carried on about the detective. "A man that good-looking, honest, and dependable is walking around in tiny little Harmony Falls without a wife or a girlfriend. Well, he has an ex-wife, but who cares?"

I gaped at my sister. "Then you date him."

"Oh, come on. What's the harm in sharing a dinner with him?"

"With my entire family looking on? No harm at all."

"It's the perfect chance for you to tell him what you know."

"I tried to tell him and he didn't want to hear what I had to say."

Kylie picked up a damp rag and wiped down the already immaculate counter. "I mean, you should tell him about what you do and why he should work with you. You're a great asset."

My phone vibrated with a call. Wallace and Reed. "I have to take this. I'm sorry."

"Are you sure you can't get back?" Grace asked, her voice tight with strain.

"I'm stuck here."

"Do you want me to try to reschedule the client meeting? I might be able to push it to Monday." The strain in her voice said that was the last thing she wanted to do.

"No, Mr. Reed would have a coronary. Just see if you can stall him a little."

"I'll do what I can, but you need to get back here as soon as you can."

"I know."

"I can't hold him off forever."

"I know."

"Good." She hung up.

"That didn't sound good," Kylie said, tossing her rag into a bucket.

"It's just something for work. I'll take care of it."

"You'll pick me up at six for dinner?"

My phone vibrated again. "Oh, geez, what is it now?"

I checked the caller ID. It was a local number, but I didn't recognize it. "Hello?"

"Ms. Abbott, it's Detective Matthews."

I stared at Kylie in shock. Talk about timing. The man had it in spades.

"Who is it?" Kylie's smile turned to a worried frown.

I covered the phone with my hand. "It's the detective, probably calling to arrest me."

"They don't arrest you over the phone." She laughed, and it made me want to laugh too.

I uncovered the speaker and said, "Detective, what can I do for you?"

"You said you wanted me to let you know when you could get into your office. Forensics has released the crime scene. You're free to go back."

"Thank you, Detective. I appreciate the call."

"You're welcome, and Ms. Abbott?"

"Call me Kate, please."

"Kate?"

"Yes?"

"Stay out of trouble."

I frowned before I realized he'd hung up.

"What did he want?" Kylie bounced with excitement.

"He said they've released the office, and it's safe for me to go back." I switched off my phone. "I have to go get those files."

# Chapter Ten

The door to Harmony Wealth Partners was open when I arrived. Expecting to be greeted by a mess of papers, I was caught by surprise to discover someone had cleaned the office. All the papers were gone. The front lobby was tidy, the furniture straightened, and even the magazines had been removed from the coffee table between the two chairs.

Off to the side of the lobby stood a worn metal desk heaped with file folders, and Hannah sat behind it, sorting through a pile of papers. Dressed in a fuzzy pink sweater over a pink flowered dress, she had her blonde hair swept behind her shoulders. Her eyes were rimmed red, a clear sign she was still distraught over Larry's murder. She looked up from her work when she noticed me standing in the lobby.

"Good morning, Ms. Abbott," Hannah proffered a cheerful greeting, her smile forced, as if she'd practiced it so many times she could do it without injecting any feeling. Despite her pink dress and her smile, the office lacked warmth. "We wondered if you'd be coming today."

"What happened to all of the files?" I couldn't believe my eyes. Hannah and Damon worked fast. How long had they been back before I got the detective's call?

"What files are you looking for?" Hannah angled her head, her eyelashes fluttering in the ends of her wispy bangs.

"The files that were all over the floor when we found Larry dead," I reminded her. "Those files."

Damon emerged from Larry's office and stood beside Hannah's desk, hands stuffed in the pockets of his black dress pants. "I cleaned them up this morning." He flashed a debonair, movie-star grin. "I got here right as the forensics team was finishing up, so I thought I could make myself useful for a change. We really should get rid of all this paper and go electronic."

I swallowed, my mouth suddenly dry as I watched my only plan skid off the rails and crash at the feet of two possible murderers. Damon and Hannah looked pleased with themselves for putting the office back to rights. I, on the other hand, wanted to scream. How was I going to get access to the files with Hannah guarding over them?

"If we did get new software, it would make the files more secure," Hannah added.

"Do we even have a way to account for everything, or to know if anything is missing?" I asked.

"Just little old me." Hannah typed something on her keyboard and her computer screen flashed. "I have a database listing all of our clients. There's software we could buy that would let us rebuild the files and scan them into a program on the computer that works with the database. It's super high-tech."

My brow rose on its own.

"You see?" Damon said. "Hannah's got it covered. We make a good team, so if you need to get back to Los Angeles, you're free to leave anytime."

I met his stare. What gave him the right to start taking over the office? "I haven't decided when I'm going back to LA. I have some things I need to handle and, while we're on the subject, why are you here?"

Damon recoiled, like he was taken aback by the question. "What do you mean?"

"Why did you come here?" I stalked toward him. "Larry was murdered shortly after your arrival, and now you own his share of the business. It's quite a coincidence, wouldn't you say?"

"My uncle called me." Damon lowered his brows, his look turning fierce. "He said he was in trouble and that he needed my help. I would have come sooner, but I had some business to wrap up in Seattle."

"If you say so." I didn't buy his answer.

"Look, we should probably talk about what you want to do with your share of the business, seeing as how we've become partners. If you plan to stay, and we're going to be working together, I'm open to discussing a merger." He waggled his brows suggestively.

I ignored his double meaning, though he looked delighted to have come up with a snappy comeback. "What if I wanted to buy out your share?" I tested him, curious to see if he'd take the bait.

"I'm not interested in selling," he said. "This town is starting to grow on me. I might stay awhile."

He needed to figure out how to get his hands on the money. It had to be why he wanted to cozy up to Hannah. I'd bet a million bucks that's what he was up to.

Hannah stopped her typing long enough to look up at him, and they shared a tender smile.

Oh, what tangled webs we weave.

I wasn't finished with them yet, and I took the envelope containing Nick's lawsuit papers out of my bag. "Seeing as how we're unwitting partners in this, I suppose you should know we're being sued." I held the envelope out to him.

Damon tore into it, and as he read the complaint, his nostrils flared, and the corded vein in his neck bulged. "What's the meaning of this? Nick Callahan has no right to sue us! It's bad enough he killed my uncle. Now he wants to take his business? Over my dead body!"

"Actually, he does have the right to sue us. It would seem that Hannah here used to work for Nick, and she took his client list when she left."

Hannah's shoulders drooped, and she hunched forward, a guilty look on her face.

"Big deal." Damon rushed to her defense. "People do that all the time. He can't sue us over it."

The fact that Damon had no clue how this implicated us confirmed he had no real understanding of the basic rules and laws regulating financial advisors. "Hannah signed a contract preventing her from going after Nick's clients, and then she and Larry went after his clients," I explained the situation in plain terms. "She violated the contract. That's grounds for a lawsuit."

"It wasn't like that," Hannah said in protest. "The clients wanted to switch over to Larry. We never asked them to do anything. They came to us."

"It doesn't matter," I said. "The moment you took that client list, you violated your contract. The law will side with Nick, and he wants someone to pay."

"I'm not giving him any money," Damon insisted.

"He said he'd take the business if we wanted to settle out of court."

Damon cracked his neck from side to side. "I know what he's after. My uncle told me about Nick pressuring him to sell the business. He wants to be the only act in town because he can't handle the competition." He looked at me, a feral wildness in his eyes. "What did you tell him?"

"I told him I had to discuss it with you." I felt a chill that made the hair on my arms rise. His powerful reaction proved he could be very threatening.

"He's not doing this to me." Damon hurled the papers into the trash bin beside Hannah's desk. "Find me the best lawyer in the state."

"Don't you mean find us the best lawyer?" I ventured.

"What?" Damon looked at me, confusion scrunching his face.

"Since we share the business, this lawsuit affects both of us, not just you."

"Oh, right…of course. What was I thinking? Do you know a good lawyer?"

It was the second time I'd heard someone bring up a lawyer today. I was beginning to think I might need to find one. Just in case.

"Do you want me to take care of finding someone?" Hannah made a note on her pink notepad.

"You're a doll." Damon winked at her, his earlier rage subsided.

"What should I tell Nick?" I wondered.

"Tell him we'll see him in court." He stormed into Larry's old office and slammed the door behind him.

"Right." I had to bite my tongue.

Damon acted like he owned the place with no regard for my thoughts or feelings on the matter. Used to dealing with male arrogance in the business world, I regained my composure and took a confident walk into my father's old office, flipping on the light switch and dumping my bag unceremoniously on the chair in front of the desk. Since Damon had taken over Larry's office, I guess I was left with this one.

A shiver trickled down my spine as I pictured what had been in the other office only a day ago. Larry's body, shot twice in the chest, blood everywhere. How could Damon work in there? Did the carpet have a blood stain? Would the office be forever haunted by Larry's unavenged spirit? It was all very *Macbeth*.

Happy with this office, I took off my blazer and draped it over the arm of the chair. My father's office was considerably smaller than Larry's. A tall, narrow window adorned with clean white blinds and a group of wilted green plants on the sill made the focal point. The wooden desk was neat and empty, aside from the phone.

I took a seat in the office chair behind the desk. The same one Alex had been sitting in before the police arrested her. Curious, I began pulling out drawers, finding the clutter of pens and notepads and an old phone book in the bottom drawer. There was a tall file cabinet on the back wall and a bookcase lined with financial reference books. I got up and opened the small coat closet, which held a suit, fresh from the cleaners with the plastic bag still draped over it, and a pair of leather loafers on the floor below.

I tried the file cabinet next, expecting to find it locked, but the top drawer rolled open without a struggle. It was empty. As was the next drawer and the next. If I'd been hoping to find a clue of some sort, I wouldn't find it in there.

I went back out to the main office, intent to get my hands on some of the files Hannah was sorting, when the main door swung open and an older gentleman dressed in a red buffalo plaid coat and khaki pants stepped inside, bringing with him the fresh scent of the outdoors. "I hear Larry Stone is laid out dead as a doornail down at the morgue! Who's going to talk to me about my account?"

"Good morning, Mr. Taylor," Hannah gave her standard greeting and fake smile. "Did you have an appointment? I—I didn't see anything on the calendar."

"Who would I make an appointment with?" His gruff voice filled the tiny lobby. "Everyone's dead."

"Just a moment." Hannah shot up from her desk and scurried into Damon's office.

I took advantage of the opportunity and walked over to the man, extending my hand in greeting. "Hi, I'm Kate Abbott."

"John's kid?" He looked me over, his eyes assessing and shrewd. "You turned out all right, I 'spose."

"Could I possibly help you with something?" I offered.

The files could wait. I had a real-life, living, breathing client. An obviously upset one. Just what I was looking for.

"I don't know," he said. "Can you find my money?"

"I'd like to try, Mr. Taylor, is it?" He looked to be in his late sixties, with graying hair and a few well-placed wrinkles, most of them around the corners of his eyes.

"Hank Taylor." He grabbed my hand and gave it a nice, firm shake, his hands roughened, but warm. "I was sorry to hear about your father. I would have come to the funeral, but I just got back into town last night."

"Would you like to come to my office?" I asked. "We could discuss your accounts in private."

"I'll go anywhere with a pretty young gal like you," Hank said, a sparkle twinkling in his eyes. "If you're smart, it's all the better. Larry Stone was useless."

No disrespect to the dead, but I couldn't agree more.

"Mr. Taylor, good to meet you." Damon strode out of his office, with Hannah scurrying behind him to slide back behind her desk. "I'm Damon Stone, Larry's nephew. We can talk in my office."

"Nah, thanks, but I'll take my chances with the lady here."

"I'm happy to take care of Mr. Taylor," I said.

"He's my client," Damon argued.

"The way I see it, we're in this business fifty-fifty." The office belonged to me as much as it did to him. "I'll confer with you after I've spoken with Mr. Taylor."

"You can't come in here and act like you own the place," Damon said.

"Why not?" I challenged back. "You did. Now, Mr. Taylor, would you like to accompany me to my office?"

Hank grinned, seeming amused by the back and forth. "Yes, I believe I would."

I led the way to my newly acquired office, and behind me, Hank clapped Damon on the shoulder. "I love talking business with beautiful women. It really gets my blood pumping." He made a fist and pumped his arm.

Trying not to laugh, I closed the door on Damon's furious face and scooped my bag and blazer out of the guest chair so Hank had a place to sit. After tossing the items in the coat closet, I took my seat behind the desk.

I wanted information, and I had a distinct feeling Hank Taylor had something of interest to share.

"Let's get straight to the point, shall we?" I folded my hands on top of the desk. "What are you trying to learn about your accounts, Mr. Taylor?"

"Call me Hank." He flashed me a wry grin. "About a year back, I got wrapped up in this real estate deal, and it's gone nowhere. I want to get out. I want to sell."

"How do you know how it's performed?" I probed for more information. "Do you have any statements or market trend analysis?"

"No, that's just it," he said. "I never got anything. I wrote a check, they cashed it, and then nothing. I've been patient for a year. Where the hell is my money?"

"That's what I'd like to know." I took a notepad and pen from the desk drawer. "How much did you invest?"

"One and a half million."

My gaze shot up from the notepad. Hank didn't flinch. His smile had faded, and his look was all business.

"That's a large sum of money." I was no stranger to dealing with large sums of money, but most people in this town were not in Hank's situation. They were regular, middle- and working-class families who couldn't afford to lose what little money they'd set aside in a risky investment. How much money had Larry taken from the people of Harmony Falls? And where had it gone?

"I should have listened to Callahan." Hank leaned back in the chair, rubbing a hand over his knee. "He's been on to Larry from the moment that snake rolled into town."

"Nick Callahan?" I asked to clarify. "What does he have to do with this?"

"He's running defense," Hank explained. "When Larry started selling shares of this real estate venture, people left Nick and moved their accounts here. The kid wasn't too happy about losing the business."

"So I've gathered," I muttered. "Did you get lured in as well?"

"I regret it now." Hank heaved a sigh. "That kid is good and honest, and boy, can he throw a football. He's the one I want to put my money with. If I can find it."

A plan began to take shape in my mind. "Do you trust me, Mr. Taylor?"

"Hank." His grin returned. "I guess I'm gonna find out."

"I plan to find your money," I said. "But first, I have to do a little housekeeping."

"I like a good intrigue," he lowered his voice to a conspiratorial whisper. "Just say the word, kiddo. I'm all yours." He flashed me a wink.

"I'll be in touch." I led Hank out of my office and saw him out the front door.

Damon didn't wait a second longer and burst forth from his office. "What was that all about? How dare you embarrass me in front of a client!"

"We were just going over some concerns Mr. Taylor had about his account." I gave a noncommittal shrug and turned to head back into my office.

"You can't do this," Damon warned. "The rest of the business is supposed to go to *me*. My uncle was going to buy you out."

"Plans have changed." I ignored Damon and Hannah's surprised expressions.

Now that I had a new lead, I had no intention of walking away. Not only for Alex's sake, but I couldn't leave my father's clients adrift and penniless at the mercy of Damon Stone. A man who was turning out to be just as greedy and callous as his uncle. Kate Abbott, numbers expert, never backed down from a challenge. I was on the case. And I always got my man.

"This isn't over," Damon said. "Not by a long shot." The pure rage twisting his face and the upset coursing through him should have been my first warning. A clear sign I was in over my head. That it might be best to tread lightly.

Instead, I went in for the kill. "Hannah, I'll need you to get as much of Hank Taylor's file pieced back together as you can. I'd like to see exactly what Larry sold to him."

# Chapter Eleven

I closed my office door with shaking hands. The confrontation was handled, but a commitment to keeping my share of the business for the immediate future had me shaken. I had no idea what would happen once I went back to LA. I saw a lot of video calls and excess emails creeping into my already busy life.

In a panic, I sat at the desk, opened my laptop, and got to work on the report for my boss. No matter what happened, I wanted to keep my job in LA. The work was familiar; it grounded me and gave me a purpose and an outlet for the numbers in my head. And if I could finish the report, it would be one less thing to worry about. My boss wanted that in his hands more than he wanted me at my desk. I didn't imagine I'd be asked to attend the client meeting, so what did it matter if I was in the office, or here in Minnesota?

By mid-afternoon, my stomach rumbled, just in time for my mother to stop by with a sandwich and a cup of soup. I suspected it was more an excuse for her to get a proper gander at the place and ferret out some fresh gossip than to feed her eldest child. While we chatted over lunch, she managed to casually—in her mind—slip into the conversation that Jake Matthews was not only handsome, but single.

"Are you looking for a new boyfriend?" I asked her.

Vivian pursed her lips in a tight line. "I meant for you, dear."

"You seem to forget I don't live here, and I already have a boyfriend in LA."

"This is the first I've heard of any boyfriend."

"We're keeping our relationship secret because we work together," I said, though as soon as the words left my mouth, I didn't like the way they sounded. Who was really the one benefitting from an invisible relationship?

"The detective would make a real catch. He's safe, dependable, gainfully employed."

"Some other woman will have to scoop him up." I wadded up my sandwich wrapper and threw it in the trash bin. "I don't do long-distance relationships."

"What if you did live here, though?" Vivian ventured out on a limb. "Wouldn't he be perfect for you?"

"How would I know? In the brief amount of time I've spent with him, I was giving details about a murder because I'm trying to save my best friend from going to prison for the next twenty to life."

"He's not going to stay on the market for long."

"Thanks, Mother, but I don't need you to set me up with a cop who thinks I'm interfering in his investigation. That will only make things worse."

"Why would he think you're interfering with his investigation?" Her voice got that excited shrill to it, like she was ready to fly off the handle at any moment. "Only four days back home and you're already in trouble?"

"No, mother, no one's in trouble. I'm just trying to help him understand how an investment fraud could drive someone to commit murder."

"Well, you'd know that better than anyone. It's what you do."

"Try telling him that," I said, grumbling under my breath. While I realized Matthews had an important job to do, I didn't see where it would hurt him to at least consider the investment was connected to Larry's murder.

"Tell me about this boyfriend in LA," Vivian said. "Is he handsome? Kind?"

"He's very handsome." I had no problem admitting that detail. Brandon was probably the best-looking man I'd ever been with. And the most unavailable.

"Can't you tell me anything else about him?"

"I'm not sure what else to say."

Vivian seemed perplexed by my admission, her smile fading. "Surely, there must be something that makes him stand out from the rest. If all you're going on are good looks, the relationship will fall flat on its face. I'd like to think you'd want something better for yourself."

"I do want something better." The confession had formed itself into words before my mind had a chance to censor it. "I don't think it's fair to just give up on him. We've been dating for two years."

My mother's face softened, and she asked, "Do you love him, honey?"

"I don't know." I felt lost. Or maybe I'd been found.

"Well, there's your answer." Vivian hopped to her feet. "A wise woman once said, 'Never make someone a priority, when all you are to them is an option.'"

"Maya Angelou said that."

"Yes, a wise woman, that's what I said."

I smiled at my mother as she cleaned up her sandwich wrapper and napkin, dumping them in the trash bin before picking up her cup of iced tea and getting to her feet. In her own Vivian-like way, she always made me feel a little better about life. She leaned down and planted a kiss on my cheek. "I've got yoga in twenty minutes. I'll see you at dinner tonight. Please don't wear jeans."

After she buzzed off to her yoga class, I was left alone with my jumbled thoughts. I couldn't help but think of Brandon and how we'd been in this place many times before. To get back into his good graces, I'd have to apologize, but I didn't think I had anything to apologize for this time. Why should I be the one to grovel at his feet? If he couldn't see the value in me, maybe it was time I did. I spent so much time focused on Brandon and maintaining our relationship that I never stopped to question if the relationship had been working for me.

A bump at the office door shocked me out of my rumination. What now? I'd been holed up in the cramped office for most of the afternoon. Was Damon getting twitchy? I had dropped quite a bomb on him by refusing to give up my share of the business.

When the noise came again, I went to open the door. A carpet cleaning service had descended on the office, and workers in matching hats and uniforms dragged plastic hoses and buckets of cleaning supplies through the lobby and into Damon's office. I guess that answered my question about the carpet situation.

When the cleaners fired up the machines, the noise became almost unbearable. My nerves were frazzled, and it had officially become one of those days. This was the last straw. It was time for me to leave and start fresh tomorrow. Stuffing my laptop and cell phone into my bag, I maneuvered my way over the obstacle course of hoses covering the floor. I'd have to finish my report at the house. It offered one thing the office didn't. Quiet.

"Leaving for the day?" Damon asked over the noise as he hovered in his office doorway.

"I think it's best for me to get out of the way and let them clean."

"Will you be coming in tomorrow?" he asked. "We should discuss the plans you and I have for this business and where we see it going in the future."

"I look forward to it." I kept my tone upbeat, while in my head I was dreading that discussion.

I didn't have to be a genius to know we had different visions for the office, and it was going to be hard to find any common ground on how we should proceed with Nick's lawsuit. The only thing we did seem to agree on was not letting Nick get his hands on the business.

"What if I came over to your place later?" Damon hopped over the hose blocking his path and came close to me, his big body invading my personal space, his green eyes growing soft and languid. The stubble on his jaw had thickened since yesterday, and it gave him even more sex appeal. "We could relax with a bottle of wine and talk about the future, or whatever you want. Do you have a fireplace? I love a good, cozy fire."

From her desk, Hannah craned her neck around to tune in on our conversation. Out of jealousy, or curiosity, I couldn't be sure. I wouldn't stand in the way if Hannah was interested in Damon. Only someone who was blind wouldn't find him good-looking, but like Brandon, that was all I could say about him. Then, I had my suspicions. No killer was getting me alone in my house after dark.

"I thought you wanted to discuss the business," I said. "I think it's better if we wait until tomorrow. I have plans tonight."

"What about after your plans?"

Did I sense desperation? It was not an attractive quality in a man. "After

108

sitting through dinner at my mother's, all I'm going to feel like doing is going home to open a bottle of wine and take a bath."

"Don't be so boring," Damon chided. "Where's your sense of adventure? Let's get to know each other better if we're going to be working together. I'd like a bath for two."

Hannah was in danger of falling off her chair if she angled her body another inch in our direction. She had nothing to worry about. I intended to keep Damon at a safe distance.

"Let's save the fun for another time. Tonight, I choose to be boring." I patted the hard muscle of his bicep as I strolled past him and sent Hannah a friendly wave on my way out the door.

My suspicions about Damon were growing. He was definitely hiding something. How did I get it out of him without putting myself in danger? I could picture him acting as an accomplice to Larry's crime, here to cover up any traces of evidence that could lead back to him. To tie up any loose ends.

Was I now one of the loose ends?

I was almost glad to be having dinner with the detective tonight. I'd get the chance to share my theory with him before Damon did something desperate. And with Matthews close by, I knew I'd be safe.

A warm, Indian summer breeze wafted over my face as I came out onto the street, carrying with it the earthy scent of fall. I breathed it in. A row of young red Maples lined the street, their tender branches reaching for the clear blue sky, and I felt lucky to be alive. I wondered if that's what Larry had been thinking before he died.

Dinner at my mother's house was never a casual affair. I decided to gratify my mother by wearing a dress, and I pulled the heels out of my suitcase. Even my auntie Linda had traded out her duck boots and waders for slacks and a knit sweater. My mother's sister had come down from her cabin life up North while she had some renovations done and a new dock put in before winter.

The detective was already there when Kylie and I arrived, and he stood in the kitchen with a cold beer in his hand. I marveled at how seeing him in plain clothes instead of his uniform made him feel more approachable, like I was privy to an inner secret life very few people were allowed to glimpse. The intensity of his stare hadn't softened, I realized, as his gaze sought mine out. The inner authority remained alert behind his civilian mask. What had brought him all the way from New York to my small hometown? I could admit he intrigued me and found I was suddenly looking forward to this dinner.

No one mentioned the murder as plates of roast beef, red potatoes, and green beans were passed around the table. It was like my mother's cooking became a balm to soothe the hurt we'd been through, and instead inspired us to talk of hobbies and interests, and much to Kylie's aggravation when she and Logan were going to get married. After finishing dessert, a simple raspberry torte, my auntie Linda helped with the dishes and left to enjoy the quiet of her hotel room and a good book.

Relieved no one had asked when Jake and I would be getting together—if my mother seating us next to each other wasn't obvious enough—I thought it wise for Kylie and I to leave before the conversation veered off into things none of us wanted to talk about. Least of all with law enforcement present.

"I'll walk out with you," Matthews offered after politely thanking my mother for the meal and the company.

Kylie moved like a flash to get out the door, leaving me behind with the detective. We walked down the porch steps in tenuous silence. The edge of the horizon glowed with the soft orange of the fading sunset, while above, the sky had darkened, glittering with a few early night stars.

He'd parked his Blazer behind Kylie's SUV, and the closer we got to leaving, the more I couldn't stand it any longer. "Did you have a nice meeting with Nick Callahan?"

"Ahh, there it is." He stopped short beside me. "You really can't help yourself, can you?"

"I'm just asking if you talked about anything I might find interesting."

"How hard was it for you to sit through that entire dinner without pestering me about the case?" He didn't sound angry, but his voice held a soft warning.

"I only want to help." I dropped my voice low. "The fact that you met with Nick tells me you're considering the financial side of the crime, which is something I know all about. Did I mention I was a forensic accountant?"

"You did mention that, yes." He looked away, scrubbed a hand over his face, then came back to me. "That still doesn't change the fact that I don't want you involved in this case. Murder is a far cry from a few stolen checks."

"A few stolen checks?" My voice jumped high. "Have you even looked at the files on my father's laptop? Because the last time I added it all up, it came to just under five million dollars. A lot of people would kill to have that kind of money."

His expression flickered, but he didn't back down. "It would appear someone did kill, and unless you want to be next, you'll sit back and let me do my job."

Sensing I'd get no further with him, I strode over to Kylie's car, yanked open the driver's door, and slid behind the wheel. "Sit back and let him do his job. *Hmph!*" I cranked down on the key and fired up the engine.

Kylie was shaking her head, looking down at her hands in her lap. "It went that well, huh?"

"Don't you start in on me, too." I heard the irritation in my voice. "I'm surrounded by amateurs. How am I supposed to make them understand?" I shifted the car into reverse.

"I don't think backing into him is the solution." Kylie watched Jake's car begin to back out of the driveway in her side mirror. "Although it might feel good."

"Don't tempt me." I watched the rear-view mirror to wait for Jake to drive away. The poor guy had no idea what he was dealing with.

The warm bubble bath in the old claw foot tub in the upstairs bathroom was just as luxurious as I had anticipated. A sea of foamy bubbles engulfed me, and I inhaled the fragrant scent of lavender, letting it calm my mind. The warm water hugged my body and relaxed my limbs and joints. Time slowed down, and I grew lazy, peaceful. Dim candlelight flickered off the tile walls of the bathroom, and soft, instrumental music drifted from the speaker of my phone.

Beside the tub, on a little wooden stool, sat a coffee mug full of Pinot Noir, along with a flickering lavender candle and some squares of dark chocolate. I reached for the mug and took a long, slow pull of the wine, then chased the notes of cherry and spice with a bite of chocolate. I leaned my head back against the tub, pulled a warm washcloth over my eyes, and delighted in the simple pleasure of the quiet evening I'd curated for myself. I couldn't remember the last time I'd felt so relaxed.

No phone calls. No texts. No boss. For one hour, it was just me and the water. I held my breath and ducked my head under the surface. As a child, I'd always been fascinated by the way sounds were quieter under the water, yet so magnified at the same time. I let my long hair float around me like a halo and shook my head from side to side, feeling the strands move like gentle feathers through the water.

I slid back to the surface and reclined again with the damp washcloth draped over my eyes. Inhaling a deep breath, the heady scent of lavender flooded my senses, then I slowly exhaled out. My inner peace felt restored.

Now that I had most of my father's belongings boxed up and ready to sell or donate, I'd worried returning home to an emptied-out house would seem desolate and lonely, but the emptiness had the opposite effect. All the space felt liberating. This weekend, Kylie and I could load up the SUV and drop off the donations at the thrift store. The dumpster was full and scheduled to be hauled away. The estate sale was the last project left to coordinate before the house sold.

I'd also started to view the lawsuit Nick Callahan had so inconveniently slapped us with in a different light. It might provide the perfect cover for me to review the books and financial records for Harmony Wealth Partners. How could I possibly consider any offers to buy out my share or make an equal trade to Nick without knowing where the business stood financially? I also had no idea how far Larry had taken his scheme. Harmony Wealth Partners could be bankrupt for all I knew. It would serve Nick right to trade him a worthless business. A girl could dream anyway.

Truthfully, the fact that everyone thought it would be so easy to buy me out made me want to dig in my heels and stay. My father knew I was headstrong and stubborn enough to get what I wanted. It had to be why he'd left his share to me and saved the evidence on his laptop for me to find. What made him decide to secure it all in a safe deposit box in the first place? And how had he planned for the lawyer to give me the key? Was it possible he'd known he was in danger? Like in the movies, where one of the characters gets a mysterious letter. An "if you're reading this, I'm dead'" kind of thing.

I hadn't been prepared for any of this to unfold. For my life to take such a drastic turn in such a short amount of time. In my mind, I planned to return home for the funeral one day and be back on a plane the next. I never imagined I'd inherit a business involved in a possible fraud, have to fend off buyers for my share, face down lawsuits, and expose a cold-blooded killer. Part of me expected I'd be missing LA, but the longer I stayed in Harmony Falls, the less I wanted to leave. That had to be the most unexpected side effect. This was my home; it's where I'd grown up. I had memories, friends, and family around every corner. The only real ties I had to California were Brandon and my job.

Grounding myself back in the moment, I savored the bath and the stillness that came with an almost empty house. The percussive melody of "You're So Cool" by Hans Zimmer filled the room, and I drifted until the song ended. The music left me hopeful and optimistic that everything would work out for the best.

Eventually, like all good things, my bath came to an end. The water in the tub cooled and the bubbles had dissolved. My playlist ended on its final tune. I slipped under the water one last time and washed my fears and worries away.

A fierce banging noise traveled through the water and jostled me out of my reverie. I shot up like an arrow, sloshing water over the edge of the tub. I wiped my eyes with the washcloth. Blinking away the water from my lashes, I stared at the closed bathroom door, my heart kicking up its beat against my chest. The familiar stab of fear crept back in around the edges. In the mirror, the yellow reflection of the glowing candles danced in the eerie quiet.

I'd distinctly heard a noise. Or maybe it was only the random sounds of an old house with old pipes. Sitting motionless, I held my breath, waiting in a strange, silent limbo for the noise to come again. Downstairs, a loud bang echoed through the house. Was someone trying to get in? Or were they already inside?

I pulled the chain for the stopper in the tub and scrambled out to stand dripping wet on the cushioned bathmat. In a hurry, I worked my wet body into my nightshirt and a pair of socks, then twisted a towel around the wet mess of my hair and picked up my phone. The time was 9:09. The number of endings. Hopefully not mine.

Racing into the spare room, I grabbed the box cutter from the dresser and readied my phone to call the police as I crept down the stairs. I'd made it halfway down the stairs when the noise persisted.

*Bang! Bang! Bang!*

I realized its source was the demanding pounding of a fist. Someone was at the front door. My thumb hovered over the slide button to eject the blade on the box cutter. Who could be at the door so late? My heart thundered in my ears, pumping blood through my veins as fear gripped me in an iron hold.

"Hello?" I called out from my perch on the stairs. "Who's there?"

"Kate Abbott?" A deep, male voice came through the closed door. "I'm Agent Mason West with the U.S. Treasury Department. I need to speak with you."

# Chapter Twelve

I mouthed the words *U.S. Treasury Department* to myself as the reality sank in. What had prompted the agent to come all the way to Harmony Falls rather than simply returning my phone call? Was it worse than I thought?

Curiosity winning out, I put the box cutter down on the step and hurried up to the front door. I turned the deadbolt and whipped the door open, only to realize how little clothing I had on and that I was still dripping water from my bath.

Mason West arched a clever, interested brow as he took in the sight of me. "I take it you weren't expecting company."

I blinked as I stared at the agent. Mason West was far from nerdy. No glasses. No pocket protectors here. He was all broad shoulders and dashing good looks put together in an expensive blue suit. What was with all the handsome guys in Harmony Falls lately? It was an interesting time for me to come home.

"I'm Kate Abbott," I said, my voice gravelly.

A soft chuckle rumbled in his chest. "I know."

"Oh, right, because you didn't ask me anything—or anything—I mean—yes?" I stumbled over my words. Agent West had thrown my mind into a tailspin. "I wasn't expecting you."

"I realize it's late, but I wanted to speak with you about the message you left for me yesterday." He looked over my shoulder into the house, his gaze scrutinizing and intelligent. "Is this a good time?"

I glanced down at the nightshirt clinging to my wet body and the rivulets of water running down my bare legs. "I just got out of the bath."

His stare darkened, if that was possible, a glimmer of male interest behind his eyes. "I can wait if you'd like to put something more on."

My thoughts exactly. I didn't think I could have a serious talk with him wearing nothing to cover my bottom half. Could the guy be any hotter?

"Or should I come back later?" he asked.

"No, no, please, come in." I waved him into the house. "I'll run upstairs and change."

As he stepped into the house, he pulled open his suit jacket and reached into the inner pocket, withdrawing a slim leather wallet. He flipped it open to reveal his federal identification card and silver badge. It was official. His presence here meant big trouble.

"You can wait in the kitchen," I said. "I'll just be a minute."

He looked past me, through the den, and into the dark office. Then his gaze met mine again. Dark, brooding, filled with suspicion, he scrutinized me heavily before he turned toward the kitchen. My heart galloping a staccato in my chest, for entirely different reasons this time, I bounded up the stairs, stopping to retrieve the box cutter before clambering into the bedroom. I dropped everything in my hands on top of the dresser and pulled out a pair of jeans and an ivory button-down cardigan from my suitcase. I had to dress fast, because every moment he was downstairs, alone, was a moment for him to find or see something that might be taken out of context.

Unwinding the towel from my hair, I combed my fingers through the wet locks and clipped a messy bun into place on top of my head. I raced back downstairs and into the kitchen. The agent wasn't there. I found him back in the office, his fingers hovering over the keyboard for my laptop.

He casually turned to look at me, his eyes glittering in the dark like a predator. Mason West was unlike any financial agent I'd ever met. He looked more like James Bond, ready to pull out a Glock instead of a calculator.

"We can talk in the kitchen," I said, turning to lead the way.

Behind me, I sensed his gaze on my body, taking in every inch of my person. I understood what it felt like to be under a microscope. Uneasy with his looming presence, I picked up the pace and scurried into the kitchen.

Right on my heels, he came to stand at one end of the island counter while I stood at the other end. We stared at each other for several moments, each taking the other in, neither of us wanting to be the first to speak. Finally, I couldn't take the silence any longer.

"So, Agent West, what brings you all the way to Harmony Falls?" He couldn't have come simply because I'd called him.

"I'm investigating a case, and I got a lead."

"What lead is that?"

"Your phone message."

We stared each other down for another moment; then I anxiously cleared my throat. "Were you investigating my father?"

"No."

I was only slightly relieved by his answer. "Are you investigating me?"

"Maybe."

What could I ask him to get more than a one-word answer? "Why did you show up at my door at nine o'clock at night?"

He reached into one of his inner suit jacket pockets and took out a photo he then placed on the counter. A black and white shot of Larry Stone. "What can you tell me about this man?"

My gaze went from the photo back to his dark stare. "Larry Stone was my father's business partner."

"And?"

"And what?" I crossed my arms over my chest in a huff. I knew what he was trying to do. "Why don't you tell me what you want to know instead of playing this silly game?"

He pursed his lips with the hint of a smirk. "What made you call me?"

"My father left your card in a safe deposit box."

"Only my card?"

"That, and a laptop computer. I think he was gathering some kind of evidence on Larry because he suspected him of defrauding their clients."

"Your father actually called me a few months ago. He told me he had evidence of a Ponzi scheme Larry Stone was running out of the office. He was supposed to get the evidence to me, but I never heard from him again.

When I tried to track him down, I found out he was dead, along with Larry Stone."

I looked down at my feet, regret tearing at my heart. "That's right."

"I'm sorry about your father," he said, his voice imbued with sincerity. "I'm here to investigate Larry Stone and his Ponzi scheme. I believe the murders are related."

Finally, someone who agreed with me.

"Wait, what do you mean by murders?" I searched his face for confirmation. "My father died of a sudden heart attack."

He shrugged a casual shoulder. "Maybe he did, maybe he didn't. It's been my experience that when people start turning up dead around large sums of money, it's all related."

I couldn't argue with him on that point. It's what I'd suspected all along. But to conclude someone had gone to great lengths to murder my father and make it look like natural causes was hard to wrap my head around. Not impossible, but even as I knew it might be true, I didn't want to believe it. "None of this makes sense anymore."

"Let me help you figure it out." He put his hands in his pockets and paced the length of the room. "Larry Stone pulled off a similar scheme in a small town in northern Washington. He got away with over two million dollars, claiming the missing funds as losses in his client's accounts. He then moved to Harmony Falls, yet another small town, and I caught wind he might be trying to do the same thing again, only on a larger scale. You see, greed makes people sloppy. They get away with one scam, so they up the stakes again and again, getting braver, taking more money, but eventually, they slip up. That's when I find them."

"You're too late to find Larry." I snorted delicately. "He's dead."

"His nephew is here." He stopped his pacing and pulled another picture from his jacket pocket. This time, he stood a little too close to me as he placed the black-and-white photo on the counter. "Damon Stone is one of his accomplices."

He smelled really good. Manly and warm with a hint of spice, like expensive leather. His suit was made from quality fabric. A watch peeked out from under his sleeve, but I couldn't see the brand. Judging from his suit, I had to guess it was designer and worth a small fortune. Agent West wasn't just good at his job; he excelled at it.

"If I had to guess, I'd bet Hannah also has something to do with all of this," I said. "She has access to the computer and all of the files. She and Damon are probably planning to ride off into the sunset together and leave me to deal with Nick Callahan and his stupid lawsuit."

"Someone has to stay behind and cover the tracks." He leaned back against the counter and crossed his ankles, hands stuffed in his pockets.

"Hold on." I held up a hand. "Do you think I murdered my own father to get my hands on the money?" I stared at him in disbelief. "How could I have done it? I was back in LA when he died."

"That doesn't mean a thing," he said. "You could have had someone else kill him. You could have killed Larry Stone and planted the murder weapon in your friend's car to make her take the blame. You could be the mastermind behind the whole operation."

I gritted my teeth and met his scrutinizing gaze with my own. "If that's what you think, then you don't know me at all."

"I know you have a background in securities and finance and that you work as a forensic accountant for Wallace and Reed Consultants in Los Angeles. In learning how to search out financial crimes, you've also learned all the ways to commit one. In my experience, the dumb ones are never the masterminds. I go after the brains. It's much more satisfying to outwit your opponent, don't you agree?"

I stared at him, aghast, and at least remembered to close my mouth. "You are insane."

He leaned in close, and his gaze searched mine. "The way I see it, you've only got one way out of this, unless you want to serve time in federal prison as an accomplice."

"I won't sleep with you, if that's what you're after." He might be sexy, and he smelled damn good, but he thought I was a mastermind killer, and his presumptions about my character were incredibly annoying.

"You're not my type." He backed off. "What I want from you is help gathering the evidence I need on Larry and Damon Stone, and Hannah Younger, if she's involved. I want to close this case."

"Let me inform you of something, Mr. Federal Agent." I jabbed a finger at his lapel. "I'm already investigating them on my own. Why do you think I called you? I need some backup."

"What are we, Starsky and Hutch?" He grunted. "I'm the one who calls for backup here, not you."

"Well, then, you'd better call them because you've got two dead bodies and five million in missing client funds."

"How do you know it's five million?"

"I have the evidence my father left behind."

"It might help your credibility if you could be as forthcoming with me as possible."

"Why should I?" I'd had enough of his intimidation. I was glad I wasn't his type. Agent West was the most annoying man I'd ever met.

"For one," he said. "It might keep you out of prison."

I paced away from the counter, then spun around. "I'm not worried about prison. You need to prove I killed two men, and since you can't because I didn't do it, you have nothing on me."

He snorted a disdainful laugh.

"And if I'm such a criminal mastermind, how come I don't have access to the business account or any of the money? Why would I call you and draw attention to myself?"

"It's called misdirection," he said. "Classic novice move."

"First, I'm a mastermind, now I'm a novice?" I shook my head. "Why am I even bothering to defend myself to you?"

"Guilty conscience? Who knows? People try anything when they're backed into a corner." A clever smirk played across his lips.

"You are impossible!" I threw up my hands. "You've accused me of murder, threatened me, intimidated me, and you want my help? Unbelievable."

He pushed away from the counter and walked up to me, looking down into my eyes as he towered over my scant five-and-a-half feet with his height. "I can make the lawsuit go away."

We stared at each other with hesitation.

"I don't trust you," I said.

"Same."

I retreated a few steps and folded my arms. "How would you make the lawsuit go away exactly?"

"I can't reveal all my secrets." For the first time, he smiled.

If I'd thought he was sexy before, seeing him smile practically made me swoon, but he was too arrogant and annoying to have any redeeming qualities. And I wouldn't give him the satisfaction.

"What do I have to do?" I asked.

When I contacted Mason West, I'd expected a nerd with a badge who'd let me call the shots. The agent standing in my kitchen would not be so easily swayed. I'd called for backup and ended up digging my hole even deeper. For the sake of my father's business and my reputation, I needed the lawsuit to go away. In a roundabout kind of way, I needed Mason West.

"I was hoping you'd come to your senses," he said. "Why don't we start with you giving me the evidence you got from your father?"

"Done." I marched back into the office and pulled the flash drive from my laptop. I'd gone over the files enough times to know what was there. I handed the drive to him. "What now?"

"I'll be in touch." He tucked the flash drive in his suit pocket, along with the two photos, and strolled out of the kitchen and up to the front door. "Hopefully I'll catch you in the bath again." He flashed a clever grin, opened the door, and left, closing it behind him.

It was a good thing he was so annoying, or I might be inclined to like Mason West.

I stood in the entryway, staring at the door after Mason when my cell phone vibrated from the kitchen counter. I'd left it next to my notebook, and I picked it up. A text message from Brandon.

His text message was one word: *Hi.*

"That's it?" I stared at the message, waiting for more to follow. "Seriously?" I didn't respond to his message. I needed more than one word.

The next message came: *Miss U.*

I knew he wanted something. Why couldn't he pick up the phone and call? Giving in, I responded. *That's sweet. Thanks.*

He came right back: *Client meeting is tomorrow. Still need your report. Grace says you won't be back in time. Want me to help?*

I found myself caught between wanting to prove my worth to the client and wanting to keep my job. I wouldn't make the meeting, and I knew I had no other choice but to let Brandon submit my report. My name was on it, at least, so they'd know who'd done all the work. It would have to be good enough. I shot off a reply: *Emailing it now. Let me know how it goes.*

His text back was basic: *Glad to help. See you when you get back.*

I waited a few minutes for another message from him. Something personal. Something a boyfriend would say to the woman he claimed to be missing.

I got nothing.

*And there was my answer.*

Deflated, I trudged into the office and emailed my completed report to Brandon. I started to type a message about how much I missed him and couldn't wait to see him, and then I wondered why I should bother. If someone wanted to salvage what was left of this relationship, I needed it to be Brandon. I erased my words and sent the email with no message, only the attached report. I had a feeling that was all he cared about anyway.

I closed my laptop and went into the kitchen for a drink. I took my new favorite coffee mug from the few I'd left unpacked on the counter. Across the front it declared *"dads are dope."* It had to have been a gift from Kylie for some random birthday or Father's Day.

I still had some leftover wine from the funeral, and I poured a Cabernet into the mug to take upstairs with me. It seemed a shame to drink Logan's wine in such a primitive way, but it still tasted the same. Logan hailed from Napa, so his wine was excellent, and I wasn't the only one who lusted after his vintage. Kylie's catering company had become the exclusive supplier in the tri-county area, and people requested her services solely to serve Logan's wine at their events. Our father would have approved of the vintage and the boyfriend. I was the one he'd found lacking. The rebel, always doing things my own way. I had to wonder why that was a bad thing.

Leaning back against the counter, I sipped the wine and checked the time. 9:55. Time for bed. I took another drink from the mug and made a quick inventory of the boxes I'd finished packing. The kitchen items had fit into nine boxes, which I'd stacked into three even rows of three. Now, there were four stacks of varying height, and the boxes weren't straight and even. My gift for numbers came with a tendency to be particular with some of my habits. Or as my therapist had labeled it, obsessive-compulsive.

OCD or not, someone had moved those boxes. The hairs on the back of my neck stood up, and I rubbed my hand over the spot, trying to calm the warning vibe. The numbers weren't matching up, and double 5s on the clock signaled change.

Something had definitely changed with the boxes. I hadn't moved them, and the last time I checked, boxes didn't move on their own. So, who moved the boxes? Had someone been in the house looking for something?

I kept all the doors locked, a habit ingrained in me from living in a big city. No one else had been in the house aside from Kylie. No one else had keys. If, by chance, someone had broken into the house, wouldn't I have noticed? And what would they want with some boxes of pots and pans and mismatched silverware? Unless they were looking for something else. My father's laptop perhaps. A piece of evidence. Maybe one of those loose ends. I told myself it had probably been Kylie, and I was worrying for nothing.

Then the phone rang. The landline in the office. I went to answer it, and no one spoke, but I heard a light breathing on the other end.

"Hello?" I said.

More breathing.

"Is someone there?"

Breathing.

"Who is this?"

*Breathing.*

I hung up the phone, a twinge of uneasiness creeping in, settling in my gut like a hard knot. I prayed the phone wouldn't ring again. But it did.

The caller ID flashed with an unknown number. I didn't want to answer it, but I also didn't want to run and hide from whoever was harassing me with these phone calls, or they might never stop.

"Hello?" I heard the annoyance in my voice.

Silence.

"Who is this?"

Nothing but silence.

I waited, thinking the person on the other end might eventually say something. Anything.

Nothing.

I hung up the phone. No sooner had I placed the receiver down, the phone started to ring again. This time, I unplugged it.

That's when my mind started doing its thing. Spiraling down into chaos and catastrophe, looking for danger around every corner. Unable to calm my anxiety, I walked through the house, turning on lights in every room and conducting a thorough inspection of all the doors and windows. They were all locked tight. I didn't find anyone hiding in the shower, under the beds, or in any of the closets, waiting to attack me. I hesitated at the door leading down to the basement. The water heater and furnace were the only things down there, along with a maze of cobwebs. There's no way I'd go down in the dark, dirty space without a flashlight and some type of weapon. I'd watched too many episodes of *Criminal Minds*.

Instead, I braced a dining chair under the doorknob to be safe. Beginning to doubt my sanity, I went back into the kitchen to straighten my stacks of boxes, restoring order in rows of three by three. If they moved again, or if the harassing phone calls persisted, I'd ask the detective to tap the phone and do a professional sweep of the house. Maybe he'd be able to see something I'd missed.

One the chance someone had been in the house, did that mean they would be coming back? Or had they found what they were looking for?

I drew in a deep, calming breath, slowly let it out, and vowed to put the worry out of my mind. They were only boxes. There could be a simple, logical explanation as to why they were moved. No psycho killers were hiding in the basement. The phone calls were probably nothing. A wrong number, or maybe a glitch. All I needed was a good night's rest.

I left all the lights on downstairs, and at the front door, I checked the deadbolt one more time. That's when I saw the car parked out in front of the house. A chill raced down my spine. My stomach tightened, the fear renewed.

Was someone watching the house? It could be the same person making the calls. Were they getting a kick out of watching me?

I couldn't see well enough through the darkness to tell if anyone was in the car, but I knew what it felt like to have a pair of eyes on me. I'd had the feeling ever since I'd gotten back to town. The voice in the back of my mind told me now would be a good time to call the detective. I wasn't hallucinating.

I leaned closer to the window, peering through the darkness in an attempt to make out any shapes inside the car. The headlights flipped on and the car sped away from the curb. I couldn't make out the color in the dark, and the license plate was impossible to read from my distance. I did notice the shiny silver hubcaps. Nothing else stood out.

I felt some ease with the car gone, but what if they came back? What if they didn't? What if they were a friendly neighbor? Or a murdering thief? How long was I going to obsess about it?

I made sure the house was locked and secure, and no one could get in without making some noise. I went upstairs, put my flashlight by the box cutter on the nightstand, and then settled into the downy pillows and went to bed. I didn't remember falling asleep, but when I did, it was a deep, dreamless slumber.

I awoke remarkably early and in serious need of coffee. I climbed out of bed and wandered into the kitchen to make myself a cup. Not worried about calories this morning, I added a generous pour of cream before heading to the front window and checking for the car from last night. It was still dark out, but no cars were parked on the street. I gazed out the window while I sipped my coffee. The caffeine chased away the rest of my grogginess and I went to take a shower.

After savoring another cup of coffee, I blow-dried my hair and got dressed in a black skirt, a lavender short-sleeved blouse, and my black ballet flats.

I checked my reflection in the mirror, then finished with some blush, a swipe of lipstick, and mascara on my lashes before heading back down to the kitchen to grab the last blueberry muffin from the box. Between the coffee and the sugar, I felt strangely refreshed and ready to face whatever the day would bring.

It was a quarter to six when I locked the front door and made the short drive from my father's house to the office downtown. Leaves fell from the trees overhead and crunched under my feet as I made my way across the deserted sidewalk. The September morning was brisk, the air fresh and clear, and I regretted not putting on a jacket.

This early in the morning, I got to be the first one to make it to the office. I locked the door behind me, turned on all the lights, and put my things on my desk. The chemical smell of the shampoo coming from the freshly cleaned carpets saturated the office, and I cracked a window open for some fresh air. Not sure how much time I had before anyone else got there, I grabbed a stack of files from Hannah's desk and got to work.

# Chapter Thirteen

Two hours later and my search turned up nothing. No account forms. No checks. No investment records. In the same way the documents copied to my father's laptop didn't indicate a crime, their absence in the files didn't escape my attention. I'd gotten through a large portion of the paperwork, changing out the stacks on Hannah's desk for her to deal with later. Unless the Feds came and took it all first.

Hannah arrived promptly at eight and had a hard time hiding her shock when she saw me working. "You're here early." She powered on her computer, stowed her purse in the bottom drawer of her desk, then came over to hover in the doorway of my office. "What time did you get in this morning?"

"Around six o'clock," I said, not looking up from my stack of papers. "I couldn't sleep."

"What are you doing?" Her gaze shifted to the piles of paperwork on my desk then darted quickly away, like she didn't want me to think it bothered her to see me wading through the files.

"I'm trying to figure out how many assets this office has under management and where the clients have their money invested." I folded my hands on the stack in front of me. "If Nick Callahan wants to take my father's business, then I want to know what we stand to lose." I prayed she'd fall for my act. Part of it was true.

When she turned sharply and walked back to her desk, I took it as a good sign and kept on working. Damon came in close to nine and spent most of his time in the lobby amusing Hannah. Or rather, distracting her from getting any work done. I secretly spied on them, though they weren't exactly being discreet. Damon sat on the edge of Hannah's desk and leaned in close to whisper something in her ear. She giggled and swatted at his roaming hand as he reached for one of her perky breasts. Not easily deterred, his other hand slipped behind the desk, and I had no idea what he was reaching for, but Hannah squealed when he found it.

Big surprise. Damon was just as lecherous as his uncle. Had he already seduced Hannah to get her into bed? To find out what she knew about Larry. Was Hannah that dumb? Grief could make people do stupid, crazy things. To her credit, Damon was gorgeous, so it couldn't have been a difficult feat. If Hannah wasn't opposed to theft, why worry about murder?

Another round of giggling ensued, and I rolled my eyes, trying to concentrate on sifting through the stack of papers that only produced more and more of the same. Then I came across something interesting.

A holdings statement for the Real Estate Investment Group.

*Bingo!*

My first thought was that the document looked fake. Printed on thin, cheap paper, some of the margins didn't even line up. I could safely assume these were not professionals I was dealing with. The contact information listed a brokerage firm outside of Virginia and a toll-free number. It was a place to start. I snapped a quick photo of the document with my phone and tucked the statement into my bag. That should keep Mason West busy and out of my hair for a minute.

Unable to take any more high-pitched squeals, I came out of my office to break up Damon and Hannah's amorous frolicking.

"Kate!" Damon swiveled around on Hannah's desk. "I see you're getting settled in your office. I have to say I'm excited we're going to be working together. You've got a lot of impressive credentials after your name. That's got to be good for business."

It appeared he'd done his research. Curious, I asked, "Which one impressed you the most?"

I hoped my Certified Fraud Examiner designation struck a chord of fear somewhere in there.

Hannah turned back to her computer screen and pretended to ignore us.

"It occurred to me that I might have overreacted yesterday when you said you didn't want to sell your share," he said.

Yep. The CFE got people to change their tune all the time.

"The more I think about it," he continued. "The more I like the idea of a partnership. We should discuss the future of the business, and of you and me, together. Maybe we could go out for dinner tonight."

Hannah suddenly regained interest in the conversation.

"If you want to discuss the future of the business, let's do it now," I said. "Should we meet in your office?"

"I don't have much free time today." Damon glanced at his watch.

Even from a distance, I could see it was a cheap Rolex knock-off. Someone who wore a watch like that wanted the finer things in life but couldn't afford them.

"My next appointment comes in ten minutes," he said.

It irked me that Damon had set up meetings with some of the clients. I couldn't imagine what they were finding to discuss. My only experience was with an irate man who'd lost one and a half million dollars. "Let's get together after your meeting." I checked my genuine Cartier watch. "Eleven o'clock work for you?"

"Eleven works great." He should look worried, like a lion pacing a cage, instead of standing there with a stupid grin on his face.

If he wanted to play this through to the end, I was game.

I went back to my office, got settled at the desk, and opened my laptop. I started an internet search. Damon had done his research; now it was my turn. I typed in his name and hit enter. I wanted to see what kind of skeletons I could find in his closet.

The first things to surface confirmed he'd worked at an investment firm in Seattle, but the firm no longer listed him on their company website as an employee. It tied in with what Mason West said about Larry running a previous scam in Washington, leading me to believe Damon and Larry did, in fact, work as a team.

Next, I used a standard industry online broker check to research the status of his professional financial background. It gave me a listing of the licenses he held and the states where he was registered to do business, along with any disciplinary action he might have received. Damon had the two licenses he was required to obtain in order to legally sell investments. The bare minimum. No surprise there. I personally held seven financial licenses, along with my many accreditations and professional affiliations.

According to the broker check, he had no disciplinary actions. No violations or complaints on his record, but he did have one disclosure for a bankruptcy three years ago.

I found that interesting. Damon went bankrupt, became a financial advisor, and inherited a book of clients in a relatively short period of time. With Larry out of the way, there was a possibility Damon now had access to millions. I hated to call it coincidence. Maybe it was luck. My intuition still wanted to go with murder.

Continuing my search, the only public record I found was for the bankruptcy. Nothing criminal. No marriages or divorce. Lastly, I checked social media and found several photos of Damon working out and lifting weights. He'd posted some close-ups of himself, his muscles, or some girl he had on his arm. He appeared to like blondes. Hannah fit nicely in that category.

And what about Hannah? She'd stolen Nick Callahan's list of clients, gone to work for Larry, who then proceeded to steal Nick's clients, and their money. How long before she was posing on Damon's arm in a photo? Did she know about the money? Was she an accomplice? Or was Hannah motivated by pure jealousy?

Armed with more information, I went out to the lobby at eleven, ready for my meeting with Damon. I planned to ask for access to the business accounts and bank records. Damon would probably make up an excuse not to give them to me. There wouldn't be much left to say after that. Guilt came in many forms.

Hannah worked at her desk, smiling and humming as she typed entries into the computer and scribbled notes on her planner. It was the happiest I'd seen her all week. Damon's office door was closed, so I seized the opportunity to dig into Hannah. "Did you know Larry had an argument with Nick Callahan at my father's funeral?"

Our gazes failed to connect, with Hannah's nervously landing on Damon's closed door. "Larry told me about that, but it wasn't the first time they've argued."

"Because Nick wanted the business," I said.

"No, he was mad about something else."

This was news. "What was he upset about?"

"I don't know." Hannah shook her head, her eyes avoiding mine. "Larry wouldn't talk about it."

I went with my hunch. "Did it have to do with the investment Larry was selling?"

Her eyes locked with me, and the silence said it all.

"What do you know about the investment?" I asked.

Damon's office door opened and he strode out, looking refreshed. Not at all like a killer with a heavy conscience. "Are you ready to plan our future?"

"I'm ready," I said. Short as that future would be.

I tamped down my nerves and followed Damon into his office, taking the chair closest to the door. I couldn't avoid a quick glance at the freshly cleaned carpet. I didn't see any bloodstains, but I knew they were there, lurking underneath the surface. They'd always be there.

I brought my focus back to Damon as he settled into the leather chair behind his late uncle's desk. He picked up a large envelope from atop a pile of folders and tossed it on the desk in front of me. "I took the liberty of having a new set of papers drawn up now that my uncle is no longer with us. His offer to buy you out was extremely generous, considering your father didn't generate a lot of business for the firm. I'm willing to double it."

It wasn't that he was willing to double the offer that caught my notice. "All of the business was generated by my father before Larry got here. Where do you think all of the clients came from? And how would you know how much business my father generated without seeing the company records?" I asked. "My father started this business. If it wasn't for him, your uncle wouldn't have a share of anything."

131

Damon's head jerked back as if he'd been slapped. "Are you saying the offer isn't good enough?"

"I'm saying my share is not for sale. To be honest, I couldn't even consider an offer until I see the books and financial records." It was time to play my cards. "With Nick Callahan's offer to take the business as settlement for the lawsuit, I'd like to see if the numbers add up before taking a stance on the issue. Where can I find the information to access those accounts?"

Damon's nostrils flared like an angry bull, and he wadded his hands into tight fists. "I am not considering Nick Callahan's settlement offer. He's not taking my business!"

"You mean *our* business, I think."

"Do you really want to hand something your father worked so hard for over to the competition?"

"I thought you said my father didn't do any work around here," I parried back, having a little fun with him. "But he did work hard to build this business. Harmony Wealth Partners has a solid client base because of my father. People trusted him."

"People invested their money—their *real* money—with my uncle because he knew what he was doing. He was an experienced businessman. Your father was small time. His name might bring people in the door, but my uncle got them to open their checkbooks."

I lost the subtle tether on my anger and shot back at him. "At least my father wasn't a crook!"

"What did you say?" Something flashed behind his eyes, something sinister and dark, and he made for a frightening opponent.

I thought it best not to push my luck. Underestimating Damon would be dangerous. I didn't know for sure if he'd murdered Larry, but thanks to Mason West, I knew he wanted the money. I pinned the envelope under my finger and slid it back across the desk, refusing his offer. "I want to see the business accounts and the financial records."

The one thing I could be sure of was that I'd find the truth in the numbers. Then Mason West would make the lawsuit go away and take Damon along with it.

Damon opened the envelope and pulled out the check. "That's a lot of zeros. Are you sure you don't want to reconsider?"

"You said it yourself. How can I hand over something my father worked so hard to build?" My lips spread into a sly smile. I could bluff with the best of them.

"I'm not the competition," he argued.

"I want to see the business accounts and the financial records," I repeated my request.

As part owner, I had as much right as he did to see those accounts, and the fact that he didn't want me to see what was in the records only strengthened my resolve.

"You don't want to play games with me." His words came laced with a warning. "Not all of us have the luxury of a steady paying job to go back to. This is my living we're talking about. My uncle worked just as hard as your father to create this place. I'd hate to see all that work amount to nothing because you want to play financial planner to a bunch of backwoods hicks."

"Be careful, someone might be listening, and we wouldn't want the clients to know what you really think of them, would we?" Ignoring his insult, I pinned him with my professional, deadpan stare. "I want to see the business accounts. I won't discuss my share until I've had a chance to review all the books and records."

Damon stuffed the check back inside the envelope and tossed the whole mess into his top desk drawer. "Hannah will get you the files once she's sorted everything out."

Exactly the answer I'd expected. "What about online access to the business account?"

"I can handle the accounting." He side-stepped the question. "Once you get your feet under you and start bringing in some business, we can talk numbers."

"It's got nothing to do with bringing in clients," I said, my frustration growing. "I have as much right to access the business account as you do."

By the look on his face, Damon didn't agree. "I don't have time to discuss this with you right now."

"Are you saying you only scheduled five minutes to meet with me?"

"I assumed you'd take the check. If not, I'm a very busy man, and this meeting is over." Damon leaned back in his chair with a smug smile on his face. He'd won this battle.

But I intended to win the war.

The door swung open, and Hannah stuck her head in the office. "Your eleven o'clock called, and they're running late, but they should be here in a few minutes."

I couldn't believe it. He'd actually booked an appointment for the same time as our meeting.

Damon checked his watch and nodded his assent at Hannah before looking back to me. "Is there anything else you'd like to discuss?"

"Apparently not." I stood to leave, careful not to step where we'd found Larry's body.

"Thanks for the chat." He came out from behind his desk, crossed his beefy arms, and sat on the edge of his desk. "I'm looking forward to doing business with you, partner."

Partner, my ass. I was going to nail him to the wall. Without another word, I stormed out of his office, channeling all of my anger into slamming the door.

"Ms. Abbott?" Hannah stopped me on my way past her desk.

"What is it?" I snapped at her.

"I found most of Hank Taylor's file, if you still wanted to see it."

Slightly taken aback, it took me a moment to find some calm. "Yes, I've been looking for his file."

Hannah fished around through some paperwork until she produced a manilla file folder and handed it over. "Here's what I've been able to find."

I flipped through the file, not seeing anything of interest. "What about his investment statements? Did you find any of those?"

"I'm not sure what you mean."

I didn't have time to explain as my cell phone rang from my office. I hesitated, but didn't think Hannah would be forthcoming with more information. "Excuse me, I have to get that."

The screen on my phone flashed with Wallace and Reed.

"Are you sitting down?" Grace's somber tone told me she did not have good news to relay. "I'm getting the agenda ready for the meeting with the client today. You're not going to like what I found."

"I'm not getting fired, am I?"

"No, it's much worse," Grace said. "Brandon stole your report."

"He's only presenting it for me," I said, relieved Grace had my back. "I emailed it to him last night since I won't be able to make the meeting. He offered to help."

"Is that why he has his name all over your report, trying to pass it off as his own work?"

"That lying snake." I sank down into the chair behind my desk. "After everything I've done for him, how could he do this to me?"

"Because you're not here to stop him," Grace remarked coolly. "This is what happens when you take time off."

My priorities flashed before my eyes. Thirty years left until retirement, with no vacations or time off out of fear someone might get ahead of me while I stepped away from the office. "I don't know if that's the kind of life I want."

"I'm sorry, what did you say?"

"I don't know what I'm doing anymore," I mumbled, talking more to myself than to Grace. "Is this how it's always going to be? Scrambling to get ahead, then getting left behind by the one guy in that office I trusted?"

There was a long silence before Grace said, "Maybe you've put your faith in the wrong place."

Had I mistaken Brandon's interest in my research skills for an interest in me? Had he been using me the whole time?

"This is my job he's messing with." I shot up from the chair and paced my small office, cursing Brandon under my breath. "I could kill him!" I fisted my hand in emphasis.

From the corner of my eye, I saw Hannah sit up and take notice of my conversation.

"I think it's too late to save this one," Grace said. "The damage has been done, and you know how the good ole' boys operate. Patting each other on the back while groping your ass and staring down your shirt."

I dropped my head in my hand. "How did I get here?"

"You got where you are because you're brilliant." Grace started one of her pep talks. "Brandon can put his name on your work all he wants, but at the end of the day, it's your mind, your research, and your work. Where would *he* be without *you*?"

"Sharing the fourth floor with the mailroom."

Grace's laughter came through the phone. "I know one fitting punishment."

"Yeah? What's that?"

"You need to dump his sorry ass."

She was right about that. "I have an even better idea."

"Well, out with it. Are you going to come back and make a scene?"

"I'm going to teach him not to mess with Kate Abbott." Filled with a renewed sense of purpose, I sat behind the desk and opened a file on my laptop to pull up the report I'd emailed Brandon. "I'm sending you an email. Tell Brandon I made a mistake in my report and had to send over a corrected version. Make sure he gets it before the meeting."

"What are you up to?"

"If I know Brandon, he hardly looked at the details of my report. He's going to trust I made it easy for him and hand out copies at the meeting. He'll let Mr. Reed take the lead and go over the specifics."

"I think I know where you're going with this, but aren't you afraid you'll get in trouble if the data is incorrect and Mr. Reed is embarrassed in front of the client?"

"Why would I get in trouble if Brandon's name is the one on the report?"

"That's devious," Grace said. "Remind me never to get on your bad side."

"Turnabout is fair play."

After hanging up with Grace, I created a fake report for Brandon, removing the specifics he'd need for probable cause. I didn't know if my plan would work, but leaving Brandon to flounder in front of the client would teach him to steal someone's work. Hopefully, it would also send the message that we were through.

With that out of the way, I decided to handle another issue that had been bothering me and fished the fake statement out of my bag, and marched up to Hannah's desk. Done playing games, I slapped the statement in the middle of her desk. "Can you explain this to me?"

"Where did you get that?" Her pretty blue eyes fluttered.

"What was Nick really mad about that day at my father's funeral?" I demanded, knowing I had Hannah backed into a corner.

"I don't think you want to know."

"I absolutely want to know because it's what got Larry killed. Most likely by your new boss!" I said the last part in a whisper while pointing to Damon's closed door.

Hannah slanted a nervous glance at Damon's office, then back to me. "Damon didn't kill his uncle."

"What makes you so sure?"

She bent forward and spoke in a quiet voice. "Look, if you want to talk, we should do it someplace a little more private." She cast another wary glance at Damon's office.

"Do you know something about Larry's murder? About the money?" I braced my hands on Hannah's desk and brought my face in close to hers. "Do you know who would want to kill him?"

"Meet me at my apartment later tonight. I have some information that will help you, and maybe it will help Alex, too." She picked up the statement and handed it back to me.

"I know Alex didn't kill Larry." I snatched the paper from her hand. "Maybe you're the one who killed him. It seems awfully convenient that you swept in the front door right after his murder, and then the cops found the murder weapon in the back of Alex's van. It would have only taken you a second to get rid of it. Why should I believe anything you tell me?"

"I didn't kill Larry, and I have no idea who did, but I want to help you. I want the cops to find Larry's killer and make them pay." Hannah picked up a notepad and a pen. "I'll give you my address."

# Chapter Fourteen

They say the road to hell is paved with good intentions. Or, in my case, potholes. The dips and craters in the gravel road leading out to Hank Taylor's place were as abundant as the lakes in Minnesota. Kylie's poor SUV was better suited for a trip to the mall than it was for any off-road adventures. I gritted my teeth and swerved to avoid as many of the holes as I could. When I called Hank to tell him I wanted him to look at the statement I'd found, he gave me specific directions from the highway, indicating his house was about a mile down the country road. As the A-frame log home with a green roof came into view and I reached the mailbox at the start of his driveway, it was exactly one mile. The odometer reading changed to 34,333. My triple digit sign that I was being led by a higher power and things would work out.

I turned down the driveway, which, like all country driveways, was mostly a combination of packed dirt and gravel. A wooden fence and pockets of birch trees ran along both sides of the drive and led up to the massive log home. A skirting of rocks wrapped around the base of the entire structure, and the covered porch, partly enclosed by a railing, extended across the front and sides of the home. The glass windows sparkled under the green roof, and a stone chimney stretched up from the back. It was a beautiful home, the property meticulously landscaped with shrubs and flowers, along with a rock garden where several bird feeders dangled from metal garden hooks.

I grabbed my bag from the passenger seat and walked up the wooden stairs and onto the front porch. I reached out to press the button for the doorbell when a deafening crack echoed from somewhere on the property. Instinct kicked in, and I ducked against the front door. A born and bred Minnesota girl, I knew the sound of gunshots. Was someone shooting at me? Maybe I'd misjudged Hank, and he was the killer, having lured me out to his house with the intention of making me the next victim. He had plenty of space to hide the bodies.

Behind me, the front door swung open, and a bald, middle-aged man in dark trousers and a white-collared shirt stood looking down his arrogant nose at me. "Ms. Abbott?"

I slowly rose from my crouched position and gave the man a sheepish grin. "Yes, that's me."

"I'm Orson, the caretaker. Mr. Taylor is out back with the dogs. He's expecting you."

Orson led me through the house, and I took in the high, wood beam ceilings, the hulking stone fireplace taking up an entire wall, and the chandeliers made from deer antlers. Glass windows along the back of the house overlooked the green backyard, complete with a pond at the edge of the tree line, and further back I could see the Straight River. Another booming gunshot rang out, and as Orson and I reached the back wall of windows, Hank Taylor came into view down on the back lawn.

Dressed in khaki pants, a flannel shirt, and a gray fishing vest, he brought a shotgun to his shoulder and took aim as a trap thrower on the ground, flung an orange target high in the air. He fired off another shot, hitting the target, the broken fragments raining back to the earth.

Two Irish setters barked and romped around the yard as Orson announced our approach down the back flight of stairs. "Ms. Abbott to see you!"

Hank lowered his weapon and rested the long barrel over his arm, his wrinkled face stern, but an amused twinkle in his eyes. The pair of dogs bounded up to me, their rich red coats long and glossy, and they sniffed ardently at my pant legs, their bushy tails wagging with excitement.

"Rascal! Brody!" Hank called after the dogs. "Heel!"

The red dogs trotted over to him and sat flanking his boot heels, their panting tongues lolling out. Orson went over to the trap thrower and switched it off before disappearing around the far side of the house.

"Let's see what you brought me," Hank said, switching on the safety for his rifle and leaning it against the trap thrower.

"It's the best lead we have at the moment," I said. "Larry did a good job of covering his tracks before someone stopped him for good."

"It's probably not the killing he was hoping for." Hank walked up to me as I waited at the bottom of the stairs, chuckling at his own humor.

"I hope you'll take this seriously," I complained. "Someone was angry enough with Larry to kill him and destroy all the files. I think his murder is connected to one of his clients. Like you, perhaps?" I squinted against the late afternoon sunlight.

"I appreciate the vote of confidence, kiddo, but I'm too old to go to the trouble of killing someone," he said. "What reason would I have to kill Larry?"

"I can give you one and a half million of them."

Hank shook his head, looking down at the ground. "I never invest money I can't afford to lose. The same with gambling." He looked me in the eye and, without flinching, said, "I didn't kill him, but his murder might be related to his extra-curricular activities."

"You mean with the women?"

An artful twinkle came to his eyes. "It always comes down to a woman."

"Where were you on the night of the murder?" I took the liberty of being blunt with Hank. He seemed to like it.

"I have an alibi, but I'm sworn to secrecy."

"You won't tell me?"

"I made a promise," he said. "To a woman."

"If you were with a lady friend, why can't you tell me? Is she married?"

"Give me a little credit, kid. I don't dip my nib in another man's ink." He winked.

"Without a solid alibi, you could be a suspect."

"I'll worry about that when the cops are standing on my doorstep. Now, do you want to show me this statement you drove all the way out here for or not?" Behind him, the dogs panted and wagged their tails.

I withdrew the statement from my bag and handed it to him. Overall, I hadn't been impressed with the document, and didn't think Hank would be either. "According to the statement, the initial investment has out-performed the market and netted a return of thirty-eight percent for the year to date. Have you ever seen one of these for your account?"

"Never." Hank scrutinized the statement. "So, if I wanted to sell my share today, I'd get back over two million dollars?"

"In theory, yes, but first, we have to prove the investment actually exists."

"What does that mean?"

I'd come up with a plan, and this was where I needed Hank's help. "I can't find any evidence the investment was registered with the SEC, or any other regulatory agency. I believe Larry was taking money for a fake product. All the checks the clients wrote were paid to Harmony Wealth Partners and deposited in the business account. What I don't know is where the money went from there. If you look at the statement right here, they normally include several legal disclosures, and this one doesn't have any." I pointed the section out for Hank. "It looks like somebody printed this off in their basement on a cheap laser printer."

"You're saying this is a fake?" Hank held the paper up to the light, looking for what, I had no clue.

"I've seen thousands of statements in my career, and never have I seen one like this. It's a very bad attempt, whether it's legitimate or not."

"You came all the way out here to bring me a counterfeit statement and tell me my money might have gone into Larry Stone's pocket?" His dark brows furrowed.

The Irish setters pricked their ears and waited expectantly for my answer.

"If I'm being honest, then yes," I said, knowing I wasn't doing a good job of winning his trust. "I also came to tell you I have a plan, and I need your help."

"I told you," he said, his smile crinkling the corners of his eyes. "I'm all yours."

He might be an older man, with salt and pepper hair and weathered skin, but I could see where he'd once been attractive. An older woman might certainly think so. "I want to try to cash in your investment. There's a phone number listed on the statement, and I want to call and request they liquidate the asset and send you the funds directly. Best case scenario? They'll liquidate and send you a check and you'll have made over half a million dollars in profit. Worst case? The phone number is a dud, or I'll get someone who will give me the run around because there's no investment and no money." I hated to tell him the call I'd made on the drive out had gone unanswered.

"You're gonna call their bluff?" Hank raised a thoughtful brow. "It's a good plan. You need me to be the guinea pig?"

The dogs pricked their ears again, looking up at Hank, as if they understood every word of the conversation.

"That's what I was hoping. You said you wanted your money back, and trying to sell your share will tell me if the investment is legit, or if it's a scam."

"You think Larry Stone's murder is also related to this investment, don't you?"

"That's what I'm trying to find out. The police found the murder weapon in my friend's car, and she wouldn't hurt a fly." Was I the only one who could see Alex was innocent?

"I hope you're right." Hank reached down and patted one of the dogs. "Alex is a good kid. She made over my new billiards room." He looked wistfully at his home. "It's my favorite room in the house."

"Alex didn't have anything to do with Larry's murder. I've known her for most of my life. She didn't have a strong enough motive to kill him, and she hates guns."

"Money's a pretty strong motive." Hank squinted one of his eyes as the clouds parted and the sun peeked through. "She can't be too happy about her mother losing all that money to Larry."

My mind struggled to register the significance of his words. "What do you mean her mother lost money to Larry?"

Alex never mentioned her mother investing with Larry. She'd known I planned to go after Larry and needed all the evidence I could find. Why hadn't Alex thought to mention something as obvious as her mother giving money to Larry Stone?

"Lillian Monroe was one of his clients," he said. "Invested her entire life savings with the guy. Of course, Alex didn't find out until after she'd done it, and by then it was a done deal. The annuity he sold her tanked, and now her mother has nothing left to live on."

I wavered, unsteady on my feet as the world around me spun out of control. I tried to comprehend what I was hearing and make sense out of it. Alex never mentioned the fact that her mother might have lost her entire life savings. Why keep it a secret? Was she embarrassed? Or was she hiding something?

"How do you know for certain her mother was an investor?" My mind swirled with doubts. It appeared everyone had something to hide. What was Hank hiding?

"I saw her in the office," he said. "We talked while we were waiting. Lillian was a real looker in her day, just like Alex."

Wasn't this just what I needed? If Hank was right, he'd given Alex a clear motive. I didn't know up from down anymore. Here I was, trying to get Alex off the hook for a murder she now might have actually committed. "I wish I'd known this sooner. Maybe Alex really did kill Larry." Even I didn't believe the words, but nothing was as it seemed.

"If you're looking for suspects, I could name at least a dozen, like his nephew, Damon. I hear he inherited the business. I'd put him at the top of the list, and I'd check out that pretty Hannah as well. She was more than just the receptionist." Hank waggled his bushy brows.

"I've already heard about Hannah and Larry," I said, knowing why Hannah might have been so quick to take up a flirtation with Damon. If she knew about the money, with Larry gone, Damon was her next best bet if she wanted to see a dime.

"And with Larry taking Alex's mother for everything," Hank said.

"Alex may have actually killed him," I finished, feeling like a traitor as soon as the words left my mouth.

"I wouldn't rule it out. That girl's got a temper as fiery as her hair." He picked up a stick from beside the stairs and threw it out across the lawn, sending the two dogs chasing after it like red blurs.

A heavy, hollow feeling settled in my stomach as I watched the dogs racing around the lawn. I wanted to believe in my friend's innocence, but Hank's revelation put me back at square one. What if Alex had killed Larry Stone? The idea was unlikely, but I'd promised I wouldn't rule out any possibilities. What other secrets had Alex been keeping?

"If I had to guess, I'd put my money on Damon Stone," Hank said. "He had the most to gain by his uncle's death."

Damon was my main suspect, especially after my little chat with Mason West last night. My new business partner had his own brand of temper, a bit scary at times, along with a grandiose sense of entitlement. I absolutely believed he was capable of murder, so much that I didn't feel safe owning half of the business he wanted to control.

The pair of dogs came bounding over to Hank, one proudly holding the stick in his mouth, the other hanging onto the opposite end as he got dragged along. Hank waited for them to drop the stick before picking it up and hurling it off again. "What are you going to do if you find out Larry took everyone's money?"

If I was smart, I'd let Mason West take over the investigation. "I'm hoping the money can be recovered, but I'll have to turn any evidence over to the authorities and let them handle it. In my experience, people rarely get all their money back, but I figure something is better than nothing. The faster I get to the bottom of this, the more likely we'll have a positive outcome."

Hank muttered a curse under his breath. "I knew I was taking a gamble on that investment. I guess that's what I get for believing anything that came out of Larry's mouth. It was too good to be true."

"I'm going to do my best to get the money back. Not just for you, but for everyone in Harmony Falls who made the mistake of trusting Larry Stone."

We said our goodbyes, and the dogs barked after me as I walked out to the car. I might not be any closer to finding Larry's killer, but I was closing in on the investment and the whereabouts of the money. As I drove away from Hank's house, I hoped I'd have some good news for him. I hoped someone at the other end of the toll-free number would answer my calls, but I had the nagging sense that wasn't going to be the case. If I had to use my best guess, Hank's money was long gone.

And Alex might actually belong in jail for murder.

Hannah's apartment was a corner unit located at the back of a three-story Victorian home that had been converted into multiple apartments. I parked on the street, left my bulky bag in the car, and strolled quietly down the paved driveway leading to the back of the property. A pink flowered wreath hung on the door, and a flowerpot brimming with bright pink fuchsia sat on the cement stoop, leaving no doubt I was at the right apartment. Hannah loved pink.

There was no doorbell, so I knocked on the door. It was precisely six o'clock, and she was expecting me. Inside, footsteps got closer to the door until it swung open. Hannah stood in the doorway in jeans and a white T-shirt. "Come in, come in." She waved her hand, then cautiously looked down the driveway before she closed the door.

It was dark in her apartment, even with the curtains open and two table lamps glowing in the living room. Hannah took a seat at the round kitchen table, and I joined her.

"We have to make it quick," Hannah said. "I'm meeting someone for dinner later, and I want to have time to get ready."

I didn't need to ask who the date was with, given her and Damon's earlier display at the office. It was clear they were becoming more than friends. "You said you had information on Larry and that it might help Alex. What did you want to tell me?"

Hannah fidgeted with her fingers, almost as if she'd changed her mind about talking to me, but then she lifted her gaze and said, "I know Larry's investment was illegal. He took money from clients and deposited the checks in the business account. We're not supposed to do that."

"What did he do with their money?" I asked. "Did it ever get invested?"

"I don't think it did, but I never had access to the business account, and I wasn't allowed to open the monthly bank statements when they came in the mail. All of that went directly to Larry. It was all very secretive."

So far Hannah wasn't telling me anything I hadn't already suspected. I'd called the phone number listed on the investment statement after leaving Hank's place, and no one ever answered the call, nor did it get routed to voicemail. It appeared to be a dead end.

"What was Larry's behavior like before he was murdered?" I asked.

"The way he'd been acting for those last few days, I knew something was wrong," Hannah said.

"How was he acting?"

"Anxious, paranoid. He didn't trust your father. Before he'd leave the office, he'd look out the window. It's like he thought someone might be watching him."

"Do you know what was going on?"

Hannah shook her head. "When I asked him, he said not to worry, and it would all be over soon. I knew Alex was making a lot of noise about her mother's investment, and she started meeting with your father. I think they were trying to gather evidence against Larry. He asked me to spy on them, but I didn't feel right about it."

Hannah had a conscience. Who knew?

"I can't believe Alex was working with my father and didn't say anything to me." Yet one more secret of Alex's I'd uncovered. Weren't friends supposed to be honest with each other?

"I think Larry found out about what they were doing, and he panicked. He'd done something your father didn't want to go along with, and when your father started going through the business records and making copies of statements, that's when people started dying."

"What do you mean 'people started dying?'" We were back to the question of my father's death being mistakenly ruled as natural causes.

Hannah fidgeted with her fingers, then clutched at the clasp for her gold necklace. "Your dad died first."

"My father died of a heart attack," I reminded her. "Do you have any reason to believe he might have been killed?"

"I think Larry had something to do with it all," Hannah responded with confidence. "He didn't seem upset when he heard the news. He was in a better mood than usual, like he was happy your father was gone and out of the way. When he got paranoid, I think it's because someone else knew what he'd done."

"Why are you telling me all of this?" I didn't consider Hannah an ally, and I trusted her even less. What was her angle?

"I don't owe any loyalty to Larry. I know he was sleeping around."

"I bet that made you pretty angry," I said.

"For three years we worked together." Hannah leaned back and crossed her legs. "You'd think that would mean something. Not to Larry. He got greedy."

"Is that why you killed him?"

Hannah scrunched up her pert nose. "I told you, I didn't kill Larry."

"He cheated on you. That had to be pretty embarrassing to find out. Something like that would make me pretty mad."

"That's not a reason to kill someone," Hannah said, as if she were the one teaching me about morals.

The quick turnaround shocked me. "Do you have any idea who else might have wanted Larry dead?"

"No," Hannah said assuredly. "That's why I need your help. I'd hate to see something bad happen to Damon because of what his uncle did. He could easily become a target if someone out there still wants revenge. I know you've been looking for more evidence, and back when all this started, I made copies of all the bank statements and the checks Larry took from the clients. Everything matches up."

"I thought you said you didn't open the bank statements."

"I said I wasn't allowed to open them, but the more paranoid Larry got, the more I wanted some insurance in case things went sour, you know? He got me to steal Nick Callahan's client list before I went to work for him, and with his cheating, I didn't really trust him very much."

Hannah had definitely woven a tangled web by falling prey to Larry's supposed charms, just like everyone else in town. The only good thing to come out of her thievery was the evidence she had hidden away. It was the last piece of the puzzle I needed. "I really need those copies."

"That's why I asked you to come here," she said. "I'll actually be glad to be rid of them."

"That was a really smart thing to do, with all that's happened. It's too late to make Larry pay for his crime, but we might be able to get some of the money back to the clients."

"I don't want anything to do with the money. It's better if you take it all back." Hannah slid out of her chair and disappeared into the back of her apartment.

Was it possible I'd misjudged Hannah? I seemed to be floundering in that department. While her methods might be questionable, in the end she'd chosen to do the right thing. It wouldn't change the fact that she could be perceived as an accomplice to Larry's crime, but she might get a lighter sentence for helping recover the money. Help or not, I had no intention of warning her what fate might await her on the other side of all this.

Finding it hard to be patient, I distracted myself by gazing around Hannah's small kitchen. It was clean and uncluttered, with pink chiffon curtains over the window above the sink and round pink magnets on the refrigerator. She even had a pink oven mitt and potholder on the stove. I wondered if Hannah had entertained Damon in her apartment. It was evident they were forming some sort of relationship. Was she blind to the fact he was following in his uncle's footsteps? Or was I?

"I don't get it," Hannah said as she came back into the kitchen. "All the evidence is gone. Every last scrap."

My unease resurfaced. Was this all a setup? It was evident I knew too much. Had Hannah lured me here only to make me the next victim? I had to stop putting myself into these situations. The worried expression on Hannah's face generated more concern than distrust, and I rose from the chair. "Someone must have taken the copies. Did anyone else know you had them?"

"No, I didn't say a word. I made the copies in secret when Larry was out of the office. No one could have known."

"Obviously, someone knew." I instantly suspected Damon. "Has anyone been in your apartment recently?"

Hannah blushed, her cheeks coloring a bright red. "Damon was here last night, but he wouldn't have done this. He's not anything like his uncle. He's honest, and he cares about the clients and the business. He wants to make things right."

Poor, gullible Hannah. Damon must have used his act on her, and she'd fallen for it and slept with him, even as he openly flirted with me right in front of her. "Would he have had the chance to go through your things?"

"Maybe when I was in the shower this morning." She twisted her hands with worry and paced the small kitchen. "I can't believe he would do this to me."

That made one of us. I had my reservations about Damon's character, and knowing the proof of Larry's crime was suddenly missing and Damon had been inside Hannah's apartment was too much of a coincidence.

"How dare he!" Hannah grew more agitated as she paced faster. "Those were *my* files. He had no right to take them from me."

"Where did you hide them? Were they locked up?"

"I didn't think I needed to lock them up. Damon said he wanted to help."

"What if he was only pretending so he could get the chance to search your apartment?" I suggested, bringing up the possibility that Damon had slept with Hannah in order to retrieve the copies. Another loose end tied up.

"I thought I was being careful." Hannah stopped her pacing. "He lied to me."

"Do you think Damon could have stumbled across them by accident?"

"In a Louis Vuitton shoe box?" She looked at me like I was the crazy one. "That's the last place any man would look."

She might be right. Damon had to have known what he was looking for, and it's possible he'd gotten lucky. "That only leaves one question."

"What?" Hannah blew out a long breath.

"Where is Damon hiding the copies he stole from you?"

She pursed her lips into a thin line and tossed a blonde lock of hair over her shoulder. "I guess I'll just have to find out."

"Are you still going to have dinner with him after he conned you?" I wouldn't have expected Hannah to show any interest in Damon after he got her into bed for the sole purpose of stealing from her, but people are full of surprises.

"I've faked entire relationships." Hannah stuck her hand on her hip. "I can definitely fake a date if it means getting what I want. When I'm through with him, he'll be sorry Boy, will he ever."

Her determination to exact revenge on Damon happened to work out perfectly for what I had planned. While Hannah kept Damon occupied for the evening, I was going to pay a little after-hours visit to the office. It was time to find out what Damon was hiding.

# Chapter Fifteen

I waited until after dark to drive to the office. I parked down the street in an attempt to remain inconspicuous, but it was after nine, and all the downtown businesses were closed. The only other cars parked on the street were in front of The Corner Pocket, the oldest dive bar in Harmony Falls. The twang of a country guitar floated out to the street as patrons congregated out front and smoked cigarettes before going back inside to shout at each other over loud music and cheap beer.

On my way downtown, I'd driven past Hannah's apartment and made sure Damon's car was parked out front. Knowing he was sufficiently occupied, I should have plenty of time to search his office. Not exactly proficient at breaking and entering, I'd put on all the black clothes in my suitcase. Black pants, a black zippered hoodie, and my black ballet flats. Technically what I intended to do was legal, considering I had a key to the office.

No one from the bar gave me any notice as I got out of the car and crept up to the front door. The feeling that someone was watching me still had me looking over my shoulder, and I wondered if Mason West would materialize out of the darkness. If he was the one watching me, I didn't think he'd want me to know. A slight chill lifted the hair on the back of my neck, and I felt exposed, in a hurry to get off the street.

I let myself into the office, then locked the door behind me. It was ominously silent, and the only light came from the streetlamps out front. I made sure my phone was set to do not disturb one last time before I switched on the flashlight mode and crept up to Damon's closed office door. This was my only chance.

I turned the knob and pushed open the door. The scent of carpet shampoo and Damon's astringent cologne lingered in the stale air, and I cautiously ventured inside, giving a wide berth to the area where Larry had expired. It didn't feel right to step there, like walking over someone's grave. It felt even more unnerving, entering the office of a possible murderer. But the suspicion that Damon had taken a life for his own selfish purposes was greater than my fear and compelled me to stick with my plan. I stood behind his desk and looked around, wondering where to begin my search.

The furniture in his office resembled the pieces in my own office, with a bookcase on the wall straight ahead and a wooden file cabinet nestled into the far corner. There was no coat closet. Seeing as how I was on a quest to locate the missing copies, I tried the first drawer of the file cabinet and found it was locked, as were the others. I sighed in silent frustration. Lock-picking skills were not my specialty, and I doubted he'd left the keys where I could find them.

I went back behind the desk and sat on the edge of his leather chair. I opened the first desk drawer, finding the envelope with the paperwork and check to buy out my share. The second drawer had a box of Larry's unused business cards and some fancy pens, while the bottom drawer was empty. None of them contained what I was looking for. I sat back in frustration, trying to think of where he might keep the file cabinet key.

The room didn't offer much in the way of hiding places. Across from me, the bookshelves were lined with reference manuals and framed certificates of achievement. An idea came to mind, and I went to the bookcase and felt along the top edges for a strategically placed key. Nothing but dust came off on my fingertips.

Back out in the lobby, I sat perched in Hannah's office chair and pulled at the top desk drawer. It didn't budge. I tried again, but it was obviously locked. The second drawer slid open smoothly and was stuffed with lipstick tubes and mascara, along with a disorganized mess of pens, highlighters, paper clips, various rolls of stamps, and some battered envelopes. In the bottom drawer, I found a stack of fashion magazines and a pink cardigan. All innocuous things I'd expect to find in Hannah's desk.

I pushed the drawer closed. My search hadn't turned up a single clue. I was going to have to get better at snooping or learn how to pick a lock. I sat in the chair, out of options, when my gaze landed on Hannah's desktop computer. Did she have access to the business records and accounts? She said Larry didn't want her seeing the bank statements, yet she'd secretly made copies. The hairs on my neck bristled. There was no doubt I'd find some clue or lead stored on Hannah's computer.

For security purposes, the computer had to be password protected if it contained access to sensitive client information, and I didn't know Hannah well enough to have the first idea what magic combination of letters and numbers would unlock the computer. Turning to look at the area where the copier was stored, I saw nothing that could offer any help. I went over to the paper shredder and opened the bin. It was empty.

There had to be a clue somewhere, waiting to be found, if only I knew where to look. Determined, I went back into Damon's office and sat down in his desk chair, scanning the room more closely now that my eyesight had adjusted to the darkness. My foot banged against the metal trash bin, and I inspected it closer. It was stuffed with crumpled-up wads of paper. I got on my knees and dumped the contents out on the carpet. They were always going through the garbage in the movies; maybe I was on to something.

Using the flashlight on my phone, I began to rifle through the wads of paper. A dry cleaning receipt. A candy bar wrapper and an empty bag of Cheetos. Not a very healthy lunch. A chamber of commerce monthly newsletter. And a phone message.

From Hank Taylor.

I held the phone message slip closer to the dim flashlight. Hank's name and phone number were written on the slip in Hannah's rounded script. Why would Hank be calling Damon?

Suddenly, I heard the unexpected jangling of keys, turning in the lock for the main office door. Someone else was here. Peeking my head over the top of Damon's desk, I could see into the lobby, and I gasped as Damon opened the door and then locked it behind him.

I crouched under his desk and turned off the light on my phone. I hurried to put the contents of the trash bin back and return it to its place, then pulled in the chair to conceal my location.

Above me, something hit the top of the desk, giving me a start. I held my breath, afraid to move, afraid to even breathe. I was alone, locked in a dark office with a potential murderer. My mind raced, and I scooted further under the desk. I didn't want to imagine what he'd do if he caught me searching through his office at this time of night.

I strained to listen for the direction of his footsteps and curled into a tight ball, hugging my arms around my legs and stuffing myself as far back into the opening under his desk as I could manage. It sounded like he'd gone out into the lobby, and then the paper shredder whirred to life, hungrily sinking its teeth into whatever documents Damon began feeding through the blades.

My gut twisted with a sense of doom. He had to be shredding the copies he'd stolen from Hannah. First Larry had tried to get rid of evidence, and now Damon was doing the same thing. In the movies, that was the last step before the crook absconded with the money and ended up on a beach in Barbados.

Had Damon let his uncle do the dirty work, only to swoop in at the last minute, kill him, and make off with a tremendous fortune? I might be running out of time to catch the killer.

The seconds stretched into minutes as Damon fed more and more paper through the shredder. I remained curled up under his desk, trying to ignore the cramp in my leg and praying he wouldn't come into his office and find me hiding there. I had nothing to defend myself with and no way to escape. I could use my phone to call the police, but how long would it take them to rescue me? They'd never make it in time. I'd be sharing a bloodstain on the carpet next to Larry's.

After what seemed like hours, the humming of the shredder stopped. From the rustling around, I deduced that he'd emptied the shredder bag, replaced it with a clean one, taken the shredded documents out to his car, and then came back inside. All the evidence, wiped clean.

His footsteps came closer, growing louder, stopping beside his desk. I took in a shaky breath and held on to it. I closed my eyes, as if the action would further assist in my concealment. On top of the desk, Damon moved something around, then walked back out into the lobby. I let my breath out, my hands shaking as I checked the time on my phone. Time of death: 10:10 p.m. The number of miracles, which was good, because I needed a miracle right now.

Next came the clacking of keys on Hannah's keyboard. Did Damon know the password for her computer? Or was he trying to guess? He pulled out her desk drawers, searching through them just as I had earlier. Giving up, he came back into his office and a set of keys rattled, then he opened his file cabinet. He took whatever was on top of the desk and moved it to the cabinet. Before he closed the drawer, a phone rang.

I jumped, slapping a hand over my mouth to stifle the gasp of surprise. It wasn't my phone ringing. It didn't sound like the office phone either. It had to be Damon's cell phone.

"What do you want?" he almost growled the words, clearly not happy with whoever was calling him. He pulled out his chair and sat down, turning his back to the desk and leaving my hiding place wide open.

I slowed my breath to listen, but my heart pounded so wildly in my ears it was difficult to hear. Only a few inches from me, if Damon turned around and looked under his desk, my cover would be blown.

"Yes, I have it." His tone remained harsh and impatient. "I don't know what you think you'll accomplish with this. I know of a better way to take care of her if you'd just let me handle it."

I froze in fear. Take care of *her*? I hated to think I might be the *her*.

"Fine, have it your way," Damon said. "I'll be there."

I would've given anything to be able to hear the person on the other end of the phone.

"Yes, we need to take care of that problem too," he said. "One hour." He sprung out of his chair and banged the file cabinet drawer closed, then slammed his office door shut.

Soon, I heard a car start out on the street and peel away from the curb. Releasing the breath I'd been holding, my entire body went loose with welcome relief. I was alone, and Damon had left the office in such a hurry, he'd forgotten to lock his file cabinet.

I crawled out from under his desk and hurried over to the file cabinet. Throwing open the top drawer, I think I half-expected something to jump out at me. Some major surprise. Damon's black gym bag was not it. I lifted the bag by the nylon handles, surprised by the heavy weight. Setting it on top of the desk, I grasped the metal pull for the zipper. Anything could be inside. I prayed I wouldn't find any bloody body parts and peeled back the zipper. As the sides of the bag fell open, stacks of banded cash oozed out.

I could hardly believe my eyes. Crisp hundred-dollar bills were banded with paper straps, indicating each stack contained ten thousand dollars. There had to be over a hundred stacks stuffed into the nylon bag. What was Damon doing with a million dollars stuffed into a gym bag?

The first thought to cross my mind was blackmail. Murder. The secretive phone call. A mysterious bag of money. Someone knew Damon's secret. It could also be payoff money for Nick Callahan. Or hit money.

An edge of panic crept into my gut. Just holding the bag of money felt wrong. I now understood what was meant by dirty money. It could even be blood money. Was this what the killer had been looking for when they'd tossed the office? Files and statements suddenly seemed like small-time evidence.

With paranoia sinking in, I zipped the bag closed, afraid Damon could return at any time to retrieve it. He could be on his way back right now, remembering he'd forgotten to lock the file cabinet. If I'd been afraid of what he might do if he found me searching his office, he really wouldn't be happy about finding me with his bag of cash.

Where did he get this kind of money?

My best guess was from Larry and the swindled clients. Come Monday, I would demand access to the business account, or I'd have to bring in Mason West. The SEC had strict rules about financial advisors having cash in their office. Serious Code of Ethics stuff. I didn't anticipate Damon would cooperate no matter what the stakes. In fact, the more I thought about it, I needed to acquire some leverage on Damon. He wouldn't respond to empty threats and legal entanglements. How did the old saying go?

CHAPTER FIFTEEN

Money talks, bullshit walks.

My next move was so foreign to my nature, so out of character for me; it was like I was watching myself from outside of my body. With a calm steadiness, I took the duffel bag by the handles and closed the file cabinet drawer. I closed Damon's office door and let myself out the front door, careful to lock it behind me. The dark street was quiet and deserted, except for a few patrons mingling out front of the bar, all of them looking at the glowing screens of their cell phones.

No one had seen me come, and no one saw me leave. If someone had secretly been watching me, they couldn't know what was in the bag. Back inside Kylie's car, I gently placed the duffel bag on the passenger seat and hit the button to lock the doors. I stared at the bag of money. How long before Damon discovered it was missing?

My guess was not long. I would have to be extra careful until I turned the money over to the police. A person couldn't just steal a million dollars and walk away free. Damon would be coming after me, and I had to be ready.

I wasn't afraid, though my mind screamed at me that I damn well should be. In any case, I wasn't putting the money back. Without knowing what had happened to the money Larry took from his clients, this might be the only portion to get recovered. As part owner of the business, I also had a legal obligation to report any wrongdoing. My career was on the line. And if Damon planned on skipping town, using the money to fund his getaway, he was now stuck in Harmony Falls. Taking the money was the right thing to do, and I had to trust my instincts on this one, as crazy as it might seem.

My cell phone vibrated in my pocket, scaring me half to death, and I almost dropped it between the seats trying to answer it. With my heart racing, I answered.

"They just released me." Alex's voice was like a blessing through the phone. "Can you come and pick me up? My car is at home, and it's too late to call my mom."

# Chapter Sixteen

Relief flooded every cell in my body, and I felt the tension between my shoulders release. Alex was going free, and as happy as seeing her cleared made me, it also meant I'd been right. The killer was still out there. "I can be at the station in two minutes."

"That's quick, where are you?" Alex asked.

"I'm at the office."

"We're staying late these days now, are we? When did you become a workaholic?" Alex's teasing laugh was a true sign she hadn't been broken. The killer's evil plan to see her take the fall for Larry's murder had been thwarted.

"I've taken on a side gig," I said. "I've been trying to find Larry's killer."

"Are you insane?" Alex shrieked. "Do I have to tell you investigating a murder on your own is dangerous?"

"So is living in Harmony Falls."

"I've started getting used to having you around," Alex said. "I'd really miss you if you got yourself killed."

I hadn't even told her the best part about my night. "I'm on my way to the station now, and you're never going to guess what I just found."

"A tall, dark, and handsome stud with a million dollars?"

I froze. How did she do that? Alex was kidding, but she had no idea how close she'd come to the truth. "I'll tell you about it when I get there."

Two minutes later, I pulled up to the police station, and Alex waited out front, her mess of red hair piled on top of her head.

All was right with the world again.

She hurried to climb into the passenger seat and I locked the doors after she was inside the car. "What did you find?" Alex dumped her leather purse on the floor by her feet.

"Gee, it's nice to see you too," I said, my tone somewhere between sarcastic and annoyed. "What happened to all that talk about missing me?"

"I meant every word. Now tell me what's been going on."

"I'm not sure you want to know. You've had enough to deal with." I took a moment to study my friend, looking for any signs of torture, or hunger, or any physical distress she might have suffered during her short incarceration. Aside from the dark circles under her eyes and her messy hair and wrinkled clothes, Alex looked unmolested.

"Why are you staring at me? I'm fine," she insisted. "They were waiting for the paraffin test to come back negative before they let me go. The first test was inconclusive, so they had to run it again, or I would have been out sooner. It was like being stuck in a bad episode of *The Andy Griffith Show*, with Barney Fife losing my fingerprints. Most of the time, the detective brought me bad coffee and asked me the same questions over and over again."

"You never should have been there in the first place." I pulled away from the curb and headed for Alex's house on the west side of town, wondering how I was going to break it to Alex that I knew her secret.

"What's going on with that dreamy Damon?" Alex wondered. "Have you taken him for a test drive, or are you saving him for me?"

I filled Alex in on what she'd missed while she'd been in jail. The only thing I left out was my little chat with Hank.

When I'd finished, Alex toyed with the sloppy, tangled bun on top of her head. "I can't believe all this happened while I was in jail. Man, the moment you came to town, all hell broke loose. Warn me if you come home for Christmas."

"I wish none of it had happened at all." I'd only come home for a funeral. A day later, I was tracking down murderers, interfering with police investigations, and evading federal agents.

"Where's the money?" Alex asked.

I gave a nod. "In the backseat."

Alex whipped her head around to look at the duffel bag. "Don't you think you should hide it?"

"Where do you hide a million dollars? It's not like I can put it under the mattress."

Alex tapped a finger against her lips as she worked through her thoughts. "What about the basement at your dad's house?"

"No good." Although I had no evidence, I got the distinct feeling someone had been inside the house. Boxes didn't move themselves. "Kylie has the realtor showing the place to buyers, and I think someone might have broken in a few days ago, but I don't know for sure."

"What do you mean you don't know if someone broke in or not? Isn't it kind of obvious?"

"Some things were moved around, that's all. The doors were all locked, nothing had been forced or broken, and nothing was stolen. It could have just been my mind playing tricks on me."

Alex gave me a droll look. "Am I to guess it does that often?"

"Just trust me. We shouldn't hide the money there."

"If the house isn't safe, you shouldn't be staying there either. Let's go to my house so I can get cleaned up, and we'll think of something. Right now, I need a drink, and I want to wash the jail out of my hair."

It was only a few short minutes until we pulled into Alex's driveway. I parked beside her white van, still wondering how I was going to bring up the fact that she'd lied to me. Hopefully I could think of something while she was in the shower.

Once inside, Alex poured each of us a glass of brandy from the collection of liquor bottles on the sideboard in the dining room. She handed one of the short-stemmed glasses to me. "Help yourself to another one if you need it."

I took a sip of the Remy Martin, grimacing at the strong hit of alcohol, but then the back notes of vanilla and honey settled in, and I remembered why I liked the drink. It warmed my belly and made a soothing balm for my frayed nerves. I didn't realize how much of a fright I'd had searching Damon's office earlier, and as I reflected back on my subterfuge, I'd been lucky to get out undiscovered. Not to mention alive.

160

With the bag of money in one hand and my glass of brandy in the other, I made my way out into the living room. I loved being in Alex's house. It was like sitting in the finest pages of an interior design magazine. All the rooms were stylishly arranged and filled with green plants and colorful artwork on the walls. Tons of oversized books on travel, interiors, and photography were stacked neatly on shelves and tabletops. The living room was my favorite area because of the white, single-cushion sofa. I settled back into the plush cushions and put my feet on the coffee table, covered with candles, sparkling crystals, and a deck of tarot cards.

I didn't realize I'd dozed off until Alex came back from her shower, saying, "I know where we can hide the money." Dressed in silk pajama pants and a matching camisole, she sat in one of the armchairs opposite the sofa and dried the ends of her hair with a white bath towel. "I have a storage unit for my overflow inventory. I can't believe I didn't think of it before. It's the perfect place."

"We'd better take it there tonight," I said. "I don't want either of us becoming a target when Damon finds it missing."

"How could I be a target?" Alex plopped the towel in her lap. "I've been in jail."

Not mincing words, I came right out and asked, "Why didn't you tell me your mother lost her life savings to Larry?"

Alex looked like a deer caught in headlights, her eyes wide and filled with astonishment. "I wondered when you'd find out."

I came forward on the sofa. "Why didn't you tell me? I had to find out from Hank Taylor."

"That old coot? What would he know about it?"

"He seems to know a lot of things, like how you were talking to my father about Larry taking money from your mom."

"I was afraid to tell you." She resumed drying her hair with the towel.

"Why?" I asked plainly. "We're best friends. We tell each other everything." Didn't we?

"I didn't know how to tell you this, so I guess I'll just come out and say it." Alex draped the towel over the arm of her chair. "It's my fault your father is dead."

I shook my head to clear it. "That's ridiculous, you couldn't have killed him."

"I might as well have," she said. "I asked your father to look into my mom's accounts, worried Larry had done something shady, and then he turned up dead. If I hadn't gotten him involved, none of this would have happened."

I had a feeling it would have happened regardless.

"Why didn't you just tell me the truth?" I hated that Alex had kept such a huge secret from me, or to think we'd drifted apart more than I realized.

"I didn't want to lose you," Alex implored, her eyes watering with the start of tears. "I thought if I convinced you to keep your share, you'd eventually find the records and figure out what Larry was doing on your own. You're so busy with work, I didn't want to bother you with my mom's financial problems, and we haven't seen each other in such a long time. I wasn't even sure it would matter."

I went over and squeezed into the chair beside her, placing a hand on her knee. "You will always matter. You're like family to me. You've always been a part of my life, and I hope you always will be."

Alex nodded, a tear streaking down her cheek, and I pulled her into a tight hug. "This wasn't your fault."

"I was so worried you'd hate me if you found out." She sniffled and pulled back to swipe at her tears.

I rested a hand on her shoulder. "I hate that you didn't tell me all of this from the start."

"I'm sorry."

"No more secrets?" I asked.

Alex nodded emphatically. "No more secrets."

I went back to my seat on the sofa and looked down at the bag of money. "What do you think Damon is doing with all of this money?"

"What if he isn't the one being blackmailed?" Alex said, her expression turning thoughtful. "What if Damon paid someone to kill Larry and frame me for the murder? What if this is payoff money?"

"It's not a crazy idea," I said. "On the phone call he said he would take care of *her*. I'm assuming *her* means me, or maybe it means you. The killer might not be finished. It might not be safe for either one of us."

Alex went pale, absently dabbing at her hair with the towel. "Do we need to go into hiding? I should have stayed in jail where I was safe, no matter how bad the coffee is."

"Hannah told me Larry was acting paranoid before he was killed. She said he thought someone was watching him. I think someone is watching me, too. Have you noticed anyone lurking around the studio?"

"I think we should tell the police about the money."

"Who should I call?" I wondered. "The detective or the agent?"

"I don't know how much help the numbers nerd is going to be. I think we should call Detective Matthews."

"Don't underestimate Agent West," I said. "He's very intimidating, and he carries a gun."

"I'll let you sort that one out on your own." Alex poured another sip of brandy in each of our glasses and handed one off to me. "Now drink this, and let's go hide the money."

I choked down the strong drink in one swallow. "If it'll make you feel better, I'll call the detective." I winced as my throat burned. "But if he throws me in jail for obstruction of justice, I'm going to be really pissed."

Alex rose from her chair and dropped the towel on the floor. "You know, he'd be a good guy for you to date."

"My mother is already going down that road. I don't need you to join her. Besides, I can't date someone from here."

"Why in the hell not?" Alex held out her hand to me.

I took her hand and let her haul me up off the sofa. "Because now that you're free, I can get back to LA and back to work. I can go home."

"Funny," Alex said, fixing me in a stare. "I thought you were home."

# Chapter Seventeen

Alex pulled the metal roll-up door for the storage unit closed with a clattering bang. As she secured the padlock, I thought about the bag of money stashed away in the secret compartment of a storage ottoman. Neither I nor Alex would be safe with Damon out there. He was going to want his money back.

"Do you think Damon is out there right now, looking for us?" I asked.

"Probably, and after what I've just gone through, I'll never forgive you if he kills me next. I just got out of jail." Alex led the way through the maze of hallways in the storage warehouse.

"Maybe I should stay at your house tonight since Damon will probably look for me at my father's place. He doesn't know you're out of jail yet. We'll be safer together."

"You know I don't own a gun," Alex said.

"I have pepper spray and a personal alarm in my purse," I told her. "And you have a great set of kitchen knives."

"I also keep a baseball bat under my bed, and I think I have some wasp spray out in the shed."

"Is it too late to call Matthews tonight?" I checked my watch. It was after midnight.

"Well, that depends." Alex pushed open the door leading outside, and we walked over to Kylie's SUV, parked alone in the dark, empty lot. "Do you think we need personal protection? I mean, if we're going to wake him, we shouldn't let him go to waste."

I hit the alarm button on the keychain to open the car doors. The headlights flashed on and off. "Is that all you ever think about?" I bent down and looked under the car.

"What are you doing?"

"Checking for psycho killers under the car, waiting to grab us by the ankle."

"Did you find any?" Alex joked.

"All clear." I inspected the empty backseat and the trunk area next. "Nothing back here either."

Alex yanked open the passenger side door. "What would you do if you did happen to find a killer in the backseat, or under the car?"

I shuddered at the thought. "Scream and run like hell."

Once inside the car, I hit the lock button for the doors. Having the money hidden in the storage unit was our insurance policy. Damon couldn't kill us until he knew where we'd stashed the money. We just had to survive the rest of the night.

"Let's hope the money isn't a set up," Alex said. "I don't want to go back to jail."

"Why would the real killer want to frame you anyway?" I asked, curious if Alex had discovered any other leads. "Why come after you?"

Alex shrugged. "Maybe because I was on to Larry's scam?"

"Or maybe Damon is innocent, and he's trying to clean up the mess his uncle made."

"If Damon isn't the killer, who could it be?"

I shared another theory. "What if Nick Callahan had something to do with it all? What if he was blackmailing Larry? So, Larry agrees to pay Nick to stay quiet about the scam, except maybe Larry decided he didn't want to pay up, so Nick killed him and planted the gun in your van in order to silence you—the only other person who might know about it—and get you out of the way. Nick could be blackmailing Damon now that Larry is dead. It's no secret Nick is after our business. If he's the only one who knows the truth, he gets to solve the crime and expose the fraud, all while becoming the town hero again. Now there's a solid motive."

"I don't know if Nick is capable of doing something like that," Alex defended him. "He seems like an honest guy."

I disagreed. "How well do you really know him?"

"I don't know." Alex sighed. "How well do you ever know anyone?"

I started the car. Damon. Hannah. Nick. Hank. All of them had motive. Any one of them could be the killer. I only hoped we'd be able to find out who it was before someone else ended up dead.

"Are you going to call Matthews?" Alex asked. "Or should we wait until morning?"

"Let's go back to your place and hide out for the rest of the night, and I'll call the detective first thing in the morning. There's not much he could do this late anyway."

"I could definitely use some sleep if I want to open the studio in the morning." Alex rested her head against the back of her headrest and closed her eyes.

She had to be exhausted. Sleep was probably the best thing for both of us. On the drive back to Alex's house, I kept one eye on the road and one eye on the rearview mirror.

We had an uneventful night, though neither of us had slept all too well, knowing a killer might be after us, but I'd managed to drift off to sleep sometime after three a.m. When I smelled the coffee brewing, I helped myself to a cup and decided to make breakfast while Alex was getting ready for work. After a hearty bacon and cheese omelet and toast, Alex wanted to open her studio and work on quelling all the rumors and speculation as to why it had been closed for the past few days.

"Once everyone finds out you're innocent, this will all blow over," I said while I cleared the dishes and loaded them into the dishwasher. "People are going to want to know, if you didn't kill Larry, then who did."

"If I'd had someone to open the studio and help me out, it wouldn't be an issue." She drank down her orange juice. "I need to hire an assistant."

I rinsed a plate before loading it in the rack. "I could've helped you at the studio if you'd asked me to."

"I thought you were flying home right away. You were in such a hurry to get back to LA that I didn't want to bother you with my problems."

"Helping you was more important to me than rushing back to my job. Anyway, they seem to be getting by without me."

"Except for your loser boyfriend stealing your work."

"Ex-boyfriend," I reiterated. "I'm sure giving him an unfinished report sent the message we were through loud and clear."

A fierce fire came to her green eyes. "I would've put a curse on him."

"Do you think you could do that to the killer? Maybe turn his hair green so it makes it easier for us to find him?"

"It doesn't work like that, and you know it." She took the dishrag from the soapy water in the sink, wrung it out, and wiped down the counter. "Spells have to be very specific, or they can end up backfiring on you."

"If I need some stronger mojo to take care of Brandon, you're the first one I'll come to."

We finished cleaning up the kitchen and Alex went off to her studio, while I decided to head to the farmers' market downtown. I thought I might be able to pick up some gossip among the locals and that it might be wise to be out in public where the killer couldn't get me without attracting notice.

The area around Central Park was crowded, but I found a parking space a block away. The gray sky was heavy with clouds, threatening rain. The weather report predicted an eighty percent chance of precipitation. I had an umbrella ready, but the wind was picking up, and most of the vendors were bundled in warm coats, bracing for some volatile fall weather. For the moment, I was content to remain warm and dry in the car.

Until I saw him.

Mason West.

He looked sorely out of place in his designer suit, browsing tables filled with homemade baked goods, fall-colored mums, and jarred tomatoes. I didn't think he was there to shop, and I braced myself against the cold wind as I crossed the street and headed over to talk with the agent.

He smiled when he saw me approaching. Not a friendly smile, but more of a sneer. "If it isn't my pal, Starsky."

"Oh, please," I said. "I'd be Hutch. The smart one."

His mouth twisted in a wry grin. "I was hoping I'd run into you. My day wouldn't be the same without your mocking wit."

"Really? Because my day was going swell until I saw you."

"No one made you come over here."

I wasn't getting pulled into another roundabout confrontation with him and came right out and asked the question that had been bothering me. "Are you following me?"

"I follow lots of people. It goes with the job."

"Did you follow me last night?"

"You're the smart one," he said. "You tell me."

I knew someone was watching me, but I couldn't say for sure it was Mason West. I sized him up, and he drilled a stare right back at me. He knew I was keeping secrets, and the way he looked at me, all predatory and hungry, I might lose my head and give all of my secrets away if I wasn't careful. He was gorgeous as all get out, but it didn't change the fact that he believed I was an accomplice to a crime, or even murder. Though I wasn't surprised to find myself attracted to Mason West, I couldn't engage in any sort of flirtation with a man who thought I was capable of killing someone in cold blood.

"In case you're wondering, I didn't find anything in Damon's office last night," I informed him. Except for the bag of money, which I was going to tell the detective about as soon as I left the market.

"What were you hoping to find in his office?"

"Passwords for the business account or something useful. I did find this." I handed him the fake account statement, then wandered over to the table with the garden-fresh salsa.

"It looks like they're falsifying account statements." Mason walked with me. "This could be useful as evidence down the road, but based on the files you gave me the other night, I don't have enough to request a warrant. I need something more concrete. The way I see it right now, this is a job for the local authorities. Maybe the U.S. Attorney's office."

"Some help you are." I handed five dollars to the salsa lady and took a jar from the group on the table. "It's proof they had intent to commit fraud, but I guess the only real proof is going to be in the business account. I need to find out where the money went after Larry took those checks. It would be easier with a warrant."

"Make Damon give you access."

"How do you expect me to do that?"

Mason's hard demeanor softened. "Use your charm."

It was hard to tell if he meant to be sarcastic, or truly genuine, given his fondness for being contrary. A gust of wind picked up, the chill going right through my sweater, and I started heading back to the car.

He continued walking with me. "Did you find anything else in his office? Any clue, no matter how big or small?"

"I know he's getting rid of all the evidence. He gave the shredder a good workout."

Mason's jaw clenched. "He won't get away that easy."

As we stepped out into the crosswalk and started to cross the street, I heard an engine rev up, followed by squealing tires, and when I looked over, a red sedan came racing down the street right toward me. I didn't have time to scream as Mason threw his arms around me from behind and hauled me back onto the sidewalk. The jar of salsa flew out of my hands and smashed to the ground.

"What the hell?" I tried to wrest myself free of his hold, and that only managed to turn me around in his arms so I faced his chest. The manly smell of him filled my senses, and I rested my cheek against the soft wool of his jacket as what just happened had some time to sink in.

"Are you okay?" Mason still held me close.

All around us, people gasped and pointed at the car racing to the other end of the street, where it peeled around a corner and disappeared.

"I'm alright," I said, then looked up at him. "Aside from the fact that someone just tried to kill me."

# Chapter Eighteen

Mason walked me back to Kylie's car, keeping a protective hand at my waist. "That was too close to be an accident."

"You don't have to tell me. I thought it was all over." My hands shook as I unlocked the car door. It was hard to tell if the car that tried to run me down had been the same one parked out front of my father's house, but if I had to guess, I'd bet it was.

Mason held the door open, and once I was inside, he closed the door. I put the key in the ignition and rolled down the window.

"I didn't get a look at the driver, and I only got a partial plate," he said. "I'll run it and see what comes back, but I'd stay off the streets for the next few days."

"I don't think I'll ever be able to cross a street again." I managed a half-hearted smile. "I'm glad you were there."

"Just doing my job." He took a few steps back from the car. "I'll let you know if I find anything."

I doubted he would get back anything in time to be useful. Someone had been bold enough to try to run me down in the middle of the street in broad daylight. I felt vulnerable and wondered if I'd ever feel safe again. Being in Mason's arms made me feel safe, like he'd kill anything that tried to hurt me, but I was not letting him get through my defenses. He was here to work a case, and then he'd be gone, and I'd never have to see him again.

Back in the park, people were gathered together, talking and pointing, and someone was cleaning up the big red splotch on the street where I'd lost the jar of salsa. It reminded me of the blood stain on Larry's chest. I saw the dark bullet holes in my mind and couldn't help but wonder if I might be next. I'd almost been run down in the street. Taking the money from Damon had most likely decreased my probability of survival. The move hadn't been thought out, I'd acted purely on instinct, and no matter the danger, I still felt it had been the right action.

Considering Mason was still hanging around, I thought I should put him to good use. How often did a girl have a federal agent at her disposal?

"Maybe you should get in the car," I said to Mason. "I have something to show you."

Mason stood in the opening to the storage unit and looked from me to the money a few times. "This might be the first time in my career I've been speechless."

"Really? It happens to me all the time."

That earned me a look. "I'm going to spare you the lecture because you're a grown woman, but what in the hell were you thinking?"

"If I'm right, I didn't want Damon to get away with murder *and* the money. I thought I could use it as leverage."

"For?" Mason dragged a hand over his mouth.

"To make him give me the business records."

"I'm the leverage." He pointed at his chest. "Me. The man with the badge and the gun."

"You said this is a matter for the local authorities, and they don't want to listen to me."

The detective's determination to do all the leg work on his own killed any hopes I'd had of a consulting relationship with the police. I feared if I waited for him to connect all the dots, Damon would be long gone, and so would all the money.

"The longer you hold onto this money, the worse it's going to look. You need to get rid of it."

"That's why I'm giving it to you. You wanted me to find some evidence."

"I can't take it." Mason backed out of the storage unit. "Not like this. Give it to the detective on the case. Let him figure out how to handle it."

I zipped up the bag and hoisted it over my shoulder so I could draw down the metal door for the storage unit. "What should I do about Damon?" I knew he was a threat and that he'd be coming for me. He was going to want his money.

"Stay away from him." Mason gave me an exasperated look. "And don't go breaking into any more offices."

I trailed behind Mason as he led the way out of the storage facility. "I hope the police will take me seriously this time. Damon already killed one person. I don't want to give him the chance to kill again."

Mason's phone chimed loudly. He stopped short to check his message. "You might not have to worry about that."

I continued past him and pushed open the door leading out to the parking lot. It had been raining steadily since we got to the storage facility, and the dark gray clouds showed no signs of letting up. I huddled under the tiny awning over the front door, waiting for Mason to catch up, but the rain fell at an angle and pelted the side of my face with cold droplets. When Mason joined me outside, his expression was as dark as the sky. "Damon isn't your killer."

"What makes you so certain?" I asked in a rush. "Did something happen?"

"I just got a call. The police found Damon's body in the Straight River. They're on the scene now."

Shock and disbelief coursed through me. Damon couldn't be dead. He was my main suspect, and if he wasn't the killer, scary as I'd seen him get, it meant someone even worse was out there. The weight of the bag on my shoulder grew heavier. "I can't believe there's been another murder."

"I'm going to head to the scene and see what I can find out."

"Where in the river did they find him?" I asked out of equal parts curiosity and concern. Had Damon returned to the office last night for his money, only to find it gone? Would he still be alive if I'd left it alone?

"They set up a scene a few miles west of County Road forty-five. Out behind a property owned by Hank Taylor. Do you know the place?"

My body stiffened in shock, my heart pounding.

*Hank.*

The phone message.

"I know the place," I said. "I'm going with you."

Mason held his hands up, fending me off. "Oh, no. No way." He shook his head. "You're dropping that money off at the police station, and then you're going home."

"I'll only give this money to the detective who is probably at that scene, so I have to come with you," I said, rain still pelting my face. "And I remembered something else I have to tell you."

"There's more?" He looked less than pleased by my admission and crossed his arms. "Tell me now."

I had no intention of playing fair. "I'll tell you if you take me with you."

"I can't take you out there. This is a police matter."

"You're not the police."

He reached into his suit jacket and held his badge up to my nose. "As long as I have one of these, I can enter a crime scene. No badge. No crime scene. *Comprende?*"

I pushed his hand away. "I only want to help. Besides, if you don't drive me out there, I'll drive out there on my own and have a talk with Hank. He is my client, and I know exactly where he lives. I remember every stinking pothole."

I became increasingly uneasy under his scrutiny. His dark eyes were hard, his jaw clenched. I could tell taking me along was the last thing he wanted to do, but I wasn't giving him a choice. I felt a responsibility to my father, my town, and the people in it. This mystery had been dumped on me, and I was determined to solve it.

"I'm going with you." I refused to back down.

Mason gritted his teeth, clenching his jaw tighter. "I can't take you out there. It wouldn't be safe. I've seen cases where killers have returned to the scene of the crime, and I don't want you anywhere near the person who did this."

His concern made my insides go all mushy and warm, a feeling I hadn't known in a very long time. It didn't mean I would back down. "What if I promise to stay in the car?"

The silent curse he bit out told me he didn't believe that any more than I did. "I'm driving." He held his hand out for the car keys.

"Just promise you won't go jumping over the hood, Hutch." I handed the keys over, a triumphant smile on my face.

"Don't make me regret this." He marched away toward the car.

I wasn't making any promises.

We pulled up to the riverbank behind Hank Taylor's property, and Mason parked the SUV behind a row of cop cars. All around us, blue and red lights flashed through the gloom and the sheets of pouring rain.

The Straight River ran along the north side of town and boasted an interesting history. It was said to have healing waters. As rumor had it, a Sioux Chief had a daughter who was very frail, so he moved his tribe to the banks of the river. The Princess drank from the magic waters daily and recovered her health. Unfortunately for Damon, one had to be alive for the healing water to work its magic.

I took in the frenzied scene outside the car window. Yellow tape stretched between trees. Medical personnel and police officers draped in black rain ponchos. Apprehension fluttered through me, tightening in my chest. The killer had taken another life. How many more lives would they take before someone stopped them? If I wanted to, I could leave this whole mess behind and head back to LA, where I was safe. But I couldn't leave the people I cared about most. I had to stick it out. No matter how crazy or dangerous it might get.

Up ahead, Hank and his two dogs came into view by the water's edge. He was talking animatedly with two officers, making motions with his hands, while his dogs watched with perked-up ears, again as if they were listening and understanding the conversation.

A tense silence enveloped the car as Mason and I stared out the windshield at the scene unfolding outside. Neither one of us was in a hurry to go out into the cold, rainy afternoon. Mason looked over at me, his face closed, and my determination faltered. He'd brought me along because he trusted me, and I didn't want to betray that trust, but I did want to question Hank. Like

I'd told Mason on the drive over, he'd left a message for Damon. He might have been the one on the phone last night. Hank might be the killer, trying to cover up his crime by calling in the murder.

Why did I have this compulsion to track down the truth? Why didn't I trust Mason and Detective Matthews to handle it?

"Wait here." Mason pushed his car door open, the overhead light illuminating the lines set into his brow. "I'll be back."

I watched as he stopped at a pair of officers guarding the scene, flashed his badge, and continued on to where the other officers were questioning Hank. Not a moment later, the detective appeared, and my stomach churned with anxiety and frustration. What would it hurt for me to talk with Hank? He was one of my clients, not some stranger off the street.

I took a deep breath and tried to relax my nerves. The car still smelled like Mason. Like spice and whiskey and wood. Masculine. Sensual. And arrogant as could be. Though for all his posturing, there was something that made me like the agent. A warmth that sometimes managed to get through his rough demeanor. I could be imagining it, but I didn't think Mason was as hard-ass as he wanted people to think.

Outside, Mason and Detective Matthews talked with each other, while the two officers who'd been with Hank had gone and left him standing alone with his dogs. Steeling my nerves, I threw open the car door and stepped out into the stormy afternoon. My feet sank into the deep, thick mud, and cold rain lashed against my cheeks. I pulled up the hood of my sweatshirt as far as it would go, but it didn't do much to keep me dry.

I avoided the two officers standing guard and snuck onto the crime scene between the cover of two cop cars.

"Hello, Hank," I said, wading through the mud to reach the debonair older man.

His clothes were soaked through, his gray hair matted. "What in God's name are you doing out here in this rain?" He looked me over. "You ain't even got a jacket on!"

I could have used a better jacket against the rain; he wasn't wrong there. Both of his Irish setters sniffed at my muddy shoes and pant legs, then one of them nudged my hand with its nose.

I patted its head. "I think they remember me."

"Oh sure, they remember you," Hank said. "They're smarter than the average person. I should know. I trained them."

"I heard about Damon."

"A damn shame." Hank looked down at the ground, rubbing a hand over the back of his neck. "Meeting the same end as his uncle. Someone has it out for that family."

"It looks that way, doesn't it?" I pulled my hood tighter as a rush of wind changed directions and pelted me with a spray of rain. "I wonder what someone who lost a million dollars might do to get it back."

Hank looked up at me, squinting against the rain. "What do you mean by that? I hope you don't mean to say I did this. Why would I?"

"Good to see you, Hank." Detective Matthews appeared from behind us, looking like he'd seen a ghost. I suppose, in a way, he just had.

"Jake," Hank greeted him. "You picked a bad day to be out here. That river will be nothin' but mud with all this rain."

I glanced uneasily at Mason as he came to my side, his glare burning through me, anger rising in his eyes. "I thought we agreed you'd stay in the car."

"I only wanted to talk to Hank." I squatted down to pet the wet dog that had taken an interest in me and to avoid his angry stare. The dog's collar had a nametag. *Rascal.*

Matthews took charge with quiet assurance and questioned Hank. "What time did you find the body?"

"I didn't find it; my dogs did. They've got free reign around here, and I usually let 'em out after lunch to patrol the property. Once, they came up on a kid tryin' to break into my shed. Gave him a real fright. But I have to say, they've never found a dead body before."

"What time do you think they found the body?"

"It was right around noon. When I called for 'em, they didn't come. I heard them barkin' up a storm back here, and I came to see what they were so excited about. That's when I found the poor guy and called it in. You can check my phone if you want the exact time."

"No, that's all right, they'll have that at dispatch," Matthews said. "When was the last time you spoke with Damon Stone?"

As far as I was aware, only Mason and I knew about the phone message and the secret meeting. And that Hank was short a million dollars after investing with Larry. I pricked up my ears like the dogs and waited for Hank's answer.

"Gosh, it had to be the same day I met with Kate in their office."

"Are you sure about that?" I rose up, staring at Hank through the slicing rain.

Mason put his hand out to quiet me. "So, you didn't speak to Damon Stone last night?"

"No, I didn't." Hank looked between the three of us, obviously uncomfortable with where the questions were leading.

"That's not true!" I shot out. "I heard you on the phone with him. You set up a meeting. You wanted him to come alone. The million dollars was for you!" I couldn't believe I hadn't pieced the clues together sooner. Hank blackmailing Damon made sense.

"Kate, let me ask the questions," Matthews warned, clearly not happy with me going after Hank.

I only wanted the truth.

"Were you the one blackmailing him?" I stared at Hank.

"Look, we were supposed to meet and talk about my money, but he called at the last minute and canceled. He said some urgent business matter had come up."

"Or maybe when he did show up last night without your money, you killed him!"

Matthews stepped in front of Hank and fixed me in his sites. "The one thing that keeps showing up in this whole mess is you. There hasn't been a murder in Harmony Falls for decades, and now we've got two of them. I'm starting to question how you keep getting in the middle of this."

"That's enough." Mason took me by the arm and turned me to face him, his straight nose only inches from mine. "Go back to the car and wait for me. I'm handling this." He looked back to Hank. "Did Damon tell you what kind of business matter?"

"I couldn't say. He wasn't makin' much sense. He said somethin' about settling a debt. He said someone's life depended on it." Hank glanced toward the river, then back to Mason. "I guess maybe it was his."

Back in the car, I held my cold hands up to the blast of warm air coming from the heater vents. Mason left the car running with the heater on full blast to keep me warm while he handed off the bag of money to Detective Matthews and caught him up to speed. The detective seemed more willing to take the news from a fellow member of law enforcement than from a lowly forensic accountant from the land of surfers and sunshine. The story of my life.

Thanks to the rain, I was soaked all the way through, and I was cold; my teeth were actually chattering. The weather would only get colder and more unpleasant as winter inched inevitably closer, and tonight was a good reminder of how unforgiving the Minnesota climate could be. I closed my eyes and pictured the warm beaches of California, and instead of feeling warmth, the image filled me with dread.

As bad as things had gotten in Harmony Falls, I didn't know if I was ready to go back to California. I liked being home. Life here was different with my father gone. I regretted his death, but at the same time, there wasn't the constant tension with my family and the worry I'd run into him out in public and have to think of what to say to a man who had essentially become a stranger to me.

The heavy rain battered the roof of the car and tracked down the windshield, blurring the colored lights and the images of police officers and emergency personnel clearing the scene. Two men loaded a stretcher carrying a black body bag into the back of an ambulance.

*Goodbye, Damon.*

The more I thought about Damon, the more I felt responsible for his death. If I hadn't taken his money, he would've been able to pay the blackmailer, and maybe he'd still be alive. He was dead because of my meddling. I should have listened to the voice of reason and never gotten involved. Death wasn't a game, and now I might have been the reason someone had gotten killed.

Emerging from the blur of uniforms, Mason made his way back to the car. A rush of cold air and a spray of rain preceded him, and he slammed the door closed with a biting curse. "This whole case is turning into one big headache." He looked over at me, water dripping down his handsome face, his drenched hair plastered to his forehead. "I wanted to be done with it by now."

"What did Matthews say about the money? Is he considering the idea that one of the clients might be a suspect?"

"He's going to start going through the list on the computer you gave him. I think with two murders, he's desperate for a quick resolution."

"I'm sorry for not staying in the car. I didn't think it would hurt for me to talk to Hank. The two of us have something in common now. We've both found dead bodies."

Mason hung his head. "I should have cuffed you to the steering wheel. At least I'd be sure you'd stay put."

"Do you really have handcuffs?" The man was full of tricks.

He cast me a real, genuine smile. "Do you really want to find out?"

His reaction was so unexpected that it caused an odd heat to pool in my belly, like nothing I'd ever felt before. The pull was strong and frightening and exciting. This dark and gloomy day, sitting in my sister's car, was the first time I realized I wanted Mason West to kiss me.

I just didn't want him to know that, so I did what I did best when I was nervous. I rambled. "I know I shouldn't have gotten involved in any of this, but it was my father's business going down the drain, and Larry was his partner. Alex is my best friend, and I know she didn't kill him, and she definitely didn't belong in jail. I had to do something to help. I mean, who would've thought that the same type of case I work on in LA would surface in Harmony Falls? Or that I could come up with a handful of people who might be capable of murder?"

"I understand your need for truth." Mason shifted in the driver's seat to face me directly. "I'm not doubting your skills, but I think we can both agree the situation is getting dangerous. I don't want to see them pulling your body out of the river next."

A warmth seeped into me from the inside and I was touched by Mason's concern for my well-being. It was scary how quickly I was shedding my dislike for the agent. "Do you think Hank killed Damon?"

"I don't get that feeling."

"I don't know if I believe him," I said, unconvinced. "Hank likes his guns, so if his dogs were barking like crazy and he went to check on them, I'll bet you a million dollars he took a gun with him. He easily could have shot Damon and made up that story about the dogs."

"It's a good guess," Mason agreed. "But Damon wasn't shot. He was struck on the back of the head."

I absorbed the dreadful image his words brought to life. The way Damon met his end. All because of me. "I know what I heard on that phone call. He had a meeting last night with someone. If it wasn't Hank, then it had to be the real killer. Can you trace his phone records?"

"I can do a lot of things." Mason turned back to grip the steering wheel with one hand and started the car with the other. "For now, I think I should take you home."

"I don't know if I'll be any safer there." I cast a guilty look at the ambulance and the stretcher loaded into the back. "If it wasn't for me, Damon might still be alive."

"How do you figure that?" He shifted the car into reverse and began to maneuver around the random police cruisers.

"He needed that money. If I hadn't taken it, he wouldn't have been killed. Poor Damon is dead because of me."

Mason stomped the brakes, sending both of us in a lurch forward, and I reached out for the dashboard. A flash of darkness went through his gaze. "Don't you dare feel sorry for him. Not for one second."

"But doesn't it make the most sense?"

"None of this makes sense, but you listen to me, and you listen good. Damon's trouble was his own doing, and from what we found in the trunk of his car, he planned on creating even more problems."

I stared back at him, my sense of dread increasing by the second. "What did you find in his car?"

Mason looked away, sighed, then dragged his gaze back to meet mine. "A container of bleach, some heavy-duty trash bags, duct tape, rags, and chloroform."

"Why would he need any of those things? Was he going to clean something?" Fear clutched at my heart as my mind caught up to the reality. "He was planning on getting rid of someone."

Like me.

Because of the money, or because I owned part of the business, I'd become a threat to him. Whatever the reason, my instincts had been right to fear Damon.

"It's hard to tell what goes through a person's mind when they're pushed far enough. Fortunately for us, fate took care of him." Mason put the car in drive.

I focused on the side mirror, which reflected the flashing police lights. Fate was a fickle mistress. How long before my share ran out?

# Chapter Nineteen

When we arrived at my father's house, Mason threw the car into park and cut the engine, then handed the keys to me. "I'm staying with you tonight." Before I could protest, he added, "I'll sleep on the couch."

I let us into the house and went through the rooms, flipping on lights to ward off the early evening gloom while Mason stood in the kitchen checking the messages on his phone. Back in the office, I wanted to check my emails to see if I had any updates from Grace. A feeling of déjà vu radiated through me when I didn't see my laptop on the desk. I knew I'd left it there, in fact, I'd gotten much more fastidious with my habits ever since the box incident.

I looked around, checking drawers, but it wasn't there. I went upstairs and checked the bedroom. The spare room. Then back down to the living room. In the kitchen, Mason fixed me with an odd stare. "Looking for something?"

"My laptop," I said. "I left it in the office, and now it's gone. I can't find it anywhere."

"Is anything else missing?" He slid his phone into his jacket pocket and walked out of the kitchen toward the office.

"I don't think so." I dragged my hands through my damp hair to pull it back from my face. "This feels like the boxes."

He stopped at the hallway and looked back over the banister railing. "It's like the what?"

"A few days ago, some boxes I had packed up were moved around. I couldn't find any signs that someone had been in the house, but I swear someone moved them. Now my laptop is missing."

"Let me take a look around." Mason proceeded to inspect every window and door until he'd swept through the entire house.

"What did you find?" I asked when he returned, scratching his head.

"No one broke in, and everything is locked up tight. Are you sure you didn't leave it somewhere? Things don't go missing on their own."

"Yeah, and boxes don't move themselves, either. Welcome to my world."

"Does anyone else have a key to the house?"

"Only my sister. It's possible she was here before and moved the boxes, but she wouldn't come and take my laptop."

"Maybe you should call her and ask, just in case."

The idea was far-fetched, but since I needed to make some calls to check in before word got out about Damon's murder, I decided it wouldn't hurt to ask Kylie if she'd been in the house. It was the only possible explanation.

An hour later, I'd spoken to my sister, my mother, and Alex, and none of them had any reason to be in the house. While it cleared up one part of the mystery, it left a gaping hole where a logical conclusion should remain. My laptop had been at the house in the morning. I'd checked my emails after I'd left Alex's house, then I got changed and went to the market in the park. Who would want my laptop?

It would be useless to the killer without the password. There was no evidence saved to it, I'd given everything I had to the detective and Mason, and it couldn't be mistaken for my father's laptop. No man in his right mind would own a pink computer.

I sent a crazed glance out the door to the patio, beyond the security light pooling on the bricks and into the dark night. I wondered if the killer had taken it to send a message. They could get to me anytime they wanted.

The phone on the desk in the office rang, causing me to jump. I'd unplugged after the weird calls. Who plugged it back in?

"Hello?" I answered.

No one.

I slammed the receiver down.

"Who was that?" Mason came into the office.

"A wrong number," I said. "Whoever it is, they keep calling. It's why I unplugged the phone, but it looks like someone plugged it back in."

When the phone rang again, Mason answered, his deep voice booming over the line. "Who is this?"

After a few seconds, he hung up the phone. I grabbed the cord to unplug it again, but Mason stopped me. "Leave it. Let them call back. I'll answer it."

But the phone stayed silent.

"I feel like I'm going crazy," I said. "I know I unplugged the phone."

"Are you absolutely certain?"

"Yes, I am." Despite the conviction in my tone, the situation made me doubt myself.

"Let's leave it for the night," he said. "Come on."

I followed Mason out to where he'd set himself up in the living room. A football game played across the television screen, and he'd taken care of half the sausage pizza he ordered for delivery, along with two beers. The stack of blankets and a pillow I'd brought downstairs sat on the end of the couch.

He aimed the remote at the television and muted the game. "Are you hungry?"

"Not really." I'd had zero appetite since breakfast, and the chill of the day was getting to me. I hugged my arms around myself to fight off a shiver. "I think I'm going to bed."

Mason made his way over to me. It was oddly intimate to see him pad across the wood floors in his dark socks, his white collared shirt rolled back at the sleeves and untucked from his pants, the top buttons undone. He put his hands over mine and squeezed as he held my gaze. "The police are watching Alex's house, and no one will get in this house while I'm here, or they'll wish they hadn't. Try to get some sleep. I've got half a pizza to finish and enough channels to keep me entertained all night."

"I appreciate you staying with me. With my laptop missing and the phone plugged back in, I know someone has been in the house. What I don't know is how they got in."

"We can file a report with the police tomorrow and have the phone tapped. Until they catch whoever is doing this, I won't be going anywhere. Your place is much nicer than the roach trap motel I booked."

184

I managed a grateful smile. "I can't believe the Cedardale is still standing, not to mention charging for rooms." The place had been a dump when I was kid, and as far as I could tell, not much had been done to remedy the condition.

"I wish I'd known that before I came to town."

"If you had called me first instead of just showing up here, I could have told you where to stay, or not to stay for that matter."

"I like catching people by surprise." A wicked gleam came to his eyes. "If I had called first, I wouldn't have caught you in the bath."

"I wish you hadn't." My cheeks heated when I recalled the embarrassment of answering the door dripping wet, wearing only a sheer nightshirt.

"I don't."

The silence between us grew, thick with lust, and my gaze dropped to his full, sensual mouth. God, I'd bet he was a good kisser. Two steps. That's all it would take for me to find out. Wisely, I took two steps back to put some distance between us. It was rare for me to meet a man who didn't underestimate me. One who stimulated my mind as well as my desire. Mason held a dangerous power, one I was sure he was aware of, and he awakened things in me that I didn't dare succumb to. Not when I had to concentrate on unraveling the mystery my father had left behind.

"I'm glad you're here," I said, then made my way upstairs and left Mason with the glow of the television.

Once we found the killer, Mason would be out of my life, and it was just as well. The last thing I needed was another distraction. No matter how good he looked in a suit.

The storm finally let up during the night, and after a restless sleep, I woke on Sunday morning to the remnants of a gray sky. It was fitting weather for the gloominess that threatened to consume me. I'd tossed and turned all night, wondering if the business I'd inherited was cursed. Or if just Larry and Damon had been cursed. If my theory about an angry client seeking revenge was right, it most certainly meant I was next. I was the only business partner left standing. I thought maybe I shouldn't worry so much about sleeping again since I'd get plenty of it when I was dead.

I turned onto my side and listened for sounds of Mason downstairs. It would have been the perfect morning to cozy up to the warm flesh of a lover or linger over breakfast in bed. Sip from a cup of hot tea and get lost in a book. As fate would have it, the universe had other plans.

My phone rang with an incoming call from Alex. The time was 8:08.

"Hey," I answered, my voice raspy from sleep.

"Stop it," Alex said.

"Stop what?"

"I can hear those wheels turning all the way over here."

"You wouldn't be so casual if you had a killer gunning for you."

"What makes you think I'm not a target? I've got police surveillance on my house. We have no idea who the killer is, especially now that Damon is dead and gone, but we do know they hated me enough to plant the gun in my van. I've started locking my doors."

"I think it had to be Hank Taylor. He lost over a million dollars, then so conveniently happened upon Damon's dead body in the river. He's not shy around guns. How do we know the gun used to kill Larry didn't come from his collection?"

"It's not Hank." Alex's tone was exact.

"You don't know that—"

"I know," she insisted. "Trust me on this one. Hank Taylor is not the killer."

Not in the mood to argue when Alex got immovable, I jumped to my next conclusion. "I haven't ruled out Hannah. She could have planted the gun before she walked in on us that morning."

"Is Hannah smart enough to kill?" Alex dropped the question. "That part is easy, but planting the gun? I'm not so sure."

"Well, you just ruled out my best suspects, and I haven't even had my coffee yet." She was not helping to improve my mood.

"What about Nick Callahan? I thought you said he had an argument with Larry the day before we found him at the office, and he wanted to get his hands on the business. We shouldn't rule him out."

"I know he seemed like the most obvious after Damon, but he has an alibi for the night of the murder."

"Who is it?"

"His wife. He said they were home all night with the kids."

"Are you kidding me?" Alex gave a bitter laugh. "His wife loves his paycheck more than he does. She would do anything to protect him. I'll bet she'd even lie for him. The more I think about it, my money's on Nick."

I'd never thought about it from that angle. All I'd seen when I first questioned Nick was his perfect, untarnished life. I, of all people, knew life was never that easy. People fell down. Things came apart. How far would someone go to keep the image of their perfect life?

"You need to get out of your head, get up and get dressed, and meet me down at the studio. The rain cleared up, and we can go out to the country club."

I draped my arm over my eyes, still considering staying in bed all day and feeling sorry for myself. "What's at the country club?"

"Nick Callahan. He'll be on the golf course. With the way people are dropping dead like flies around here, I think we should question him again. Does he have an alibi for the night of Damon's murder?"

I was suddenly curious to find out. The phone message from Hank could have been about something else. Nick seemed more capable of blackmail and murder than he did. "I don't know how to golf."

"Well, men do it," Alex said. "How hard can it be?"

Alex was like a dog with a bone. There was no question she'd be making a visit to the country club. "Do you even have a set of golf clubs?"

"My mom has a set, she used to be on a league. We don't actually have to play the game, we only have to look the part. Do you have a polo shirt?"

"I'm not wearing polyester." Even I had standards.

"Whatever. Just try to look like you belong on a golf course and meet me downtown in an hour." Alex hung up.

As much as I dreaded digging up more trouble, I had to finish what I'd started. Finding the killer was the only way I or Alex or anyone else in town would be safe.

Kicking off the covers, I shivered from the cold. I'd gone to bed in my only nightshirt, and I refused to turn on the heat. It was only September. A hot shower would help dispel the cold, and then I'd make a cup of coffee.

I pulled on a pair of jeans before going downstairs to check on Mason. The blankets were folded up on the couch, the pizza box and beer bottles had been cleaned up, and there was no sign of him. So much for my round-the-clock protection. When I went into the kitchen, I found a paper coffee cup and a brown bag on the counter, along with a note from Mason.

*Went to the station to report your missing laptop.*

*Have a coffee and a donut, and don't worry.*

*This will all be over soon. M.*

The coffee was still warm, and I peeked inside the bag. Chocolate wasn't the healthiest breakfast, but I made an exception and enjoyed the donut on my way back upstairs to get ready.

After a steaming hot shower, a quick search through the clothes in my suitcase turned up nothing sporty to wear, so I dressed in yoga pants and a T-shirt and covered up with a warm cardigan. I hardly looked sporty, but the outfit would have to suffice. On my way out of the house, I texted Mason that I was going to see Alex and I'd let him know when I was on my way back to the house.

Outside, the sky was a gloomy shade of gray with low-hung clouds. I pulled up the hood on my coat and walked across the wet lawn to Kylie's car parked in the driveway. Wet leaves matted the ground, their colors dulled and trampled underfoot. I cheated and used the heater in the car on my short drive downtown, and the closest parking spot to Alex's studio was a full two blocks away.

Once inside the Monroe Design Studio, I could see why parking on a Sunday morning had been an issue. I wove my way around several groups of people, happily browsing through textiles and candles, and made it to the back counter where Alex was ringing up a sale.

"Hi!" Alex wore a pleased smile, then bagged up the candles and decorative fall bowl fillers for her customer, handing the bag off with a bigger smile. "Did you see how crowded it is? I haven't been able to keep up this morning. I'm even running out of stock in the back."

188

"What is going on?" I gave another incredulous look around the studio, at women with armloads of blankets and pillows and fake greenery.

"Everyone wants to gossip." Alex beamed. "People know I was the main suspect in Larry's murder, and then word got out about Damon. Now it's all anyone can talk about."

"Word has a way of doing that in this town."

"At least I'm not on the line for murder this time around." Alex came out from behind the sales counter in a flurry. "I have to get all of these people cleared out before we can go to the golf course."

"I can't imagine anyone wanting to golf after all the rain we got." I glanced out of the large front windows. A promising ray of sunshine peeked out from the gray clouds.

"You obviously don't know golfers. They'd golf in the snow if they could."

"I'll never understand the appeal of that game," I said. "The few times I played, I kept losing the ball. I spent most of my time sifting through the rough or raking sand traps."

Alex assessed my outfit with outright displeasure. "Are you seriously wearing yoga pants?"

"They're sporty, aren't they?"

"Yeah, in a soccer mom, SUV, iced coffee kind of way."

"I'm actually driving an SUV."

"You can't golf in that outfit," Alex said.

No surprise that she was dressed in a cute white skirt and a white polo shirt, looking more like she was going to play tennis than crash a bunch of middle-aged men teeing off at the golf course.

"I thought we were only going to talk to Nick again," I said. "I'm working with a limited wardrobe. This is the only thing I have to wear."

"We'll have to make it work. Maybe we can call and get his tee time and head him off at the first hole."

"I don't expect he's going to be real happy to see us crashing his game," I said when a movement of color across the street caught my eye, and I recognized the person coming out of Pickwick's Pawn Shop. "Hey, look. That's Janice."

189

Alex didn't give my father's old girlfriend the slightest notice. "I'm going to get these ladies rounded up so they can pay for their things, and then I can close for lunch. I might need two lines."

"I'll be right back to help after I go talk to Janice for a minute."

Outside, the clouds were giving way to blue sky and more bright rays of sunshine. Janice glanced over and did not look pleased to see me rushing across the street. I only prayed a psycho killer in a red car didn't try to run me over again. As I reached the other side of the street, Janice actually picked up her pace and walked faster.

"Hi, Janice." I caught up with her, slightly out of breath. "I saw you from Alex's studio. How are you doing?"

"You didn't have to come all the way over here to talk to me." She didn't look at me and kept walking along.

"I wanted to come talk to you. I tried calling yesterday to see if you were ready to get the boxes I packed for you, but I never got an answer."

"I'm sorry, dear. I've been busy getting ready for my craft circle next week. I haven't had the time to call you back." Janice increased her pace as we came to the corner, her long, colorful skirt flowing behind her. Looking much more put together than the last time we'd met, her hair had been cut, colored, and styled.

I had to walk faster in order to keep up. "Kylie wants to get the estate sale planned, and I wanted to give you first pick of the furniture before she takes out an ad in the paper."

"Maybe I can come by next week. That is, if you're still going to be here." Janice kept her gaze forward as she rounded the street corner. "With such an important job, they must be missing you in California."

"I'll be here." I tried to make eye contact with Janice. "I'm thinking of extending my stay."

"Your mother and sister must be so happy to have you around."

Janice's white hatchback was parked down the street, and I wanted to finish our conversation before she could get in the car and drive away. "Look, I know we didn't always get along, and there was the rift with my father, but I'd like for us to be friends."

"You don't want to be friends with an old bird like me." She waved her hand. "You need to get out with young people your own age."

"My dad would've liked us to be friends," I said, making my last attempt to get through to her.

Janice pulled out her car keys and hit the alarm button, the taillights on her car flashing. "I'm not so sure your father knew what was good for anyone, least of all himself."

The comment was odd, even for Janice. "What do you mean by that?"

"Never mind," Janice said as we came to her car. "I've really got to dash."

Her little hatchback was stuffed to the gills with boxes and quilts and other household items. If I didn't know better, I'd think Janice actually was living in her car.

"Wow, your car is really full."

"What?" Janice opened the driver's door. "Oh, that. I'm in the process of packing so most of this old junk is going to the thrift store later."

"Let me know if you want some help," I offered. "Moving is a lot of work."

"Right." Janice got into her car. "See you." After a fleeting wave of her jeweled fingers, she slammed the car door closed, cranked the engine to life, and sped away from the curb.

I couldn't begin to count how many ways my encounter with Janice was weird. What I found especially strange, even for Janice, was that she didn't look me in the eye once during our brief conversation. Then, there was the peculiar comment about my father.

Knowing Janice had a tendency to be flighty and flaky, I didn't take her cool demeanor personally. She'd probably been in a rush and had a lot of other errands to take care of, considering she was in the process of moving. I would bring up the issue of the furniture next week when she wasn't so busy.

On my short walk back to Alex's studio, most of the clouds had passed, leaving the sky clear and blue, the golden sunshine warming the ground and drying the puddles. It looked like it would be a good day to pay a visit to the Harmony Falls Country Club after all.

# Chapter Twenty

We reached the country club after lunch in the midst of a perfect, sunny day. The kind of warm, colorful fall day that endeared me to Minnesota. Never mind that the weather in my home state was bipolar, because the extremes could be spectacular.

Alex parked her van among the front row of stalls, right in front of the putting green where several men in trousers and bright polo shirts warmed up for their golf games. I'd never spent much time at the property. When I was young, my family struggled to make ends meet and couldn't afford exclusive membership fees so we could spend our Sunday afternoons attending brunches where everyone dressed to the nines in order to impress their neighbors. It still sounded like a mild form of torture.

"Do you see him?" Alex peered through the windshield at the group of golfers on the practice putting green.

"They all look the same." I pushed my sunglasses back on my head to get a better look.

"None of them really stand out, do they?"

A blond man exited the clubhouse through a side door, white bandages on the bridge of his nose and his cheek.

"That's him!" I pointed. "What happened to his face?"

"We know what the other guy looks like." Alex opened her car door and got out. "Let's see him try to squirm his way out of this one."

I kept up with her fast clip and ignored the curious looks from the other golfers as we headed straight toward Nick Callahan. When he saw the two of us approaching, his face twisted in anger.

"You've got a lot of nerve showing up here," he shouted. "What else do you expect to accomplish in front of all these witnesses?"

I did not like being the focus of everyone's attention, and Alex seemed equally startled by his harsh reaction.

"Are you back to finish the job?" Nick rushed up to Alex, stopping mere inches from her, his fury barely leashed.

"What happened to your face?" Alex wrinkled up her nose. "Have you been running with scissors?"

"Drop the act!" Nick shouted, stepping even closer to her. Had Alex been a man, he might have shoved her or even swung a fist.

"Calm down." Alex put up her hands in surrender. "I come in peace."

Nick breathed in heavy gusts, his chest heaving. His blue eyes were wild, savage almost. "I hope you enjoyed your time on the outside, because once the cops catch up with you, a tiny cell is all you're going to know for the next five to ten."

"What?" Alex drew back. "Why am *I* going to jail?"

"I think there's been a misunderstanding here," I spoke up. "What's got you so upset, Callahan?"

He turned his venomous stare on me. "You're probably in on it, knowing your kind. It's one thing to go after me, but my kids are innocent."

"Wait a minute," Alex said. "We didn't go after anyone. What happened to you?"

Nick's tension relaxed, his face softening. "Are you saying it wasn't you?"

"That depends." Alex flipped her long hair. "What am I being accused of this time?"

"Last night, someone tried to run my truck off the road. I had my oldest son in the car with me. We crashed into a ravine, got beat up pretty good. I had seventeen stitches. My son got eleven stitches and a broken wrist. If you were a guy, I'd knock your dick in the dirt." He stabbed a forceful finger at her chest.

"Out of all the people in this town, what makes you think it was me? I don't even know how to run a car off the road."

"How many people do you know with bright red hair?"

Her blue eyes clawed him like talons, and her temper flared. "My hair is not red!"

Nick retreated a step at her outburst, but her reaction seemed to amuse him. "Whatever helps you sleep at night, red."

"My hair hasn't been red since grade school. It's auburn now."

It was almost like grade school with these two. Knowing where this might lead, I stepped in. "Did you see what kind of car they were driving?"

"It was hard to see with all the rain, but it was a red four-door sedan. I only wish I'd gotten the full license plate."

"Someone driving a red car tried to run me over yesterday." It had to be the same person who went after Nick. There was some piece of the puzzle I was missing.

"Did you see what the driver was wearing?" I asked. "Are you sure it was a woman driving?"

The line of his mouth tightened a fraction more. "I didn't really have time to get a good look at the driver while my truck was taking a nosedive into a twenty-foot ravine. I suppose I could be mistaken."

"But you managed to notice they had red hair and get a partial plate?"

"That's what I just said, isn't it?" There was an anxious edge to his voice.

I didn't have a lot of sympathy for Nick, the guy was suing me after all, but I understood why he was shaken, and felt bad his son had been injured.

"What I think she's trying to say is you might have noticed some other detail without realizing it yet." Alex awkwardly cleared her throat. "Can you recall anything else?"

Nick reached a hand into his pants pocket and drew out a white leather golf glove. He stuffed his hand into it, opening and closing his fist as he snapped the back closure. "I told the police everything I know. Are we done here, ladies?"

Alex kicked up her chin in determination. "Not yet, actually, no. Someone framed me for Larry Stone's murder. I'm trying to give you the benefit of the doubt, seeing how we've been friends in the past, but it's looking more and more like you have something to hide."

His expression tight with strain, he said, "I have an alibi for that night."

"Your wife isn't the most convincing alibi, and while you may have been at home that night, it doesn't mean you didn't hire someone to kill Larry for you. It also doesn't look very good that you're suing Kate because she got in the way of your plans to take her father's business, or that Larry's nephew turned up dead. Maybe you ran yourself off the road to cover the truth. That's sinking pretty low, but I guess you had to come up with another way to be the town savior. Where were you on Friday night?"

"I don't have to stay here and listen to this." He brushed past Alex.

"Spoken like a man with something to hide," Alex said to his retreating back.

He stopped, turned, and spread his hands regretfully. "Forgive me for not knowing how to act when I get accused of murder on the golf course. The day is still early. Come back in a few hours, and you can ruin the rest of my afternoon."

Alex opened her mouth to shoot him another clever reply, then thinking better of it, she turned on her heel and strode for the parking lot, her auburn hair fanning out behind her like a dark flame.

"Are we leaving?" I asked, thinking we had more questions for Nick.

Alex continued walking, not stopping to explain.

"Right, we're leaving now." I avoided stares from the other golfers and hurried after Alex.

Back in the van, Alex dropped her head on the steering wheel. "That went well."

"We didn't totally strike out." I took a lesson from my little sister and refused to be anything other than optimistic. "What did we learn?"

"Never to show our faces on a golf course again." Alex groaned.

I laughed despite the tension. "In between all that stuff about Nick being run off the road by a red car—a story I believe because it also happened to me—we learned he has something he feels guilty about."

Alex lifted her head, and her face brightened. "How did you come up with that idea?"

"It was when he said it was one thing to come after him, but his kids were innocent. Come after him for what? Did he feel he deserved to be run off

195

the road? He didn't say anything to defend himself. He just got defensive."

Alex's eyes went wide, filled with realization. "He didn't actually answer any of our questions, did he?"

I shook my head, smiling. "I don't know if he's capable of murder, but he believes he's got a reason to be run off the road by a psycho killer."

Alex turned the key in the ignition with a deft flick of her wrist, the excited light vivid in her eyes. "I'm going to find out if Nick Callahan framed me, one way or another, and then I'm going to make him pay."

I paused before clicking my seatbelt. "Spoken like a true psycho killer. Maybe you did murder Larry Stone."

Alex whipped her van into reverse, backing out of the parking space, then shifted into drive and floored the gas pedal, leaving the bewildered golfers behind in a screech of tires. "What can I say? That man inspires my inner serial killer. It's not a crime if you kill them in your head."

I watched the retreating golf course out the window. "Let's hope it stays in your head."

We made the short drive back to my father's house so I could give Alex a few bottles of the wine left over from the funeral. She'd been raving about Logan's Cabernet and wanted to host a tasting event at her next business women's meeting to vote on whether to serve his wine at their Annual Gala next spring.

The moment I opened the front door, I sensed something was wrong. The energy in the air had changed.

"What's that smell?" Alex stopped in the doorway and sniffed the air.

"Gas." My nerve endings vibrated a warning, and my skin prickled with gooseflesh. It couldn't be the stove. It hadn't been used since the funeral. Had the gas line sprung a leak since I'd left this morning? Not likely.

"Don't go inside." Alex slowly backed us out onto the porch. "One wrong move, and the house could explode."

"That only happens in the movies."

"That's what I thought about finding dead bodies, but here we are."

Tears sprung to my eyes as I bounded down the front steps. Anger threatened to overwhelm me, and I wanted to hit something, or break something. I knew who had done this, and I felt my blood run cold. "Son of a bitch!"

This was no accident. Someone had been in the house for a third time. Someone vicious and vile, who had killed two people, perhaps even three. Someone who was now focused on killing me.

"Whoa, calm down, hon." Alex wrapped me in a hug and made gentle strokes along my back. "We'll call the emergency number for the gas company and they can check for a leak."

"No!" I pulled out of her embrace. "We need to call the police. There's no gas leak. The house was fine when I left this morning. Someone wants me dead."

"Okay, let's call the police." Alex went to the van for her cell phone and made the call.

I was so angry. Why was the killer after me? Had I unknowingly done something to piss them off? Was it because I took the money from Damon? Because I found Larry dead? Because of my father? Whatever the reason, I'd come closer to death than I was comfortable with.

"They're on their way." Alex came back and waited with me on the front lawn.

"Thank you for being here." I reached for her hand while blinking away tears. I refused to cry. I wouldn't give the killer that satisfaction.

"What are friends for?" Alex patted my back. "The cops should be here any minute."

We didn't have to wait long. Detective Matthews in his Blazer, trailed by a black and white cruiser, raced down the street and slammed to a sudden stop along the curb. Matthews hopped out of his vehicle before it had come to a full stop and jogged across the lawn.

"Are you okay?" His warm eyes overflowed with worry.

"We're fine," I said. "Except for the fact that someone tried to kill us. There's a gas leak in the house."

His look turned fierce, menacing almost, and I was glad to have the detective on our side. "Wait here. We'll check it out."

Matthews made a hand motion to the uniformed officers, and they followed him. The trio cautiously approached the house, went up the steps, and made their way inside. Nothing exploded, and after several minutes of waiting, they came back out on the porch. One of the officers spoke into the radio receiver strapped to his shoulder.

"The gas for the stove was left on," Matthews said, coming down the front steps. "Did you forget to turn it off this morning?"

"No," I said. "I haven't used the stove once."

"That's kinda what I figured, since all four burners had been left on without a flame. It looks suspicious in any case. We'll dust it for prints. Did you want to go inside and have a look to see if anything is missing?"

"The only thing of value to go missing recently was my laptop."

"Agent West informed me you believe someone broke into the house. When I was inside, I didn't see any signs of a forced entry. Is it possible you left a door or one of the windows unlocked?"

"I always double-check both doors before I leave the house. Whoever did this wasn't looking for something," I said. "They were trying to kill me."

"It might make sense for you to avoid the house for a bit. Is there somewhere else you can stay?"

"You're staying at my house." Alex looped her arm through mine. "But first we should get the wine. I need a drink."

The police officers finished their work later that afternoon and called to tell me they put a tap on the house phone and would file a report about the theft and the possible trespass. I would need to come down to the station to sign the report in the morning. My next call was to the only locksmith in town, but since it was Sunday and most businesses were closed, I had to leave a message.

I called Kylie next and filled her in on what happened, then had to endure a lecture about the dangers of tracking down murderers. I called my mother, who was almost hysterical and insisted on coming over to Alex's house. I assured her we were safe and promised I would call if I heard from the police or learned any new information.

By then, early evening had descended, the sun was hanging low in the sky, and Alex made dinner. While she stirred the ingredients for a chicken stir-fry in her wok, I poured the wine, and we had our own private tasting, getting rather tipsy on the local vintage. We reminisced about high school and growing up in Harmony Falls, and then I told her about my odd attraction to Mason. What was it that always attracted me to unavailable men?

"They're exciting because they're unpredictable," she said. "We all go through a phase."

"I want to be with a man who makes me feel safe."

"Cheers to that." Alex lifted her glass and finished the rest of her wine in one long swallow. "I can't believe tomorrow is Monday already. I feel like I'm missing time after the two days I spent in jail."

"I can't believe I extended my vacation by another week. Now that I got screwed over by my ex-boyfriend, why should I be in a hurry to get back?" A hiccup escaped me. "Do you know I have over four hundred hours of vacation time?"

"Haven't you taken any time off since you've been there?"

"Never." I lifted my wineglass, realized it was empty, and set it back down. "They sell you a great benefit package when you get hired, but they don't expect you to actually use any of the benefits. What's the point in having all that vacation time if I can't use it?"

"That's what I love about running my own business. I can take time off whenever I want." Alex cast an anxious glance out the kitchen window over the sink. "Do you think the killer will come here?"

"If they do, they'll be sorry. We've got the cops and Mason watching the place."

"I don't know how much longer I can live waiting for the other shoe to drop. It's exhausting." Alex cleared our wine glasses and empty dessert plates from the counter and set them in the sink. "It's getting late. I think it's time for bed."

I swerved as I stood up. "I think you're right."

We'd both lost track of how many glasses of wine we'd enjoyed, and without sleep, I'd be a wreck in the morning. Back in Alex's guest room, I climbed into the middle of the bed and pulled a blanket over me, blocking out the world. The wine made me drowsy, but sleep did not come easy that night. I wondered if it ever would.

On Monday morning, I woke up to the smell of coffee and shuffled out of bed and into the kitchen, where Alex sat, leafing through an interior design supply catalog. The morning paper sat on the table next to her, a picture of Damon on the front page and the word 'MURDER' in large block letters across the top.

"Coffee's on, and the aspirin is by the sink," Alex said. "I don't know about you, but I had a hard time getting up this morning."

I only had a small pounding headache, but my mouth felt like a desert. I filled a glass with water and chased down two aspirins before fixing a cup of coffee and taking a sip.

"You're all dressed up." I complimented Alex on her outfit, a matching cream blazer and pantsuit. "Are you going somewhere special?"

"I'm being photographed for the Harmony Falls Business Women's Association newsletter." Alex closed the catalog and took a final sip of her coffee before getting up from the table.

I gave a low whistle. "Look at you being all professional."

"It might be a small town, but what we lack in substance, we make up for in style."

"Because girls just wanna have fun." Throwing quotes from our favorite movies never got old.

"That should be our next movie night." Alex set her coffee mug in the sink. "I'd better get going. They're doing the photo shoot at the studio. You should drop by and check it out on your way to the office. You can get my autograph."

I smiled. No one deserved to be honored for her work more than Alex. "Thanks again for letting me stay."

"There's a box of croissants on the counter, and help yourself to anything from my closet."

"Have a good day, dear," I said as Alex sashayed out of the kitchen.

I decided I'd better get moving myself if I wanted to have time to stop by

Alex's studio before going to the office. Not that there was any reason for me to go to the office, but I wanted to be open. I wanted to be at my desk to show the killer I wouldn't be broken so easily.

I showered and dressed in navy pants, a white sweater, and a pair of comfortable flats I borrowed from the back of Alex's closet. In the bathroom, I helped myself to the hair dryer and some makeup, then had a croissant for breakfast and another cup of coffee. After cleaning up the kitchen, I hopped into Kylie's SUV and drove downtown to Alex's studio.

The morning had dawned crisp and clear, bringing with it a renewed sense of hope. I had experienced a setback, a minor roadblock, but I wasn't giving up. Sometimes, all a girl needed was to clear her head and remind herself of who she is, and where she's going. I trusted my instincts to continue leading me in the right direction.

Parking wasn't as much of an issue this morning, but there were still a good number of people browsing in Alex's studio. Some of the shelves were bare and most of the staged tablescapes and sofa textiles had been picked clean.

"Hey!" Alex called from behind the counter. "You're just in time."

Two women in the back of the studio were setting up lights and photography equipment.

I strolled up to the counter and watched the excitement unfold. "It's not every day your friend becomes a celebrity."

"You'd better believe it!" Alex sounded excited. "I found out I've been nominated for Business Woman of the Year. Isn't that great? You should talk to Susan Miller about joining, seeing as how you're a new entrepreneur in town."

"Don't remind me," I said, having no idea what exactly I was going to do with the office now that it was mine. "Murder isn't good for business."

Alex frowned. "Someone else hasn't turned up dead, have they?"

"Not yet, but it's still early."

A slender brunette woman with big, brown eyes and long, dangly earrings came behind the counter and touched Alex on the elbow. "I think we're ready for you."

"Kate, this is Susan Miller with the Business Women's Association," Alex made the introduction. "Kate Abbott is my best friend and she recently moved home to take over her father's investment business."

"I haven't exactly settled things at the office yet," I said, exchanging a polite handshake with Susan Miller, who, for such a slender woman, had a bone-crushing grip.

"You should think about joining the BWA," Susan said. "We could always use new members. You could join just in time for the Fall Festival next month."

"That sounds fun," I said. "What is it?"

Harmony Falls had its share of festivals, from Fourth of July and the Summer Festival to Crazy Days in the spring, and then there was the Christmas Parade and the Winter Fest, but this one I'd never heard of before.

"The chamber of commerce officially hosts the four-day event, but the BWA has had some involvement for the past few years," Susan explained. "Primarily, we sponsor the scarecrow contest, but we also ask our business owners to decorate their storefront windows with scarecrows and put up a flier for the event. It gives an overall sense of unity."

"Don't leave out the fun parts," Alex said. "They have an apple bobbing contest and a three-legged race in Central Park, pumpkin carving, and the street dance on Saturday night. Last year we had a live band. They were really wild!"

Susan lit up at Alex's mention of the live band. "The Vagabonds! We're getting them back this year. My cousin is the bass player."

Their excitement was contagious, and I couldn't resist the urge to get involved. I excelled at planning and organizing, and who didn't love a good party? "I love festivals, and I'd love to learn more about how I can help the BWA," I said. "I've done some event planning back in LA, and I'd be happy to lend a hand wherever it's needed." The way things were going with finding the killer, I might be stuck in town forever.

"I'm running the membership drive this year." Alex winked at me. "Looks like I'm off to a good start."

"I'd hate to think my own friend set me up." As confused as I felt about the

202

fate of my father's business, I was touched by Alex's determination to keep me in town.

"This is great!" Susan clasped her hands together, her smile widening in approval. "I'll get a membership packet put together and a festival assignment for you. Here's my card." She handed it to me. "Let's meet for coffee later this week and go over the details." She looked to Alex next. "Are you ready to get started?"

"Ready as I'll ever be."

"I'll catch you later." I waved and left the women to do their thing.

I wanted to get to the office and see if anyone else would bother to show up. Hannah and I were the only ones left.

# Chapter Twenty-One

When I walked through the door, I found Hannah in torn jeans and a white Florida State sweatshirt, packing the contents of her desk into a box.

"What are you doing?" My nerves tensed immediately.

Was this the end for Hannah?

"I can't do this anymore." Hannah's voice cracked, on the verge of tears. "I know I shouldn't have stolen the client list and that what Larry did was wrong, so I tried to help you, I really did. It's just that every day, someone else working here dies, and I don't get paid enough to risk my life for this job."

I'd pretty much ruled Hannah out as a suspect after Damon was killed. It's possible she may have been jealous enough to kill Larry in a fit of passion, but she'd been too enamored with Damon to turn around and kill him. She might be an accomplice to a crime, but she wasn't a killer.

"Did someone try to hurt you or come after you?" I only now thought to ask about the events of her weekend. "Should we call the police?"

Hannah gave a bitter laugh as she pitched her pink sweater and a box of tampons into her box. "The cops have been at my apartment since yesterday. First, they came to tell me Damon had been killed and ask me tons of questions. Then they wanted to put a cop car out front to watch my building. They said I could be in danger, that the killer could come after me next. All my neighbors are whispering about me. I can't take it anymore."

Right, so essentially, we'd had the same weekend. I'd had two near misses with death in the last two days. I wasn't sure my luck would hold out long enough to survive another. And though Hannah wasn't innocent in this whole charade, she also didn't deserve to be hunted down and murdered. No one deserved that horror. "Would you like to stay with me and Alex until the police solve this? We could stick together until they catch the killer."

"You're the most obvious target and the last person I want to be around." Hannah stopped emptying out her desk and looked directly at me, a mix of tenderness and exasperation on her pretty face. "I quit."

"Please don't quit." I scrambled for an excuse that might convince her to stay.

There were none.

Hannah's life was possibly in danger, and I couldn't ask her to ignore the risk involved in staying. I'd already possibly gotten one person killed. I didn't want to be responsible for ending another life. It was time to part ways with Hannah and face the uncertainty of my future alone.

"What will you do?" I wondered what life held next for Hannah.

"My parents want me to come home to Florida. They say it's too dangerous here. I've got a flight leaving this afternoon." She pulled a set of keys from her jeans pocket and twisted a small key off the ring with a pink gemstone pendant.

My heart skipped a beat as I watched Hannah turn the key in the lock of her top desk drawer and pull it open.

"All my passwords are on this sheet." She held up a pink index card.

The drawer did hold secrets.

She scribbled something on a sticky note and pressed it to her desktop. "You can mail my final check to this address. The payroll program has a shortcut on my home page."

"Are you sure this is what you want to do?"

Hannah twisted off another key from her key ring. "This is my office key." She set it on top of the sticky note.

"Did you ever find out why Damon took those files from you?"

"He said he took them to keep me safe." She gave a choked, desperate laugh. "And look what happened to him."

"None of this was your fault." Not totally, anyway.

She picked up her box, then draped her bag over her shoulder. "I want to see everyone get their money back, but it's not worth dying for. Have a nice life. If you live that long." Hannah strode out of the office for the last time, leaving me with an inexplicable feeling of emptiness.

I was all that remained of Harmony Wealth Partners. Was this what fate had planned for me all along? To leave me with nothing but a bloodstained carpet, a lawsuit that would surely bankrupt me, and a handful of defrauded clients? What else did fate have in store for me if I stayed? I wouldn't be surprised if Mason West led a team of FinCEN agents through the door to arrest me for securities fraud. At least no one would be trying to kill me while I served ten to twenty in federal prison.

My gaze drifted to the list of passwords on the pink sheet of paper. I'd finally found what I'd been looking for.

Time to get to work.

I booted up the computer and logged in. Every second the computer took to load felt like an eternity. My heart raced in anticipation, and my fingers twitched over the mouse. The truth was almost within reach.

Once I was in, the only programs on Hannah's computer were for the client database, her email, and the payroll program. There were no file folders or scanned documents. I explored the client database but it led nowhere. The computer was clean as a whistle. One might almost be led to believe it had been wiped. In the same way Damon had shredded the last of the paper evidence.

Lucky for me, I knew a few tricks of the trade. Files could be deleted, but there was always a back door. An electronic trail of breadcrumbs to follow. Once I accessed the recent files and the downloads folder, I hit the jackpot. Hannah hadn't cleared the cache to perform a hard delete.

My left ear started ringing as I went through file after file of bank statements for the past three years. It was all there in black and white. The deposits for the client checks, along with payouts to a small handful of those clients, with the rest of the money being diverted by wire transfer to Larry's personal and investment accounts, including an offshore account in the Bahamas. Words like concealment, evasion, and money laundering danced around in my mind. The numbers always led to the truth.

There were no foreclosed real estate properties. None of the money had ever been invested on behalf of the clients. He'd run a classic Ponzi scheme, promising higher than normal returns to lure investors in, then he paid profits to the earlier investors by using funds from newer investors. The rest of the money had been funneled into accounts for Larry's own personal use.

He would've gotten away with millions of dollars if I hadn't come home. The idea that my father had been killed to keep the scheme quiet wouldn't let me rest. It kept coming back around, haunting my brain, weighing on my heart.

How far would a person be willing to go to secure a fortune?

I searched deeper, finding files that went back several years. Larry had generated false statements to give his investors the illusion that everything was operating normally. The same type of statement I'd found and shown to Mason and Hank Taylor. Some of them even linked back to clients of his in Washington.

I went farther down, landing on one final piece of evidence to seal my case. Certificates of investment had been created so the clients would have something tangible in exchange for their money, sort of like a stock certificate, only no one knew they were worthless at the time. One major discrepancy stood out. In the files my father left me, there were ninety clients, but this folder had ninety-one certificates. Listed in alphabetical order, the first name was John Abbott. My father.

A rush of adrenaline spiked through me, filling me with equal parts excitement and dread. The numbers had been leading me here. Curious, I clicked on the file. The registration was held jointly, and the other name listed on the certificate shouldn't have surprised me, but it did.

Janice Murphy.

No wonder Janice was having money problems. She'd made the mistake of trusting Larry. Another jilted client left scrambling to make ends meet while he planned to make off with their money. Then, she had to watch the ex-wife inherit the million-dollar life insurance policy.

It could make a person mad enough to kill.

My throat began closing up, making it hard to breathe. My heart pounded. My hands trembled. I felt warm and a little dizzy. All the signs of a panic attack constricted around my chest, squeezing tighter as I tried to take a full breath. I closed my eyes, wanting to block out the terrible truth. Then I opened them and looked once more at the certificate on the screen.

The numbers told me what I had to do.

The locksmith was scheduled to meet me at my father's house in an hour. That would give me enough time to make some quick calls. I locked up the office, not sure when I'd walk through the door again. On my way out to Kylie's car, I called Mason and got his voicemail. I told him he didn't need a warrant and I had all the evidence he wanted at the office.

As I drove through downtown, I called Kylie, who answered right away.

"Ky!" I yelled into the phone, an edge of hysteria in my voice. I didn't want my hunch to be right.

"What's happened?" she asked. "What's wrong?"

"When Janice moved out of Dad's house, did you get the key back from her?"

Silence followed as Kylie took a moment to think. "I don't think I ever did. There was so much going on, and I was so upset about Dad I never even thought to get it from her. Do you want me to call her and get it back?"

"It's too late for that," I said. "I'll have to call you back."

I called Detective Matthews next and had to leave a message. I explained what I'd discovered and told him I was on my way to the house to meet the locksmith and asked him to meet me there.

By then, I'd reached the house and pulled into the driveway. I cut the engine. It all made perfect sense to me now. The moved boxes, my missing laptop, someone leaving the gas burners turned on. Each time I knew I'd locked the house, even got into the habit of double-checking everything, and with no signs of a forced entry, it meant someone had to have a key.

I checked my phone again for any messages from Mason. With no activity at Alex's house last night, he said he had some work to take care of this morning, and he'd call to check in with me later. I let a few more minutes pass by and got no call from him or the detective. It wouldn't be long before the locksmith got there to change out the locks.

I wondered if it was safe to go inside the house, but it was broad daylight, so I decided to take a closer look and got out of the car. The front door was locked when I tried it, which was a good sign. If Janice was inside, the door would still be open. Just as I unlocked the door and stepped into the entryway, my cell phone started to ring insistently.

All at once, my mind had too many things to process.

First was the detective's voice coming through the phone. "We've traced the calls made to Damon's cell phone Friday night. They came from your father's number. Kate, are you listening? The calls were made from inside your father's house."

*Well, shit.*

I would have answered him had I not been staring down the barrel at the end of a gun.

*Double shit.*

It would appear my instincts weren't as sharp as I'd thought.

Janice put a finger to her lips, warning me not to speak. She came forward and leveled the gun at my head, her face set in a vicious expression.

Was this the last thing Larry and Damon had seen before meeting their end?

"Get rid of it." Janice waved the gun, instructing me to toss the cell phone.

I gripped the phone tighter. Standing face to face with a killer, I wasn't about to let go of the only lifeline I had available. I tried to form the words to tell Matthews I needed help. Instead, my throat closed up, my mind went totally blank, and I froze. No words would come.

"Toss it." Janice pressed the cool metal barrel of the gun to my cheek. Her face was so close I could see the pores on her nose and the malice in her cold stare.

Knowing how easily Janice could kill, I thought it best not to tempt fate and I dropped my cell phone on the floor. Safeguarded by the protective case, it bounced, but didn't break.

"Kate!" Matthews called out in vain, his voice small and distant. "Kate!

Are you there?"

Janice kicked the phone out the front door, and it skittered down the porch steps and onto the front lawn.

"Close the door." Janice backed into the darkened house, keeping the gun trained on me.

I closed the door, my gaze going back to the gun, and felt my panic rising. The whole town knew Janice was having money problems, and rather than look deeper, I'd let guilt get the best of me and offered to help her get back on her feet. I'd befriended a killer. Janice had fooled us all and taken matters into her own hands. She was desperate. And that made her highly dangerous.

"You're a murderer." I managed to find my voice, but it was swallowed by the echo of an empty house.

"I'm a survivor," Janice said with contempt.

My gaze darted around the house in search of a weapon or a means of escape. In my efficiency, anything that could be useful was secured in the garage for the estate sale. I couldn't run without the risk of taking a bullet, and I knew Janice wouldn't hesitate to shoot. Not after she'd killed Larry and Damon in cold blood. I needed to get out of the house, but panic and fear made it difficult to concentrate.

"It's over, Janice." I was afraid it might be over for me too, but I mustered the courage to stare Janice down. "The police are on their way. They'll be here any minute."

Janice pointed the gun at me. "Then they'll be too late."

# Chapter Twenty-Two

"Are you going to shoot me?" I went cold with dread, and my body was drawn taut as a wire. The only thought I could grasp and hold onto was that I should keep Janice talking. The odds were not in my favor, but no matter the danger I faced, I was determined that this would be the end of the line for Janice. "Did my father know what kind of a monster he was living with?"

"I'm sure you think you have it all figured out, don't you?" The gun in her hand dipped slightly. "He left me nothing in his will. Nothing! Do you know how that makes me feel? After all I put up with, taking care of him, cooking his meals, washing his clothes. He said he loved me! That life insurance policy should have been *mine*."

"Is that why you went after Larry?" I asked. "You must have known my father was investigating him, that his investment was a fraud. You knew he was stealing money, so you thought you'd get in on the action. One million seems to be your magic number."

"I saw an opportunity to improve my situation, and I took it. Larry promised to deal me in for a whole lot more if I got your father out of the way. He knew Jack wanted to turn him in, and we had to put a stop to that."

I couldn't hide my shock and disgust, even as I'd known the truth. "You killed my father?"

Janice laughed, the sound of her voice icy cold. "It wasn't hard. His own doctor prescribed him rat poison for his blood thinner. I just upped his dosage a bit."

White-hot anger overrode my fear, and I took a step closer to Janice. "All this time, I defended you, and you're nothing but a murdering, scheming bitch."

"That's not a very nice thing to say." Janice couldn't be provoked. "Is that any way to talk to the person who was with him at the end?"

"What did you do, wait for him to die before you called for help?" I rigidly held my angry tears in check.

"I had to wait for his heart to stop before I called for an ambulance. I couldn't take the chance they'd revive him. By the time they arrived, it was too late. They couldn't even shock his heart into beating."

"How could you?" I was no longer concerned with making an escape. I wanted to wrap my hands around Janice's neck and squeeze the life out of her. Because of Janice, I'd never get a chance to heal the past.

"You really should not have interfered," Janice said. "All you had to do was come home for the funeral, sell your share of the business to Larry, and leave. Things could have been so much easier without you snooping around."

"I was only trying to help all the people Larry was about to screw over."

"Good little Kate." Janice kept the gun trained on me. "Always helping people. You're just like your father. You think you have all the answers, but you don't know anything!"

I dared another step closer to Janice, waiting for a chance to make my move. "Why shoot Larry? Unless he stayed true to form and tried to screw you out of your share of the money. If that's true, you murdered my father for nothing."

The gun shook in Janice's hand as her eyes grew wild. "That cheat got what he deserved! We had a deal, and I showed him what happens to people who don't keep their word. He didn't even bring the money with him to the office that night. Can you believe it? He never intended to pay me. He said I couldn't turn him in without incriminating myself."

"What I don't get is why you framed Alex for his murder."

"I needed her out of the picture. She knew too much. It was the perfect plan to take the focus off Damon as the main suspect. I had to find a way to get my money, and Alex was the perfect distraction for that handsome young detective. I knew she'd keep him busy long enough for Damon to pay me, only he changed the plan, so I had to take care of him."

Janice had gone on her own personal killing spree, and if my current predicament was any indication, she wasn't finished.

"It's time to wrap things up for the police." Janice retrained the gun on me with a firm hand. "The cops are going to find out you took my friend's car for a little joyride." She tossed a set of keys on the floor at my feet. "A red car. The same car that ran Nick Callahan into the ditch."

"My fingerprints won't be in the car," I challenged. "How do you explain that?"

"You have the keys; what else do they need? The police will figure you killed Larry to get his share of the business, and when Damon got in the way of that, you killed him next." She seemed pleased with herself. "But you didn't stop there. You wanted to get rid of Nick because he knew about Larry's scam. You wanted to keep the money for yourself and you ran Nick off the road. But the grief of what you'd done was simply too much for you to bear, so you came home and took an overdose of your father's medication. They'll find the car parked around the block."

"You can't frame me for trying to kill anyone," I said. "It will never work. I have no motive to kill them."

"You had the perfect motive to kill Larry and Damon. Besides, if you leave a suicide note, they'll believe anything it says, especially if it's in your own handwriting."

"You're crazy. You know that, right?" I felt quite certain Janice didn't care.

"We don't have much time, now get moving." Janice jerked the gun toward the kitchen. "There's a piece of stationery and a pen on the table. I'll tell you what to write."

I didn't move, instead meet Janice's gaze with a fiery stare. I was afraid, but I refused to let Janice see my fear. Panic like I'd never known before welled in my throat, and I felt like a hand had closed around it, cutting off my breath.

"Come on, I haven't got all day." Janice prodded me with the end of the gun.

I walked slowly, dragging my feet like they were made of lead, and entered the kitchen. The clock on the stove read 1:01. There would be no new beginnings unless I got that gun away from Janice. My time was running out.

"Take a seat." Janice pulled out a chair at the table.

I saw the blank sheet of paper and the bottle of pills, and despair spread through my stomach like ice. Would they really believe a confession made in a suicide note?

"Pick up the pen," Janice instructed with a wave of the gun. "I'll tell you what to write."

"Go to hell, that's what I'll write," I said, turning up to glare at her with all the venom I could muster. "You can't make me do this."

"Can't I?" Janice shoved the cold gun to the side of my temple. "Pick up the pen."

When I didn't comply, Janice slapped my cheek, the sting spreading out across the whole side of my face. "Pick up the pen!"

In a flash of brilliance, I tried to calm my hammering heart as I obeyed Janice and picked up the pen, turning it in my fingers to get a feel for the grip. I could do this. I had to do this. Janice had to be stopped.

"I hate for you to sound cliché, but I thought we'd start with 'I don't want to be scared anymore.'"

I held the pen in my hand, hovering over the sheet of paper. "I'm not writing that. I'm not scared."

Janice slapped me across the face again, harder this time. "Do it!"

"Okay!" I shook my head, the sting in my cheek now burning, causing my eyes to water. "I can't write with that thing digging into my head."

"Fine." Janice pulled out the chair to the left of me and sat down.

I couldn't have planned it more perfectly. Before Janice raised the gun, I closed my fist around the pen and drove it into her face. I aimed for one of her eyes but wasn't sure if I'd hit my mark. The pen met resistance, so I drove it in further, feeling it sink into warm, meaty flesh.

Janice's anguished scream told me I'd hit something vital. I lurched to my feet and made a grab for the gun, but Janice was quick, and I was only

214

able to lock a hand around her wrist. As Janice tried to twist away, she fell to the floor. I refused to release my hold and went down with her, and as we wrestled, fighting over the gun, Janice got me pinned to my back. In a move that surprised even me, running purely on instinct, I tore the pen from Janice's eye socket and stabbed it into the center of her throat.

Sucking in a panicked breath, Janice got no air into her lungs. She dropped the gun, and her hands fluttered up to her throat. I'd landed the pen in her windpipe. Janice's eyes flew wide with shock, and she leaned back on her heels, trying to make a seal over the wound so she could take a breath.

I rolled onto my side and scrambled to my feet. I stalled for a brief second, wanting to get the gun, but Janice had already reached it and got to her feet as she took shallow, wheezing breaths. When I turned to run, Janice pointed the weapon and fired off a shot. The bullet ricocheted off the archway leading into the living room, and a shower of white plaster rained down on me as I clamored out of the kitchen.

Janice let out a gargled scream. "Get back here!" She wheezed, her breathing labored.

I wouldn't have time to get out the front door before Janice could get off another shot. I'd seriously wounded her, but she wasn't incapacitated. I rounded the stairwell and ran into the den. Janice's footsteps moving over the hardwood floors were close behind. I hurried to the side door leading to the patio and the backyard. Numb fingers struggled with the lock. As soon as it released, I grabbed the handle and threw the door open wide. As I ran through the door, a gunshot followed me, and then another, this time planting itself in my shoulder.

I grabbed at the burning wound but never stopped running as I sprinted outside across the brick patio. Something wet and warm seeped through my fingers, and I knew it was blood. My foot caught on an uneven brick, and I fell forward, propelled face-first into the grass. I knew it would be all over if I stayed down. Pain and fear didn't register with all the adrenaline pumping through my body, and the moment I scrambled to my feet, another gunshot rang out. I had to stay up, had to keep moving. I'd heard it was almost impossible to hit a moving target and prayed it was true as I ran across the lawn, headed for the neighbor's yard.

It wasn't even close to dinnertime yet, and most families wouldn't be home, so trying to get help would only waste time. Had I been thinking straight, I would have run for the front yard to retrieve my cell phone. It was too late to change course now. Janice was right on my heels. My best bet was to get out to the street and flag down a car before Janice could shoot me again.

Another gunshot came after me, and almost immediately, something whizzed past my ear. Janice had fired five shots. How many did she have left? I tried to remember what kind of gun she had, but it was no use. All I could visualize was staring down the black maw at the end of the barrel. Another shot hit the ground in front of me, and then another thwacked into a tree as I ran past it, spraying bits of bark into the air. That was seven.

If Janice had an automatic weapon, she had plenty of shots left, and I could die before I finished counting. Not wanting to take the chance that Janice had poor aim, I ducked behind a garden shed for cover, my hand pressed over the bleeding wound in my shoulder. I flattened my back against the wall and drew sharp, ragged breaths into my lungs as I tried to plan my next move. I had to act fast. Janice would be closing in.

Peering around the corner of the garden shed, Janice was nowhere in sight. I knew that didn't mean I'd lost her.

Which direction would she come from?

I inched my way to the opposite side of the shed. I took a chance and looked out around the corner. Janice pumped her arms to race toward me, the pen sticking out of her throat, one of her eyes bleeding, the other full of fury. She got off another wild shot, and I instinctively ducked, but I slipped on the grass and went down. I used my wounded arm to break my fall and something in my wrist snapped as it made contact with the earth. I was too frightened to register the pain, or too pumped up with adrenaline to feel the injury.

Behind me, I heard the unmistakable click of a gun, and Janice was either out of ammunition, or she'd had a misfire. I rolled onto my back and saw Janice standing over me.

"You really shouldn't have gotten involved." She aimed the gun at me. "I had a plan. I would have gotten away with it if it hadn't been for you."

I knew I was a goner. This was the end of the road. At least I'd fought back and tried my hardest to stop Janice. I closed my eyes, preparing myself for the shot that would end my life before it had truly gotten started. All I could think about were the missed opportunities and the chances I'd been too afraid to take. Life was made up of bad moments, but it was made of the good ones, too. You had to embrace them all. I understood that now. I'd wasted so much time.

I heard the shot go off. Like slow motion, I waited to feel the bullet enter my body, for the pain that would be sure to follow. Nothing happened. There was no light. No host of angels. My life didn't flash before my eyes.

"Drop the weapon!" A man's voice boomed across the lawn.

It was Matthews.

Another shot fired. It was deafening. But if I could hear, that meant I was alive. I opened my eyes in time to see Janice topple to the ground in a heap of colorful fabric and gaudy jewelry.

"Kate!" Matthews came flying across the lawn.

I released the breath I'd been holding.

Matthews slid to his knees beside me and holstered his gun. "Kate, are you hurt? Talk to me."

I blinked, looking into his kind eyes, so wrought with concern. I tried on a smile, but I didn't feel like moving. All I wanted was to lie on the cool grass and look up at the billowy clouds moving across the sky.

# Chapter Twenty-Three

I'd never spent the night in a hospital. Detective Matthews had gone with me in the ambulance and wanted me fully checked out. I think he liked having me confined to a hospital bed so he could keep track of my whereabouts after I'd been shot and broken my wrist trying to escape a deranged killer. He also had a calming effect on my mother, which I appreciated when she showed up with a vase of flowers and a blood pressure reading that almost landed her in the bed next to mine. I was in debt to Jake for not only saving my life, but my sanity.

Mason showed up later, after visiting hours were over, and I could only guess how he'd gotten past the nurse's station and into my room. He spent the entire night glued to the chair at my bedside in that sterile white room. He told me about the case, how my theory had been the right one, and how the only person who would face any charges was Hannah because she was the only one left alive.

I'd drifted in and out of consciousness, the painkillers they gave me were really strong, and I distinctly remembered him telling me "well done." He may or may not have held my hand for a little while. That part was a little foggy. The part I did remember was seeing a different side of him, something tender, and the warm feeling that lit me up inside. He made me feel safe, and it felt good to hold his hand, even if it was all in my head.

Kylie brought me cupcakes when she and Alex came to pick me up the next morning after I'd been released. Alex had arranged her guest room to accommodate the needs of a woman with only one arm operational and insisted I stay with her as long as I needed the help.

"I made sure the locksmith changed the locks at your father's house," she said.

"It doesn't matter anymore now that Janice is dead."

"Maybe not." She gave a little shrug. "But it still feels better to have it done."

Jake came to visit me at Alex's house. They'd found my laptop among Janice's things and he wanted to return it to me, as well as ask me a ton of questions about the financial aspects of the case. He made a good student and seemed pleased when I told him he could come back with any more questions and I'd be happy to lend my assistance.

By the end of the week, I had to decide what I wanted to do about my job in LA. I wasn't ready to go back, but really, it came down to the fact that I wasn't ready to leave Harmony Falls. The moment of fear I experienced when I turned in my notice didn't compare to the hope I had that everything would work out for the best. I did own a business, and Nick Callahan miraculously dropped his lawsuit, though I didn't see us being friends down the road.

Alex had gone by my father's house to leave a new key for the realtor and checked the mail while she was there. I was surprised when she returned with a wrapped gift for me.

"What's this?"

"Maybe you should open it and find out."

I could tell she was just as excited as I was to know what was inside and who had left the mysterious gift. I tore off the paper to reveal a red Cartier box. Resting inside on soft black velvet was a brand new, square-faced Tank watch with blue hands and a black leather band. From Mason. When he'd been with me in the hospital, I remembered complaining that the worst part about getting hurt was breaking my favorite watch. I vowed to take better care of this one.

A week later, October arrived, and Kylie had organized the estate sale at my father's house. I offered to lend a hand, a joke my mother, sister, and Alex did not find amusing.

"It's starting to get busy again, are you coming out?" Kylie held the door leading out to the garage.

I stood in the empty living room, looking at an incoming call on my cell phone. "I'll be right there. I want to take this."

Kylie rolled her eyes before heading back out to the garage. It was 11:11 when I answered the call from Grace. The most auspicious number, and a sign of good things to come.

"How's it going at the house?" she asked.

"Things are getting cleared out. It feels good. It feels like closure, or as close to it as I'm going to get anyway. But enough about me, I want to hear your good news."

"What makes you think it's good?"

I smiled. "Just a hunch."

"I got the job!" The excitement in her voice was unmistakable. I knew if I was there, she'd be glowing with pride. "Thanks to your letter. The best executive assistant you'll ever have. Don't let this one get away. You really laid it on thick, but it worked. They offered me a twenty percent pay increase."

"You're worth every penny."

"This means I'll be able to save enough for a down payment on a house by the same time next year. I can move out of my dumpy apartment."

"You'd better invite me to the housewarming party. I might need a vacation from the cold weather by then."

"I don't know if that's such a good idea," Grace remarked. "You seem to drive people to murder."

"Ha, ha, that isn't funny."

"And the best part is they want me to start next week, which means I had to turn in my immediate notice of resignation to Mr. Reed yesterday."

I could imagine how well that went over so soon after he'd received mine. "What did he say?"

"He offered me a two percent raise to stay." Her laugh was more of an evil snicker. "I laughed all the way out of his office. I would have called you with the news yesterday, but the gang took me out for drinks, and it got late."

"I'm really happy for you, Grace. You're going to do great things in the world of corporate finance."

"You better believe it," she agreed. "I know you probably don't want to hear about him, but Brandon is miserable without you around. His team fell apart after you set him up with the doctored report, and Mr. Reed gave his promotion to the new guy they hired."

"Serves him right. I don't know what I ever saw in him." Good looks and charm had kept Brandon in my life longer than he deserved.

"Some of the people around the office wanted to know if you were hiring."

"I think I'm going to fly solo for a while," I said, ready to start planning the next chapter of my life.

After we said our goodbyes, I went into the garage to see how the sale was progressing. The large furniture items and household appliances had been the first things to go. I was hoping to see everything gone by the end of the afternoon. Out front, the street was lined with cars and people browsed through my father's old belongings and haggled with Kylie and my mother over prices.

"No one would have ever suspected someone from Harmony Falls was the killer." Connie Pearson had gathered a small crowd by the kitchen items and dishware, the feather in her hat bobbing up and down as she gossiped. "To think, I was the one who asked Janice to join the Ladies' Aid bridge club."

"Our most dangerous enemies are the ones we never knew we had," I said, pretending to arrange some items on one of the tables.

"We're just lucky you came back to town and helped the police solve those murders," Connie said, and the women around her nodded and agreed. "You're a real asset to this town."

"I appreciate the kind words." I wasn't sure the sentiment was sincere, but I would take it that way.

"Oh, good, you're out here." Vivian appeared, pulling up a folding chair so I could sit down. "How are you feeling? Do you need anything?"

"I'm fine, Mother. Stop fussing over me so much. We're all going to be fine."

"With Janice off to meet her maker, we are," she said. "I still can't believe the amount of trouble she stirred up. Your poor father, he must have suffered a terrible death." She made the sign of the cross.

"Why did you and Dad really get divorced? I know you had your differences, but you never stopped caring about him. Couldn't you have made it work?"

"We both wanted different things." Vivian gazed out on the street. "Your father wanted someone to take care of him, and I wanted someone to take me to Europe." Her smile was wistful with some distant memory.

"Couldn't you have gone to Europe without him?"

Vivian put a hand on my knee. "It looks like I'll have to." Kylie joined us then, and Vivian reached out to take her hand. "You girls are the best part of my life."

Kylie put her arms around both of us. "I love you guys."

"How much do you want for this deer?" Someone asked from the crowd.

"Please, do anything to get rid of it," I said.

As Kylie went to make another sale, Vivian swiped at her eye with her free hand. "Well, now," she said, giving a light sniffle. "I have to go inside and check on my apple cider."

When she opened the door to go inside, the smell of cinnamon drifted out. It reminded me of home.

Alex slid into the empty chair beside me. "Does it still hurt?" she asked, pointing at the sling cradling my right arm.

I fidgeted with the Velcro straps. I would never get used to wearing it. "It comes and goes, but I have half a bottle of painkillers left. I'm just happy to be alive."

"Promise you won't do something like that again. It's been nice having you around."

"It's been nice to be around," I said, because I finally knew where I belonged.

It was early evening by the time we wrapped up the sale. Only a few boxes of random items remained, and Kylie hauled them out to the curb and labeled them with a 'free' sign. They'd be gone by morning.

Along with the falling temperatures, the days were getting shorter, and I pulled on a warm sweater before joining the ladies on the front porch for some of my mother's famous spiced apple cider. After deciding to keep my father's house, I'd acquired two more black rocking chairs to match the two my father had originally purchased and added some soft cushions, an outdoor rug, and another side table to the space, creating a comfortable outdoor seating area. As the weather got cooler, I might think about adding some warm throw blankets. It was the first area of my new house I'd decorated. With Alex's help, of course. Now that the inside of my father's house was empty, we had all winter to redecorate.

"Look who it is." Alex blew on her steaming cider before taking a sip from her mug.

On the street out front, Jake parked his Blazer and climbed out. He wasn't in uniform, so it couldn't be an official visit.

"Evening, ladies," Jake said as he came up the porch steps. He wore a leather jacket over his navy shirt and faded jeans. It was a good look for the detective.

"Good evening, Jake." Vivian greeted him with a wave of her fingers.

My mother had taken an extra special liking to the detective since he'd saved my life, and she was constantly finding excuses to bring him food or sing his praises to anyone who would listen.

His focus moved to me. "How's the arm?"

"I'll live." My gaze went to the newspaper under his arm. "What do you have there?"

He unfolded the newspaper and flashed the front-page headline:

FORMER FINANCIAL ADVISOR STOLE 5.8 MILLION FROM CLIENTS.

"I got an early edition of tomorrow's paper," he said.

"Let me have a look." Vivian reached for the paper. She put on her reading glasses and started to read aloud. "The Securities and Exchange Commission investigated Lawrence Stone, a former securities broker, for stealing 5.8 million dollars from several clients."

"Can they charge a dead man with a crime?" Kylie sipped from her mug of cider.

"No," Jake offered. "But they still conducted an investigation to determine if there were any accomplices."

"The investigation alleges that Stone stole the investment funds from his client's accounts over nearly a three-year period," Vivian continued. "And used the majority of the money on gifts for several women with whom he had romantic relationships. Stone employed various methods to conceal his misconduct from his clients, including creating fake account statements, forging signatures, and embezzling funds through numerous fraudulent checks that he made payable in the name of his business and later deposited into his personal accounts."

"It was all on Hannah's computer," I said, closing my hands around the warm mug of cider. "Once the Feds got into the hard drive, they found even more evidence." I sipped my cider, enjoying the warm treat and the feeling of justice being served. Even if Larry was dead, his name would always be linked with his crimes.

"How many women was he involved with?" Alex asked. "Were they all from Harmony Falls?"

"We don't have an exact number," Jake said. "But most of them were from the area."

Alex gave me an intrigued look. I had no doubt that information would come out soon enough.

"In addition to spending the money on vacations, luxury cars, and private school tuition for his romantic partners, he also used 1.4 million to repay funds he had taken from clients in Spokane, Washington." Vivian looked over the rim of her glasses. "It seems Larry was a busy man."

"An advisor is entrusted with money belonging to his clients," I said. "Larry took advantage of that trust in the worst way. If he was alive, he'd be facing criminal charges."

"What about Hannah?" Vivian asked. "What will happen to her?"

"I know charges have been filed," Jake said. "She went back to Florida, but she'll have to come back and stand trial."

"I'll bet she regrets getting involved with Larry," Kylie said. "What a scumbag. Why did Dad ever hire him in the first place?"

"He wanted someone to take over the business when he retired," Vivian said. "I told him to ask Kate, but he was too proud."

"He could have asked me," I said, my heart constricting with disappointment. I was afraid the past would always make me sad.

"He didn't think you'd want to leave LA."

I couldn't say what I would have done back then. I only knew what I'd chosen to do now.

Vivian went back to the article. "The SEC's continuing investigation is being supervised by Special Agent Mason A. West of the Financial Crimes Enforcement Network. The SEC appreciates the assistance of the U.S. Attorney's Office for the District of Minnesota, and Certified Fraud Examiner Kathryn Abbott." Vivian took off her glasses and beamed a proud smile at me.

"Look who's famous!" Kylie set her mug down and clapped her hands over her head. "My sister, the financial investigator. Look out, criminals of Harmony Falls."

"I was just doing my job," I said, not sure I deserved the praise. Damon's death still weighed on my heart. Were he still alive, he might be facing a long prison sentence, but he'd be alive.

Seeing my long face, Alex tried to boost my spirits. "It doesn't matter that Nick got to take some of the local credit for busting Larry in exchange for dropping the lawsuit. His name didn't make the paper."

"I guess it doesn't matter who takes the credit, as long as justice is served." How many times had I said those words in my career? I was choking on them now. I hated having to downplay my role to serve another man's enormous ego, but Mason couldn't get Nick to drop his stupid lawsuit unless he got painted as the town hero. Nick wanted to keep up his image. While the golden boy might win back some of his clients, it was my name in the paper. I had Mason to thank for that. "I'll be happy when we can finally put this whole thing behind us."

"What about the reputation of your business?" Vivian asked. "It can't help that you're letting Nick take all the credit for uncovering Larry's crime. What will people think?"

"Let Nick be the hero." I put on a practiced smile. "It matters more to him."

"The lawsuit would have been worse," Alex said. "This will all die down after a while, and people will be talking about the next scandal."

"Hopefully, you won't be wrapped up in the middle of it." Vivian leaned back with her mug and crossed her legs.

"I'm not sure I want to carry any financial clients," I said, giving voice to my thoughts concerning the business. "I want to bring something new to Harmony Falls. Something no one here has ever seen before. I'm going to close down the office for the season and get a fresh start in the spring."

Kylie picked up her mug from the side table. "What will you do until then?"

"I've got an empty house to fill, a business plan to create, and the holidays to spend with my family and friends. Maybe I'll even make some new ones."

Jake locked gazes with me. It was almost as if by saving my life, we'd become inexplicably tied, somehow connected to one another. I couldn't explain the feeling, and I didn't know what it meant, but I did know it couldn't hurt to explore it further.

"Speaking of new friends, where are my manners?" Vivian jumped out of her chair and wound her arm around Jake's. "Let's get you a cup of my famous cider. I use a secret ingredient passed down from my great-grandmother." She dragged Jake inside the house, telling him all about the recipe.

"Someone should tell Mom Jack Daniels isn't a secret ingredient." Kylie took a drink of her cider. "Now that you're staying, when is the realtor taking the sign out of the yard?"

"Tomorrow." I sipped my cider, feeling the liquor spread, warming me all over, and for the first time in a long time, I knew I was home.

It only made sense to keep my father's house, and my things would be arriving from LA in another week. Alex had already started on the plans to re-decorate. In time, the house would feel safe again, and I'd fill it with new people and new memories. With the things I loved. I couldn't think of a better way to heal the past than to pick up exactly where I'd left off.

"Won't you miss LA?" Alex wondered. "Just a little bit?"

I looked over the rim of my mug. "Maybe, but there's no place like home."

# About the Author

J.L. Winters writes fun, action-packed mysteries. Her characters are clever and fearless, and you'll always find bookish heroines, dark, tortured heroes, and a dash of romance and magic.

Before she started writing, J.L. worked as an OSJ manager, supervising the activities of several financial firms. There, she not only ensured they adhered to applicable regulations and laws but also gathered lots of ideas for her stories. After that, she worked as a property manager, an event planner, and assisted the CEO of an energy company. She now writes full-time.

J.L. pens the Write Magic blog and her newsletter about astrology, books, creativity, and anything else she finds interesting.

When she isn't reading or writing her next mystery, she's probably teaching meditation and yoga, getting into deep, intellectual conversations (hello, Gemini), or dreaming of Michael Fassbender.

J.L. is best known for her Murder By The Numbers mysteries and The Lexy Alexander Files.

SOCIAL MEDIA HANDLES:
https://www.instagram.com/thebibliolass/
https://www.facebook.com/jl.winters.37

AUTHOR WEBSITE:
https://jlwintersmysteries.com/

www.ingramcontent.com/pod-product-compliance
Lightning Source LLC
Chambersburg PA
CBHW030422120726
47903CB00003B/774

* 9 7 8 1 6 8 5 1 2 6 0 9 4 *